continued on next page . . .

"*Death By Darjeeling* is a good beginning to a new culinary series that will quickly become a favorite of readers who favor this genre. The cozy and inviting setting will quickly draw readers in and a likable cast of characters will have them eager to return." —*The Mystery Reader*

"Gives the reader a sense of traveling through the streets and environs of the beautiful, historic city of Charleston."
—*Lakeshore Weekly News*

Shades of Earl Grey

Chosen as a Monthly Alternate by the Literary Guild's Mystery Book Club®

"A heart-stopping opening scene." —*St. Paul Pioneer Press*

"Delicious cozy." —BooksnBites.com

"Once again, the reader experiences the scents, atmosphere, and elegance of Charleston."
—*Lakeshore Weekly News*

Keepsake Crimes

LAURA CHILDS

BERKLEY PRIME CRIME, NEW YORK

KEEPSAKE CRIMES

A Berkley Prime Crime Book / published by arrangement with the author

PRINTING HISTORY
Berkley Prime Crime mass-market edition / May 2003

ISBN: 0-425-19074-9

Berkley Prime Crime Books are published
by The Berkley Publishing Group,
a division of Penguin Group (USA) Inc.,
375 Hudson Street, New York, New York 10014.
The name BERKLEY PRIME CRIME and the BERKLEY PRIME
CRIME design are trademarks belonging to Penguin Group (USA) Inc.

PRINTED IN THE UNITED STATES OF AMERICA

10 9 8 7 6 5 4 3 2 1

This book is dedicated to my dad,
who died a few short months before I became
a published author.

Acknowledgments

A million thanks to my husband, Bob, who urged me to pursue this scrapbooking theme; to mystery great Mary Higgins Clark who has been so encouraging with every book I write; to my agent, Sam Pinkus; to Henri Schindler, Mardi Gras float designer, historian, and author, and Stone and Joan in New Orleans who revealed the fascinating world of Mardi Gras parades, float dens, and balls; to my sister, Jennie, who was this book's first reader and critic; to my mother who always believes in me, no matter what; to Jim Smith, dear friend and tireless cheerleader; to my Chinese shar-pei dogs, Madison and Maximillian, who were the inspiration for little Boo; to everyone at Berkley who was so enthusiastic about a scrapbooking series; to all the thousands of scrapbookers out there who are so marvelously creative; and to readers of my Tea Shop Mystery series who expressed genuine excitement over my new series.

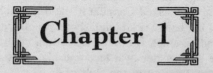

Chapter 1

CARMELA Bertrand spun out a good fifteen inches of gold ribbon and snipped it off tidily. "This," she told the little group of scrapbookers clustered around her table, "gets added to the center panel." Heads bobbed, and eager eyes followed Carmela's hands as she punched two quick holes in the scrapbook page, then deftly threaded the ribbon through.

The ladies had been asking about wedding scrapbooks, and Carmela had come up with a layout that was easy for beginners yet elegant in appearance. Color photos of a bride and bridesmaids were alternated with squares of embossed floral paper, three down and three across, like a giant tic-tac-toe board. A diamond-shaped card, perfect for personal jottings, was positioned in the center.

As Carmela's hands worked to fashion a bow, her mind was working overtime. She had about a gazillion things to do on this late February afternoon. Call her momma, pick up batteries for her camera, check with her friend, Ava, about the Mardi Gras parade tonight, figure out just what the heck she was going to wear.

But there was time, right? Sure there was, there *had* to be time.

Willing herself to calm down, Carmela pushed an errant strand of hair from her face and took a deep breath.

People always asked Carmela if she'd gotten her name because of her hair. Dark blond, shot through with strands of taffy and caramel, it offered a startling contrast to the clear, pale skin of her oval face and blue gray eyes that mirrored the flat glint of the Gulf of Mexico.

Of course, Carmela didn't have the heart to tell folks she'd been born hairless, just like a baby opossum.

Over the years Carmela had chunked and skunked her hair, as Ava laughingly called it, in an effort to shed her cloak of conservatism and adopt an image that was a trifle more outgoing and a little more . . . well, hip.

Too often, people thought her reserved. Not so, she told herself. She only *looked* reserved. Inside was a zydeco-lovin', foot-stompin' Cajun. Well, *half* Cajun anyway. On her mother's side. Her father had been Norwegian, which, when she thought about it, probably *had* given her a slight genetic tendency toward wearing beige and voting Republican.

When she was little, before her dad died in a barge accident on the Mississippi, he'd jokingly told her she was Cawegian. Half Cajun, half Norwegian.

Carmela had been enchanted by that. And as she got older, chalked up her orderly sense of design to her Norwegian side, her passion for life to her Cajun side. It made her uniquely suited for New Orleans, a city that was eccentric, fanciful, and profoundly religious, yet casually tossed ladies' panties from Mardi Gras floats.

Carmela had taken to New Orleans like a duck to water. The Crescent City, the City That Care Forgot, the Big Easy. Only lately, things hadn't been so easy.

Carmela finished with a flourish, "There," she told her group. "The amazing Technicolor wedding layout."

"How very elegant," marveled Tandy Bliss. She slid a pair of bright red cheaters halfway down her bony nose and studied Carmela's handiwork. Tandy was a scrapbook fanatic of the first magnitude and one of Carmela's regulars at Memory Mine, the little scrapbooking store she owned on the fringe of the French Quarter in New Orleans. "But didn't you mention something about using vellum?"

Carmela dug into her pile of paper scraps and came up with a quick solution. "Three-inch squares of vellum go here and here," she said as she slid the thin, transparent paper atop the floral paper. "Gabby, you want to hand me those stickers?"

Gabby Mercer-Morris, Carmela's young assistant, passed over a sheet of embossed gold foil stickers. Carmela peeled one off gingerly and pressed it at the top of the velum to anchor it.

"What a lovely, soft look," marveled Byrle Coopersmith. This was her first scrapbooking class, and she was wide-eyed with excitement. "I had no idea scrapbooks could be so elegant."

"People are always amazed at the sophisticated looks you can achieve," explained Carmela. She picked up a sample vacation scrapbook she'd created and flipped through the pages for all to see. "See . . . you can highlight a single photo by creating a gangbuster layout around it, use several photos for a fun montage effect, or turn your page into a kind of travel journal by incorporating your own personal notes and clippings. No matter what you do, scrapbooking is all about preserving memory in a very personal way." She passed the album to Byrle, who accepted it eagerly. "Think about it," continued Carmela. "Most people have snapshot collections that document all sorts of precious events: new babies, weddings, graduations, vacations. But what do they do with them?"

"Stick 'em in little plastic albums," said Tandy in her soft drawl. "Which is so *borrring.*"

"You got that right," said Carmela.

"Or toss 'em in shoe boxes like I used to," piped up a fifty-something woman with the incongruous name of Baby. Baby Fontaine was on the far side of fifty, but her tiny figure, pixie blond hair, peaches and cream complexion, and genteel accent lent a youthful aura. And Baby's friends, in no hurry to abandon the familiar, endearing moniker that had been bestowed on her back during her sorority days, continued to call her Baby.

There were five of them seated around the table. Carmela and her assistant, Gabby. And Tandy, Byrle, and Baby.

Tandy had found her way to Carmela's shop when it first opened, almost a year ago, and she was practically a fixture now. Tandy had completed elaborate scrapbooks that celebrated her wedding anniversary, vacations in Maui, and all of her children's varied and sundry accomplishments. Now she was working on a combination journal/scrapbook that documented her family heritage. Blessed with six grandchildren, Tandy had also done scrapbooks on each of the little darlings. And with two more grandchildren on the way, Tandy was now mulling over creative ways to showcase sonograms.

From out on the street came a loud hoot followed by raucous laughter.

"Parade goers," pronounced Tandy. She wrinkled her nose, swiveled her small, tight head of curls toward Gabby. Her smile yielded lots of teeth. "You going tonight?" she asked.

Gabby glanced down at her watch. "Are you kidding? I wouldn't miss it. Stuart's picking me up in . . ." She frowned as she studied the time. ". . . half an hour." Then, glancing quickly at Carmela, she asked, "I can still borrow your digital camera, right?"

"Not a problem," replied Carmela. "Knock yourself out."

"And we *are* closing at five today, aren't we?" said Gabby.

Carmela nodded again. "If we don't, we'll all be trapped here," she joked. Carmela loved her location next to one of the romantic, tucked-away courtyards on the edge of the French Quarter. With the gently pattering three-tiered fountain, overflowing pots of bougainvillea, and tiny, twinkling lights adorning the spreading acacia tree, it was a truly magical setting. But when Mardi Gras was in full swing, as it certainly would be tonight with the traditionally raucous Pluvius parade wending its way through downtown, the ordinarily manageable throngs of tourists would swell to an enormous, rowdy crowd. And that was way over here on Governor Nicholls Street. By the time you got to Bourbon Street, with its jazz clubs, daiquiri bars, and second-floor balustrades lined with shrieking, bawdy revelers, the scene would be utter chaos.

"Stuart got us an invitation to the Pluvius den," boasted Gabby.

The den she was referring to was the big barnlike structure down in the Warehouse District. Here, amid great secrecy, the Pluvius krewe had constructed twenty or so glittering Mardi Gras floats that would be revealed to appreciative crowds when their gala parade rolled through the streets of New Orleans in just a matter of hours.

The Stuart that Gabby gushed over so breathlessly was her husband of two months, Stuart Mercer-Morris. Mercer-Morris wasn't just a politically correct hybrid of their two last names, it was Stuart's family name. The same Mercer-Morris family that had owned the Mercer-Morris Sugar Cane Plantation out on River Road since the mid-1800s. The same Mercer-Morris family that owned eight car dealerships.

Baby nodded her approval. "It's a kick to visit the dens.

Del's in the Societé Avignon, so you can believe we've done our fair share of preparade partying." Baby rolled her eyes in a knowing, exaggerated gesture, and Tandy and Beryl giggled. "Lots of mud bugs and hurricanes," Baby added, referring to those two perennial New Orleans favorites, crawfish and rum drinks.

Carmela was only half listening to Baby's chitchat as she studied a New Baby Boy scrapbook page she was planning to display in her front window. Then she let her eyes roam about Memory Mine, the little scrapbooking store she had created.

Memory Mine had been her dream come true. She'd always "shown a creative bent" as her momma put it, excelling in drawing and painting all through high school, then graduating with a studio arts degree from Clarkston College over in nearby Algiers. That degree had helped land Carmela a job as a graphic designer for the *Times-Picayune*, New Orleans's daily newspaper. Once she'd mastered the art of retail advertising, she'd parlayed her design experience into that of package goods designer for Bayou Bob's Foods.

Bayou Bob, whose real name was Bob Beaufrain, fancied himself a marketing maven and spun off new products at a dizzying rate. Carmela designed outrageous labels for Big Easy Etouffee, Turtle Chili, and Catahoula Catsup. In Carmela's second year on the job, just after she married Shamus Allan Meechum, Bayou Bob hit it big with his Gulfaroo Gumbo and got approached by Capital Foods International. Not one to pass up a buyout opportunity, Bayou Bob sealed the deal in three days flat. Carmela may have sharpened her skills as a package goods designer, but she was suddenly out of a job.

She trudged around to design studios and ad agencies, showing her portfolio, schmoozing with art directors. She got positive feedback and more than a few chuckles over her Turtle Chili layouts, along with a couple of tentative job offers.

But her heart just wasn't in it.

Deep inside, Carmela nursed a burning desire to build a business of her own. She was already consumed with scrapbooking, as were many of her friends, and New Orleans still didn't have the kind of specialized store that offered albums, colorful papers, stencils, rubber stamps, and punches, the scrapbooking necessities that true scrapbook addicts crave.

Why not do what she loved and fill the niche at the same time?

With a hope and a dream, Carmela put together a barebones business plan and shared her idea with husband Shamus. Turned out, he was as fired up as she was, proud that his wife had *"gumption,"* as he put it. Shamus, who was pulling down a reasonably good salary from his job as vice president at his family's Crescent City Bank, even offered to foot the rent for the first four months.

Locating an empty storefront on Governor Nicholls Street, Carmela set about masterminding a shoestring renovation. Once the site of an antique shop, the former owners had packed up their choicest items and fled to Santa Fe, where competition in the antique business wasn't quite so fierce. Abandoned in their wake were a few of their clunkier, less tasty pieces. An old cupboard, a tippy library table, a dusty lamp.

The jumble of furniture hadn't deterred Carmela in the least. She took the old cupboard, gave it a wash of bright yellow paint, and lined it with mauve fabric. By adding a few painted shelves, the newly refurbished cupboard became the perfect display case for papers, foils, and stencils.

Likewise, the old library table, which had probably been too ponderous to transport, was also put to good use. Carmela shoved it into the back of the store, jacked up the errant leg, bought a dozen wooden chairs at a flea market, and declared the table "craft central." For five dollars an hour, scrapbookers were welcome to sit at the table and use all the stencils, punches, paper cutters, and calligraphy pens they wanted, as well as dip into a huge bin of scrap paper.

Flat files were added, as well as displays of albums, photo mats, how-to books, acid-free pens and adhesives, markers, brass stencils, scissors, and card stock. The walls were lined with wire racks that held hundreds of sheets of different papers that featured all manner of designs and colors.

Shamus had encouraged Carmela every step of the way. After all, she'd been a designer and had a real knack for teaching others how to piece together a great layout. And Shamus had been bragging-rights proud that his wife was able to demonstrate such business smarts. In New Orleans, a woman-owned business, albeit a small one, was still as scarce as hen's teeth.

But all that had been a year ago, when life had seemed as eternally bright as sunlight on Lake Pontchartrain. Because four months ago, Shamus up and left her. Had tossed his jockey underwear into his suitcase, grabbed his football trophies and camera gear, and taken his leave from their home in the rather elegant Garden District. Reluctantly (or so he said) and pleading the Gauguin precedent, Shamus left in his wake a closet full of three-piece suits, a rack of wing tips, and his rose gold wedding band.

Carmela bit her lip as she passed a piece of teddy bear art over to Tandy. Shamus's parting words still stung like nettles.

The rat had told her he craved space, that he desperately needed breathing room. He'd pleaded and cajoled, telling her he *despised* banking, that he needed a respite, a time-out from *everything* in his life. Tearfully, Shamus told her he wanted to focus on photography and that he needed to find a renewed sense of *balance* in his life.

Carmela had been stunned. She thought Shamus *loved* banking. She thought Shamus had *found* balance. She thought Shamus loved *her.*

But there was something else, something that didn't sit right. All this raw emotion from a good old boy who tended to display his feelings only in such instances as a superlative bourbon mash or a well-thrown Tulane touchdown, had seemed, well . . . forced.

Why, suddenly, seemingly overnight, had Shamus, *her* Shamus, become a touchy-feely, need-my-space, got-to-break-free-and-grow kind of guy?

Très strange.

Carmela wasn't sure, she hadn't yet found *concrete* proof, but Shamus's departing words had sounded suspiciously as though he'd been reading from a TelePrompTer. As though the words had been . . . borrowed? Had a few key phrases in Shamus's exit speech been culled from the current crop of self-help books? Yeah . . . maybe.

Carmela had even racked her brain, trying to remember if she'd heard some of those same phrases uttered by Dr. Phil on *Oprah.* Could be.

Whatever fishy circumstances had surrounded Shamus's departure, Carmela's humiliation hadn't ended there.

Two weeks after Shamus traded their large brick home in the Garden District for the bare-bones privacy of his family's old camp house in the Barataria Bayou, her in-laws had come a-knocking. Led by Glory Meechum, Shamus's overbearing older sister, the in-laws had politely yet resolutely asked her to vacate the premises of what, they explained, was technically *the family's* house.

Never mind that Shamus had also slapped *the family* in their collective faces when he renounced his vice presidency from their beloved Crescent City Bank. Blood was thicker than water and, right or wrong, the family was abiding with Shamus's decision.

What could she do? In New Orleans, the only thing thicker than blood was gumbo.

Carmela abided by her in-laws' wishes, making it clear to them that, when it came to cordiality and common decency, she regarded the Meechum family as being on a par with the Manson family.

Loading her few personal possessions into the vintage Cadillac she'd dubbed Samantha, Carmela and her dog, Boo, set off for her momma's house in Chalmette. They spent five days there. Carmela wandered the woods and piney forests where she'd grown up, sat by the edge of Sebastopol Pond, and grieved. Boo, her little fawn-colored shar-pei, kept her company, gazing at her with a perpetually furrowed brow and sorrowful eyes. And when Carmela cried long, mournful sobs, the dog with the chubby face sighed deeply as well, the picture of soulful love and canine understanding.

Like pages in a scrapbook, Carmela looked back over her time with Shamus. She worried about what was good and true and okay to keep, what should be chucked out. Or at least stored in a file in the bottom drawer.

It wasn't easy; her defeat was so recent.

On the fifth day spent at her momma's, Carmela finally came around to worrying about *her* life, *her* future. She decided that was the most important thing now.

With a heavy heart but a clear head, she assured her momma that she was okay. Not exactly great yet, but she thought she'd be able to find her way there in her own good time.

Carmela and Boo drove back to the French Quarter, sacked out on a futon in her scrapbooking shop for a few days, then finally located a tiny garden apartment just two blocks from her store. The rent was right, the atmosphere slightly decadent, and the decor showed promise. Tucked behind Ava Grieux's little tourist-trap voodoo shop, Carmela's new apartment boasted coral red walls and all the incense she cared to inhale.

"ARE YOU GOING TO THE PLUVIUS PARADE?" Gabby asked Carmela. Gabby was pretty and twenty-two, with dark hair and even darker eyes, primly turned out today in a pistachio-colored cashmere twin set and elegantly draped gray slacks. Carmela, on the other hand, with her newfound single status and French Quarter lifestyle, was now veering toward clothes with a slightly more flamboyant style. Today she wore slim black jeans and a hand-painted black denim jacket shot through with wisps of gold and mauve.

"I wouldn't miss tonight's parade for the world," Carmela assured her. "I ran into Jekyl Hardy at the French Market the other day, and he was telling me that all this year's floats have these fantastic *oceania* themes. Sea serpents and jellyfish and flying pirate ships."

Jekyl Hardy was chief designer for the Pluvius floats and a dear friend of Carmela's. They'd gone to art school together and both volunteered with the Children's Art Association.

Gabby followed Carmela the few steps over to a flat file, where Carmela rummaged for paper. "I don't suppose you're going with Shamus?" Gabby asked quietly. Gabby was a newlywed of four months and regarded marriage as a holy sacrament and the Mount Olympus of feminine accomplishment. Gabby had confided to Carmela that she prayed to Saint Jude, the patron saint of lost causes, every night to help mend her and Shamus's differences. She also assured Carmela that she would light a candle each week until the two were once again reunited.

Carmela had thanked Gabby warmly, then suggested she might want to purchase those candles in bulk.

"I only ask," continued Gabby, "since I know Shamus used to be a member of the Pluvius krewe." They were back at the table again, and Carmela slid a sheet of calico-printed paper to Baby, a sheet of rose-printed paper to Tandy.

"That's no longer an option for my dearly departed husband," Carmela told her. Dearly departed was the term she most often used in polite society.

"Oh, I'm sorry, dear," said Byrle. She looked up with a distracted air. "Your husband is dead?"

Carmela smiled pleasantly. "No, just living in the bayou." She saw that Byrle was trying to fit way too many photographs onto a single page. Reaching a hand across the table, Carmela slid three of the photos off the page that Byrle seemed to be struggling with. "Try it with just these five," suggested Carmela. "And maybe . . ." She reached behind her and grabbed a sheet of lettering. ". . . this nice blocky typeface."

"Dead, living in the bayou . . . same thing," Tandy said with an offhand shrug.

"Pardon?" said Gabby. She peered at Tandy as a frown creased her forehead. She was never quite sure when Tandy was serious or just teasing her.

"A few years back," said Tandy, "my husband's uncle, Freddy Tucker, moved to the bayou out near Des Allemands. He had some romantic notion about living in harmony with nature, if you can call alligators and snakes nature. Anyway, after a while the poor fellow went sort of feral." Tandy glanced up to find a half circle of startled faces. "You know," she explained, "Uncle Freddy started picking fights whenever the relations got together for weddings or funerals."

"Sounds normal to me," said Baby. She had cousins who hailed from down in Terrebonne Parish, also hard-core bayou country, so nothing surprised her.

"Eventually, Uncle Freddy just stopped coming to

town," said Tandy. "We never saw him again."

Gabby stared at Tandy, fascinated. She was the only one in the group "from not here," as they say in New Orleans. Which meant Gabby hadn't been born and bred in New Orleans and was sometimes overwhelmed by their offbeat brand of humor.

"You never saw him again?" asked Gabby, looking unsettled.

"Nope," cooed Tandy happily. "We don't really know what happened to Uncle Freddy. I suppose the old coot could still be out there, unless he got bit by a cottonmouth or something."

"Do you think that'll be the case with Shamus?" Gabby asked Carmela. "That he'll continue to live out at his camp house, I mean. Not get bit by a cottonmouth."

Carmela frowned as she snipped a piece of powder-blue gingham-patterned paper with her wavy-edged scissors. "No," she said. "No such luck."

AVA GRIEUX SWEPT THROUGH THE FRONT door of Memory Mine with her red opera cape trailing grandly behind her and a king cake clutched in her hands.

"Afternoon, ladies," she greeted them. Ava Grieux was tall and sinewy, with a tousled mane of auburn hair and porcelain skin. Ava Grieux, formerly Marianne Sommersby and first runner-up in the Mobile, Alabama, Miss Teen Sparkle Pageant, had been brought up to believe that a lady should never set foot in the sun without benefit of hat or parasol. That Southern notion, instilled by her mother and grandmother, had stuck with her, and now, at age thirty, Ava still had a flawless if not somewhat luminous complexion. Never mind that she'd changed her name and now ran a slightly tacky voodoo shop that catered shamelessly to tourists with its overpriced candles and herbal love spells stuffed into little silk bags and tied with ribbon.

"Have a piece of king cake, Gabby," urged Ava as she set the goody in the middle of the table. "You can afford the calories."

King cake, to the uninitiated, is basically braided coffee cake topped with frosting and liberally sprinkled with purple and green granulated sugar. It's a de rigueur Mardi Gras treat and always features a plastic Mardi Gras baby baked inside. Whatever lucky person chomps a molar down on the tiny plastic toy is then beholden to provide the *next* king cake.

"Just who are the Pluvius queen candidates this year?" asked Tandy, breaking off a piece of king cake and suddenly getting swept up in the Mardi Gras spirit.

"Swan Dumaine and Shelby Clayton are the front-runners," said Baby with a knowing smile. "The other four girls are all very pretty and sweet, but they don't count. They're not *seriously* in the running." Baby was well versed in the social intricacies and political strata of Mardi Gras. Back in their debutante days, both her daughters had been queen candidates as well as reigning Mardi Gras queens for the Societé Avignon.

Ava Grieux flashed a broad smile at Carmela. "Just for you, my dear . . . batteries." She tossed a small brown paper sack onto the table.

"Batteries," exclaimed Carmela. "Thank you, Ava, you're my saving angel!" Carmela tore the batteries out of their blister pack, then quickly inserted them in the digital camera she'd promised to lend Gabby.

"Honey, you're not eating any king cake," said Tandy to Ava.

Ava made a face, held out one of her arms. "I think I'm gettin' crepey."

"You're what?" said Baby.

"You know those little dingle bags that hang down

from the inside of your upper arms?" asked Ava. "I think I'm gettin' those."

Carmela glanced at Ava's arms. They were as sleek and toned as ever.

"Do you-all have any barbells I can borrow?" Ava asked Carmela.

"Soup cans," pronounced Baby.

"Pardon?" said Ava.

"You can use cans of soup instead of barbells. To do arm curls," said Baby. She pantomimed the exercise.

"Then, once you've worked up a real appetite, you can heat up the soup and really chow down," laughed Tandy.

"Listen," Ava said to Carmela, rapidly losing interest in her dingle bags, "I have to head back to my shop. I've got two customers stopping by to pick up masks."

In the past year, Ava had taken up the ancient art of mask making. She was hoping to eventually go legit and convert her store from a voodoo trinket shop to an upscale *atelier* that offered custom leather mask making. And she was off to a rousing good start. Ava already had more than two dozen customers who'd ordered custom masks for this year's Mardi Gras festivities.

"You come bang on the door when you're ready, honey, okay?" said Ava. "Then we'll head on down to the parade."

"Gotcha," nodded Carmela as Ava slipped out in a flurry of red fabric. The two women were going to the Pluvius parade later tonight and had plans to hopefully meet up with friends and watch the parade over near the French Market.

Carmela turned back to her group. "Remember, after today, we won't have any formal classes. Until Mardi Gras is over, that is."

They nodded sagely. They knew that from now until next Tuesday, Fat Tuesday, which was still a week away, there'd be a parade almost every night and the entire

French Quarter would be clogged with revelers.

"And we'll be closed all day Fat Tuesday," Carmela
added.

JOSTLING DOWN RAMPART STREET TWO HOURS
later, Carmela was amazed by the hordes of revelers, most
of whom were clutching little plastic *geaux* cups, or to-
go cups, purchased from the various bars. They were still
five blocks from the parade route, and already it was impossible to walk on the sidewalk.

"Come on!" Ava grabbed Carmela's hand and tried to
speed her along. "If we cut down Cabildo, then hook a
right into Pirate's Alley, we can pop out near Jackson
Square," she suggested.

Carmela was still wearing her black denim outfit, but
Ava had changed into red hip-hugger snakeskin slacks, a
skintight black nylon T-shirt emblazoned with a glitter
skull, and what appeared to be a spring-loaded bra. Her
ensemble would have drawn stares in any other part of
the country, but it was arguably a tad conservative for
Mardi Gras. Because, as the two women jostled their way
through the French Quarter, the costumes worn by the
myriad revelers and sightseers were amazing to behold.

Venetian lords and ladies clad in elegant velvets and
brocades sported gilded bird masks with hooked beaks. A
man in a swirling black Phantom of the Opera cape had
somehow engineered an enormous crystal chandelier to
hang above his head. Drag queens in full costume and
makeup were trying to outshine the leather bondage afi-
cionados, and a man wearing a suede spotted dog costume
walked a real spotted dog on a leash.

These costumed and coiffed revelers were accompanied
by legions of Peking Opera performers, swashbuckling
pirates, hooded monks, knights in armor, and even a car-
dinal in a mitered hat. They all jostled together, funneling

down the narrow avenues of the French Quarter toward the parade route, their glittery costumes sparkling under neon lights.

Carmela stopped nearly a dozen times to snap pictures, using her little auto-focus Leica, since she had lent her digital camera to Gabby. She was determined to create three or four scrapbook pages that would showcase tonight's parade and serve as a knockout window display. Hopefully, her pages would inspire others to seek out her scrapbooking know-how and help fuel a demand for all the special green and purple paper, gold lettering, and Mardi Gras stamps and stickers she'd stocked up on.

"Over here, Carmela. Quick!" Ava beckoned to her from a spot she'd commandeered directly in front of two young men who were perched atop a twelve-foot-high stepladder, with a homemade viewing platform.

Carmela slipped into place just as the first marching band blared its way down Decatur Street, the brass section prancing and strutting in true Mardi Gras style.

Behind them, two dozen flambeaus twirled their flaming naphtha-fueled torches, dancing for coins, as has been the tradition for almost a hundred years.

Then, as the first floats rolled by, strands of purple and gold beads began to sail overhead. These were traditional Mardi Gras throws being tossed to the eager crowd by Pluvius krewe members who rode atop the floats. It wasn't long before ordinarily decorous women were shouting at each other and elbowing one another out of the way, getting embroiled in heated disputes over exactly *who* a strand of colored beads had been intended for.

Cries of "Throw me somethin', mistuh!" rang out as a starfish-themed float and a giant dolphin float glided by. The soft Cajun dialects mingled with the flat, nasal sound of tourists from up North, and lilting tones of African Americans blended with the soft, easy strains that were distinctly Baton Rouge.

It's a gumbo of dialects, thought Carmela, as the parade seemed to kick into high gear and the night became a whirlwind of bright colors, loud music, and frenzied activity. Giant heads with gaping grins loomed from prows of floats that sparkled with thousands of tiny lights.

Carmela executed a deft leap and a one-handed catch and settled another strand of Mardi Gras beads around her neck. "Look," she nudged Ava, "there's the sea serpent float Jekyl Hardy mentioned."

Plumes of smoke from the carefully concealed dry ice machine billowed into the night air, and a motorized head and tail wagged from side to side as the enormous green and yellow sea monster suddenly dominated the street. The scene was kitchy, totally over the top, and truly awesome to behold. All Carmela could do was grin from ear to ear as more strands of plastic beads rained down around her.

Then, just when the massive sea serpent float was directly in front of them, it shuddered to a stop.

Taken aback, the crowd stared curiously up the steep sides of the float. Twenty feet above them, some kind of disturbance seemed to be taking place. Men in white silk robes and white plastic masks milled about, talking in urgent voices and bending down over something.

Carmela's first thought was that there might be a mechanical problem with the sea serpent. Or that the crew had run short of beads or coins.

But, suddenly, the *whoop whoop* of a police siren sliced through the din of the parade noise. A murmur rose from the crowd, and people pressed closer to the float, craning their necks upward. It was obvious something more serious in nature was taking place up top. But what?

A police cruiser, its blue and red lights pulsing, wove its way between a marching band and group of flag twirlers. With a squeal of brakes, the cruiser pulled in front of the float, and two police officers jumped out. They rushed immediately to the side of the float and extended their arms upward.

Suddenly, from high above, a body was dangled over the side.

"Someone's ill," Carmela said to Ava. "I think they're trying to get him down off the float."

The crowd, sensing a defining moment, suddenly hushed.

Ava nodded. "Must have drunk too much or took sick."

The men atop the float seemed hesitant in their attempt to pass the body down to the two police officers. The sick krewe member, still clad in his fluttering white tunic and mask, hung uncertainly over the side of the float. From street level, the police continued to stretch their arms upward, ready to catch him.

A dozen hands seemed to release the body all at once, and it appeared to hang in midair for a split second. Then the police below grappled to catch the falling man. They fumbled for a brief moment, then got purchase on the body. Gently lifting the man down, they laid him on the pavement.

Carmela edged forward to see what was going on.

One of the police officers knelt down and carefully peeled the plastic mask from the face of the injured krewe member.

A gasp went up from everyone nearby. The poor man's eyes had rolled back in his head, and only the whites of his eyes were showing. His face was literally blue.

"His breathing must have stopped," said Ava. "Or he choked on something."

"My God," said Carmela, squinting at the downed man. "I think I know that poor soul. I think it's Jimmy Earl Clayton!"

"He might be gone," Ava pronounced in a matter-of-fact tone.

"Don't say that," admonished Carmela as two more sirens pierced the night with boisterous whoops. "Here come the paramedics now. Maybe he just had too much to drink." It was no secret that krewe members riding on floats often drank to the point of complete inebriation.

"He's sure feelin' poorly," said Ava in a classic understatement.

A second police car, as well as a red and white ambulance, pulled up alongside the float.

Two paramedics, looking very polished and professional in their crisp white uniforms, hopped from the ambulance and sprinted for the man who lay sprawled in the street. The two newly arrived police officers pulled open the back door of the ambulance and unloaded a metal gurney. It jittered across the uneven road surface as they wheeled it over, stopping just short of the body.

Both paramedics were on their knees, crouched over the inert man.

Carmela strained to hear what was being said but could only catch fragments of conversation.

". . . needs an airway," said the first paramedic.

". . . so swollen, I can't see his . . ." came the panicky reply from the second paramedic. He probed at the mouth of the collapsed man with latex-gloved hands, obviously frustrated in his attempt to establish an airway.

The two paramedics remained bent over the man, working on him furiously. Then Carmela saw one of the paramedics pull a small instrument from his medical bag. A sharp glint of metal told Carmela it must be a scalpel.

"Traching him," murmured a man next to her.

Carmela peered intently at the scene in front of her and saw that one of the paramedics was, in fact, performing an emergency tracheotomy. Crouched on the pavement, a single wavering flashlight held by one of the police officers, the circumstances were primitive at best. She prayed the paramedic was blessed with a steady pair of hands.

Finally, their emergency procedure seemingly accomplished and an airway established for Jimmy Earl, the police and paramedics rolled the inert man onto a stretcher. Then they scrambled to their collective feet and rushed him to the back door of the ambulance. As they slid the poor man in, one of the paramedics jumped in beside him. Then the door was slammed shut, and the other paramedic clambered into the driver's seat. Lights flashed, the engine roared to life, and the siren gave a single plaintive *whoop* as the ambulance screeched off down the street.

Chapter 2

THE walls in Carmela's apartment were painted coral, a rich, satisfying red that matched the tumble of bougainvillea that sprang from the brown ceramic pots crouched outside her front door. Her furnishings were mostly thrift shop finds. Chairs and couches with classic lines that she'd slipcovered in crisp, natural beige cotton.

Ava Grieux had donated a couple of sisal rugs, claiming they were "too upscale" for her shop, whatever *that* meant.

The rest of the furnishings were little touches Carmela had found in the bargain back rooms of French Quarter antique shops. An ornate framed mirror with some of the gilt scuffed off. A piece of wrought iron that had once been part of a balustrade on some grand old home and now functioned as a dandy shelf for Carmela's collection of antique children's books. Brass candle holders that were so oversized they looked like they must have once resided in a church.

It wasn't the sprawling grandeur of the Garden District,

that was for sure. But her apartment *did* reflect the quirky charm and old world ambiance of the French Quarter. Punchy yet relaxed, a little bit decadent, definitely Belle Epoque. A distinct flavor that could only be found in this birthplace of New Orleans.

Carmela knew that most visitors, once captivated by the French Quarter's spell, would give their eyeteeth to live here. And all she had to do was get tossed out of her own home. Correction, get tossed out of *Shamus's* home.

Carmela was in a downer mood tonight and knew it. Then again, who wouldn't be after seeing poor Jimmy Earl Clayton get handed down from his sea serpent float and laid out pathetically in the middle of the street for all to see?

It was an ignominious moment for one of the Pluvius krewe's big muckety-mucks. And not exactly the best way to cap off their gala torchlight parade.

Had Jimmy Earl been resuscitated at the hospital? Carmela wondered. She certainly hoped so. They'd probably taken Jimmy Earl to Saint Ignatius Hospital, where they had a crack ER team.

The more Carmela thought about it, she more she figured the poor man must have suffered some sort of cardiac incident. That would account for his terrible palor, his inability to breathe, right?

Jimmy Earl was young, mid-thirties, still in fairly good shape. But in a city that dined nightly on crawfish bisque, deep-fried shrimp, andouille sausage, fried oyster po'boys, and bread pudding with whiskey sauce, early onset heart attacks weren't exactly unheard of.

Carmela grabbed a carton of orange juice from her small refrigerator and poured herself a glass. Stepping out of her shoes, she padded back across the floor to an antique wicker lounge chair that had been bolstered with down-filled cushions. She flopped down and nestled in.

Stretching her legs out, she caught the matching footstool with her toe, pulled it toward her.

Ah, that was better. Now she could kick back and relax. Carmela took a sip of juice, savoring the sweet, fruity taste, and closed her eyes.

For one split second tonight, when she'd seen that poor limp body in the white mask and tunic being hauled off the sea serpent float, Carmela had experienced a terrible moment when she'd imagined that it might be Shamus. Somehow, her mind had flashed on the idea that Shamus had been up there, riding in the Pluvius parade with his old krewe, and that something bizarre had befallen him.

But, of course, she'd known it *couldn't* have been Shamus. Shamus wasn't a member of the Pluvius krewe anymore. When he renounced his old life, he'd renounced *everything.* Gone cold turkey. Bid adios to her, his job, his social obligations.

There was no way Shamus would have been riding on that float.

Experiencing an unexpected flood of relief, Carmela was suddenly angry with herself.

Why had she thought it might be Shamus? How had *that* thought insinuated itself in her head?

Better yet, why would she even care? Wasn't she still furious at Shamus? Yes, she was. Of course she was.

Footsteps scraped across cobblestones in the courtyard outside her door and Boo, suddenly roused, let loose with a mournful howl. In almost perfect synchronization, the doorbell rang.

Carmela pulled herself out of the chair, ambled to her front door, opened it as much as the safety chain would allow.

Two uniformed police officers peered in at her.

"Ma'am?" said one.

"Yes?" said Carmela pleasantly.

The two officers continued to stare in at her.

Suddenly, reluctantly, Carmela had a pretty good idea of why the two policemen were here.

"Has something happened at the store?" Carmela asked then sighed deeply. Most business owners, the *smart* business owners, reinforced their store windows with wooden barriers and chicken wire during Mardi Gras. It was a good preventive measure that kept the party hearty hordes from trampling or pushing their way through your plateglass windows. If the police were here, it was a pretty good indication something like that had happened. That the front window had been busted in or at the very least cracked. Darn. And she'd just put in a brand-new display.

"Ma'am . . ." one of the officers was saying.

"It's the front window, isn't it?" said Carmela as she unhooked the chain and reluctantly pulled the door open. "I could just kick myself. I *knew* I should have—" she began, even as she wondered if her insurance would cover it.

"It's not your window, ma'am," said the officer whose name tag read Robineau. He hesitated. "We're here about your husband."

Carmela was so surprised she took a step backward. Boo, who'd been milling about at her knees for the past minute, suddenly pressed forward for a good, investigatory sniff of the two men who stood in the doorway.

"My husband?" said Carmela. *What could this be about?*

"Yes ma'am," said Officer Robineau as he continued in that maddeningly polite procedural manner that many policemen adopt. "You are the wife of Shamus Allan Meechum?"

"*Estranged* wife," Carmela replied. "Shamus and I are separated."

"Well, ma'am," continued Robineau, "Mr. Meechum's been taken in for questioning."

Carmela frowned. *Why would the police want to ques-*

*tion Shamus? What on earth has he done to warrant being
taken into custody by the police? Gotten drunk and prop-
ositioned one of New Orleans's social doyennes?* Carmela
cleared that thought from her mind. *No, that would be no
big deal. During Mardi Gras that kind of social impro-
priety was par for the course.*

"He's been arrested?" Carmela asked with some trepi-
dation.

"No, ma'am," the second policeman, Officer Reagan,
chimed in. "Not formally charged, nothin' like that. It's
just like my partner said. Mr. Meechum is being *questioned.*" Officer Reagan paused. "We'd like to ask you a
few questions as well."

"You want to tell me exactly what this is about?" Carmela asked, a note of suspicion creeping into her voice.

Officer Reagan, who bore the sad look of a betrayed
bloodhound said, "Your husband is being questioned concerning the apparent murder of Jimmy Earl Clayton."

Stunned, Carmela put a hand to her heart. "Jimmy Earl
is dead?"

Officer Reagan nodded slowly.

This was shocking news to Carmela. Somehow, she'd
been fairly sure the brilliant doctors at Saint Ignatius
would work their medical magic on Jimmy Earl. That
they'd EKG, EEG, or ECG him so he'd live to play the
fool in yet another Mardi Gras celebration.

*And what is this about Shamus? Why on earth would
the police think he is involved?*

"Oh, no," said Carmela, "poor Jimmy Earl. Such sad
news. I thought for sure he'd . . ." her voice faltered. "I
hoped it was something the doctors could easily fix. But
this . . ." Shaking her head, Carmela motioned the two officers in. "Perhaps you'd better come in . . . tell me all
about it."

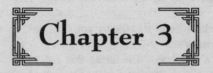

Chapter 3

THE sun wasn't up yet, but something was making a dreadful racket.

Carmela lay in bed in a half-dream state, trying in vain to figure out what was going on. Flag twirlers in spangled uniforms and shiny white boots pranced in front of a green and yellow float. Then the float ground to a halt, and a giant phone was handed down to her.

What? Oh, oh. Phone, she finally decided.

Carmela fumbled for the pale blue princess phone she'd ripped from the wall in the butler's pantry the day she'd vacated Shamus's home.

"Hello," she croaked.

"Carmela." The voice was a deep, languid drawl.

Carmela uttered a sharp intake of breath. It was the rat himself: Shamus.

"What?" she mumbled. Lifting her head, she peered at the oversized dial on her vintage clock radio. It read a big five-fifteen. She hadn't slept more than six hours. No wonder she felt tired and crabby.

"Are you insane?" Carmela groaned into the phone at Shamus, already knowing the answer. "Because it's so early the *birds* aren't awake. It's so early the morning shift of bartenders down on *Bourbon Street* hasn't come on yet."

"Carmela, I need to talk to you." Shamus's voice was soft yet insistent.

Carmela grimaced. She hated that soft, wheedling tone. It drove her crazy and got to her practically every time.

She closed her eyes, tried not to conjure up a mental picture of him. It didn't work. In her mind's eye she could still see Shamus. Tall, six feet two, and the proud possessor of a lazy smile that tended to be devastating when he decided to turn it up a notch or two. Shamus had a sinewy body, strong hands, flashing brown eyes. And a soft accent. His mother hailed from Baton Rouge, and he carried her soft-spoken ways.

"What about?" Carmela asked. She pretty much knew what Shamus was going to say, but she didn't feel like making it easy for him. She swung her legs out of bed, hit the sisal rug, scrubbed the bottoms of her feet back and forth across the bristles, as though the rug were a loofah, and she could magically rub some energy into herself. Positive energy that would fortify her against Shamus.

"You heard what happened to Jimmy Earl Clayton?" Shamus asked her.

"You know something, Shamus?" she told him. "I was *there*. I was standing in front of the French Market when the entire Pluvius parade ground to a halt and the police had to lift the poor man down from his sea serpent float." Carmela didn't know why she was suddenly so defensive, but she couldn't seem to help herself. When they were living together, she'd always thought they brought out the best in each other. Now that they were apart, Shamus most definitely brought out the worst in her.

"You're not going to believe this, Carmela," Shamus roared back, "but the police questioned *me* last night. Me!" She could hear both anger and anxiety in his voice. "In fact, they held me at the police station until almost two in the morning!"

"I've got news for you, Shamus, they came and talked to me, too," Carmela fired back.

"What?" said Shamus, genuinely stunned. "When?"

"Last night," she told him. "Around ten, ten-thirty. They came to my apartment. The exceedingly small apartment I was forced to move into after you unceremoniously dumped me. The one I retreated to after your lovely sister ousted me from our former home."

"Carmela, we've been over this," Shamus said plaintively. "I didn't dump you; I love you. You're my wife."

"Let's see now," she said. "Would that be your have-and-to-hold-till-death-do-us-part wife? Or your I'll-get-back-to-you-when-I'm-good-and-ready wife?"

"Carmela."

Oh man, she thought, *there's that insidious, wheedling tone again.*

"Carmela," repeated Shamus. "What did they want with you?"

"They wanted to know if I'd seen you last night. I told them I hadn't seen your sorry ass since you stuffed your argyle socks into your banjo case and boogied on out the door."

"Guitar. You know darn well I play guitar."

"Sweetheart, I don't care if you switched to a cello and joined the Boston Symphony. The police wanted to know if you were acquainted with Jimmy Earl Clayton."

"What did you tell them?" asked Shamus.

"I told them everybody and his brother from here to Shreveport was well acquainted with Jimmy Earl Clayton. The man was your basic Southern boy mover and shaker. Rated several column inches per week in the business section as well as a few mentions in our somewhat question-able society pages. And I use that term loosely, society being what it is today."

"That's it?"

"Of course that's it, Shamus. I even gave you the ben-efit of the doubt. I assumed you had absolutely nothing to do with this."

"You assumed right, darlin'."

Darlin'.

"So what was it that prompted the police to come knocking on my door then?" asked Carmela, more than a little peeved.

"Nothing. I was taking pictures of the Pluvius floats, for Christ sake. I suppose I was in the wrong place at the wrong time, that sort of thing."

"And you just happened to snap a few photos of the sea serpent float," said Carmela.

"Yes."

"That's it?"

"Of course, that's it," said Shamus. He paused. "Well, I might of had words with Jimmy Earl."

"Words," Carmela repeated.

"Yes, words," Shamus said crossly.

"What exactly did you say to Jimmy Earl?" asked Car-mela.

"What does it matter what I said?" Shamus answered in a huff. "It was nothing. Just because something hap-pened to Jimmy Earl Clayton later on, doesn't mean it had anything to do with me. I'm truly sorry the man is dead, but I can assure you, I had nothing to do with it."

A tiny pinprick of heat slowly ignited behind Carmela's eyes. It spread into her forehead and set her nerves to jangling. Carmela knew what was happening. She was getting one of her Shamus headaches. They swept over her whenever he acted this way. Belligerent, aggressive, manipulative. In other words, your typical Southern male.

"I have to go, Shamus," she told him. "Nice talkin' to you. Bye-bye." Carmela slapped the phone back in its cradle, flopped back into bed. She lay on her back, staring up at the lazily spinning ceiling fan.

Just when you think you're safe, she thought to herself. *Just when you think your heart won't hurt again. What was it the tin man said when Dorothy was about to leave Oz and fly back home to Kansas? "Now I know I've really got a heart because I can feel it breaking."*

Carmela pulled the covers over her head. Did she want to be married to this clod, or should she go ahead and get that divorce? Which was it going to be? Door number one or door number two?

Carmela lay there trying to release the tension from her body. If she could just relax and clear her head. Maybe catch a couple more hours of sleep . . .

Nope. No way, nohow. Try as she might, counting sheep, counting her chickens before they were hatched, counting on her own resourcefulness, she couldn't fall back to sleep. That vision of Jimmy Earl Clayton being dropped from the float and laid out on the pavement seemed burned in her memory. It played over and over in her head like a bad news bulletin on CNN.

Do the police really think Shamus had something to do with it?

She shook her head in disgust. *Preposterous. Shamus may be a louse, he might even turn out to be a sneaky two-timing bum, but no way is he a killer.*

Carmela pulled herself out of bed, crept to the little kitchen, brewed a pot of nice, strong, chicory coffee. Scrounging one of yesterday's beignets, she went out to sit in the courtyard. Wisely, Boo remained tucked in her cozy little dog bed, the L.L.Bean version that had cost way more than Carmela's down comforter.

The sun, just beginning to peep over the crumbling brick wall that separated her little slice of the world from the rest of the French Quarter, felt warm on her shoulders. The steady drip-drip of the fountain was somehow reassuring.

Sipping her coffee, Carmela tried to banish thoughts of Shamus from her mind.

Begone, she commanded, as she let her eyes take in the beauty of the courtyard garden. The wrought-iron benches, the lush thickets of bougainvillea, the old magnolia tree dripping with lacy fronds of Spanish moss. Against the brick wall, tender green shoots of cannus peeped up through the dirt, and tendrils of tuberose curled on gnarled pine trellises that had been cut and woven by hand more than a hundred years ago.

There was a powerful amount of history here in the French Quarter, Carmela told herself as she took a fortifying sip of hot coffee. Which would make it a logical place to begin one's life anew.

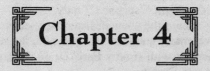

Chapter 4

"KETAMINE," exclaimed Gabby. "What on earth is ketamine?" She stared at Tandy Bliss in wide-eyed amazement.

Tandy had shown up promptly at ten o'clock. A packet of photos that showcased two of her grandchildren, wide-eyed, grubby-faced, and cooing over last night's Pluvius parade, were clutched in her hot little hands. Carmela figured Tandy must have hit the one-hour photo mill at first light.

"Sweetie," said Tandy, obviously enjoying her inside track, "don't you ever watch *Sixty Minutes*? Haven't you ever heard of *club drugs?*"

Gabby shrugged. The only clubs she was familiar with were the boisterous, rollicking clubs in the French Quarter. Jasmine's, Dr. Boogie's, Moon Glow. She assumed some drug trafficking went on there. But didn't it go on most everywhere now?

"Ketamine as in Special K," explained Tandy. "It's the stuff kids are always OD'ing on at raves."

"Oh," said Gabby as understanding began to dawn. "Come to think of it, I *have* heard of Special K. And raves. Aren't those like . . ." She searched for the right words. ". . . . *unauthorized* parties for high school kids?"

"More like *illegal*," snapped Tandy.

Standing behind the counter, listening intently, Carmela gave an involuntary shudder. How on earth did something like that connect with Jimmy Earl? *Or Shamus*, she mentally added. *Or Shamus*.

"Here's the thing," said Tandy as she waggled her index finger and moved closer to the counter. Carmela and Gabby, fascinated by her words, leaned in to listen, even though no one else was in the shop yet. "Poor Jimmy Earl had a whopping dose of this Special K stuff in his bloodstream."

The news of Jimmy Earl's death had made front-page headlines in the *New Orleans Times-Picayune*, though the story that followed was short, with very few details. Carmela knew it was only a matter of time, however, before a mix of rumors and truth concerning Jimmy Earl's demise would spread like wildfire throughout the city.

Gabby frowned. "Isn't too much of that stuff like *poison*? Where did you hear this?" she demanded. "And are you sure it was ketamine?"

"Darlings," Tandy's hyperthyroidal eyes got even bigger, "I heard it first-person from CeCe Goodwin, Darwin's sister-in-law." Darwin was Tandy's husband. "I'm not sure you-all know this," continued Tandy, "but CeCe is a nurse over at Saint Ignatius. And," she added triumphantly, "she just happened to be on duty last night when Jimmy Earl Clayton was brought in to the emergency room, all pale and white on a stretcher!"

That level of confirmation was good enough for Gabby. "Wow," she breathed. "Do they know how he overdosed? I mean, it *was* an overdose that killed him, right? Or did someone . . . what? Put it in his drink?"

"Nobody's saying anything about that yet," said Tandy. "Of course, it's possible Jimmy Earl could have taken the drugs himself. He *did* have a slight tendency to overdo."

Slight tendency, thought Carmela, *now there's an understatement.* She recalled seeing Jimmy Earl Clayton at a Garden District party one night doing the macarena on top of someone's Louis XVI table, stoned out of his mind. Then there were his so-called after work "martini races" at Beltoine's. Those were legendary. And he'd once tossed his cookies on the eighteenth green at the Belvedere Country Club in full view of the clubhouse after he'd imbibed in a few too many bourbons. *No,* she thought, *Jimmy Earl Clayton hadn't been just a social drinker; he had darn near achieved professional status.*

"I'm sure the police will explore all possibilities," continued Tandy. "They're *extremely* clever when it comes to things like toxicology screening and forensic tests." Tandy talked as though she'd just earned a master's degree in criminal justice. "They can run tests that narrow everything down to the nth degree," she added.

Carmela listened intently to Tandy. That was exactly what the police had told her last night when they revealed that Jimmy Earl had been poisoned. *No wonder Shamus had been heartsick and worried this morning,* thought Carmela. *Being accused of such a heinous crime. And poor Jimmy Earl. Dead from an overdose of a drug that was popular, easy to obtain, and so very lethal.*

Still, there was no way Shamus would ever have been involved.

Jimmy Earl had so loved to party, Carmela mused. So there was that possibility. It wouldn't be the first time a white-collar business type had been caught using drugs. Just look at the popularity of cocaine. It was not only rampant these days, cocaine was most often the *drug du jour* among executives. Jimmy Earl could have just as easily developed a taste for club drugs. It happened. God knows, it happened.

On the other hand, Jimmy Earl was also a high-test financier. He was one of the senior partners in Clayton Crown Securities. Clayton Crown was one of the few independently owned brokerage firms left in New Orleans, and they handled millions, maybe billions, in stocks, bonds, mutual funds, and corporate financing. They also engineered mergers and acquisitions. Shamus had mentioned Clayton Crown on more than one occasion and had obviously had a lot of respect for them. In fact, Clayton Crown was considered a major player in New Orleans.

But as head of a prominent company like that, it was also possible Jimmy Earl had courted a few enemies over the years. Sooner or later, investors lost money, mergers went sour, financing fell through.

The question was, would someone have gone so far as to *kill* Jimmy Earl? Carmela thought about this for moment, didn't come up with anything definitive. That would be a good question for Miss Cleo's Psychic Hotline, she decided.

"What happened to the float?" Carmela asked Tandy as an afterthought.

"Impounded," said Tandy. "Apparently, poor Jimmy Earl really choked down a megadose so they're checking *everybody* out."

The tightness in Carmela's chest loosened a notch.

"So . . ." said Gabby, unwilling to let the issue of Jimmy Earl Clayton's death go, "they *are* surmising that someone put ketamine in his drink?"

"Honey, nobody knows for sure yet," said Tandy. "But I'm not surprised that Jimmy Earl ingested so much," she sniffed. "Given the way most of those men tipple all that whiskey." Tandy gave a tight nod of her curly head, then headed for the back table to work on what would be her fourteenth scrapbook.

* * *

"GABBY, THIS COULDN'T BE OUR LAST SHEET of purple foil." Carmela stood at the paper cabinet, pulling open drawers, riffling though stacks of colored paper. She was feeling slightly discombobulated by Tandy's news as well as her obvious excitement over all the gory details.

Gabby looked up from the counter. "I think it is. Didn't you order more?"

Purple, green, and gold were the official colors of Mardi Gras, and Carmela knew that, over the next few weeks, everybody and his brother would be looking for those specific colors when they put together scrapbooks to showcase their Mardi Gras photos.

"I ordered a ream of foil paper. What's happened to it?"

Gabby frowned as though trying to recall. "I think Baby bought a hundred sheets for wrapping party favors. Then, the other day, while you were at lunch, some of the people from the Isis krewe came in and bought a whole bunch more. What with your regulars . . ." Gabby's voice trailed off uncertainly.

"I get the picture," said Carmela. "But we're going to need more. Pronto."

"Can you put an order in?" Gabby asked as she stood at the counter, arranging packets of foil stickers.

"I'll place an order on-line," Carmela assured her. "That way we'll get free shipping, and the order should be processed today."

"Good." Gabby looked up as the bell over the door sounded. "Oh, hi there," she said as Baby walked in, accompanied by one of her spectacularly beautiful daughters.

"You remember Dawn, don't you, everybody?" asked Baby as she proudly thrust her daughter in front of her. Dawn possessed the same classic features as her mother, but at twenty-five was a far younger and perkier version.

"Of course," said Carmela, greeting her warmly. "And this is Gabby, my assistant."

"Hello," said Dawn pleasantly as she pushed back a tendril of golden blond hair. "Hi, Tandy," she waved a hand toward the back of the store.

"Hi, sweetie," replied Tandy, barely looking up from her stack of photos.

"You heard about Jimmy Earl?" asked Baby.

Everybody nodded.

"Tragic," breathed Baby, "simply tragic."

"Tandy's husband's sister-in-law was there," said Gabby. It was a tangled reference, but Baby and Dawn seemed to pick up on it right away and nod expectantly. "She was right there in the emergency room when Jimmy Earl was brought in," finished Gabby with great enthusiasm.

Baby cranked her patrician brows up a notch and turned to study Tandy. "You don't say," she murmured. "Was the poor fellow still alive, do you know?"

"Dead as a doornail," said Tandy as she flipped through her stack of photos like playing cards.

"I heard they found drugs in his bloodstream," volunteered Dawn.

"Ketamine," called Tandy from the back, not wanting her inside information to be overshadowed by anyone else.

"Such a sad business," said Baby. "I think I'll make a crab étouffée to take over to Rhonda Lee." Rhonda Lee was Jimmy Earl's wife. Technically his widow now. "What do you think, honey?" She turned to Dawn.

"Crab's good," said Dawn.

"You know, the Claytons only live a few blocks away," Baby added. "It just goes to show you never know when or where tragedy's going to strike." There were murmurs of agreement from the women, then Baby shook her head as if to clear it. "On a happier note, I was telling Dawn about the wedding scrapbook pages you showed us yesterday."

"Ya'll know I just got married this past fall," said Dawn, brightening immediately. "To Buddy Bodine of the Brewton Creek Bodines. And I *still* haven't got my reception pictures in any semblance of order. Mama did my wedding album, of course, but these . . ." She sighed dramatically and held up a large fabric-covered box that presumably contained a jumble of reception photos. "I thought maybe ya'll could help," she finished with a pleading note.

"You thought right," said Carmela, draping an arm around Dawn's shoulders and leading her to the table in back. "In fact I just got a *load* of new albums and papers in. Here . . ." Carmela got Dawn and Baby seated at the table, then moved to a flat file cabinet and slid open a drawer. Drawing out an album with a thick cover of cream-colored, nubby paper embossed with tiny hearts, she passed it over to them.

Dawn fingered the thick paper. "I *adore* this cover, it's so tactile."

"That's because the paper's handmade," Baby quickly pointed out.

"And I absolutely *love* the almond color," said Dawn, "it's so much more elegant than just plain old pasty white. And those little hearts are *perfect*. So romantic."

"I've got some great papers, too," said Carmela, smiling at Dawn's over-the-top enthusiasm. "Some are mulberry, handmade in Japan. One even has cashmere fibers woven in."

CARMELA HAD ALMOST FORGOTTEN ABOUT Jimmy Earl's demise by the time Donna Mae Dupres walked in to her shop. A rail-thin little woman in her sixties with a tangle of gray hair, it was rumored that, in her youth, Donna Mae Dupres had been wilder than seven devils. But whatever mischief she had wrought and hearts she had broken had now been replaced by matronly decorum, for Donna Mae Dupres was a tireless fund-raiser and chairman of Saint Cyril's Cemetery Preservation Society.

Saint Cyril's, like all the ancient cemeteries in New Orleans, had been built aboveground back in the late 1700s. With constant outbreaks of yellow fever killing off large numbers of the population, early settlers had still found it nearly impossible to bury the bodies of their dead in the ground. The city of New Orleans, it seemed, was situated a good six feet *below* sea level. So the water table had a nasty habit of eventually returning their loved ones to them. An alternative method was hastily and cleverly devised. The aboveground tomb.

Carmela had been commissioned by Saint Cyril's Preservation Society to design a history scrapbook commemorating this historic old cemetery with its whitewashed tombs, historic monuments, and black wrought-iron gates. Quite a creative coup and the first *commercial* scrapbook project she'd ever received.

"Look what someone just donated, dear," said Donna Mae, handing a yellowed and tattered brochure to Carmela. "It's the program for the dedication of Saint Cyril's back in 1802."

Carmela accepted the fragile program. From the condition of the faded, half-shredded paper, it had obviously been forgotten for decades in someone's old trunk. And, over the past hundred years, it had been subjected to all manner of heat, mildew, mold, and insects.

"I'll get this treated with archival preserving spray right away," Carmela promised. "Like some of us, it doesn't need any more age on it."

"We located a few more black-and-white photos, too,"

said Donna Mae, handing over a large manila envelope. "And I asked some of the older folks to write down their recollections, just as you suggested."

"Wonderful," said Carmela. "That way this scrapbook can be an interesting amalgam of photos, news clippings, and written history."

Donna Mae beamed. "And you'll have a sample page or two to show the committee by the end of next week?"

"Count on it," Carmela assured her.

"Isn't that a coincidence," remarked Tandy as the door closed on Donna Mae Dupres. Tandy's eyes sparkled, and a curious smile occupied her thin face.

"What is?" asked Carmela.

"You're creating a scrapbook for Saint Cyril's," said Tandy, nodding at the packet of photos in Carmela's hands.

"Yes," said Carmela slowly, still wondering what coincidence Tandy was referring to.

"And the Clayton family plot is in Saint Cyril's," continued Tandy. "That's where poor Jimmy Earl will be laid to rest."

CARMELA WAS HUNCHED OVER HER IMAC IN her little office at the back of the store when Gabby poked her head in.

"Jekyl Hardy's on the phone," Gabby announced. She looked at the computer screen. "You got the order in okay?"

Yes, mouthed Carmela as she picked up the phone. "Jekyl, hey there," said Carmela.

Jekyl Hardy was a whirling dervish of a man who, for the better part of the year, made his living as an art and antiques consultant. When Mardi Gras rolled around, however, you could usually find Jekyl Hardy at the Pluvius or Nepthys dens, where he served as head designer and float builder for both krewes. Lean and wiry, dark hair pulled snugly into a ponytail, Jekyl Hardy was usually attired in all black. And since he was constantly overbooked, Jekyl was generally in a state of high anxiety throughout Mardi Gras—at least until the last beads were tossed and the queens were crowned on the final Tuesday night.

"Carmela, my most darling and favorite of all people," came his intense voice at the other end of the phone. "Do you know your name was mentioned in passing regarding our fair city's latest brouhaha?"

"What are you talking about, Jekyl?" She had a pretty good guess as to what Jekyl meant but still held out a faint glimmer of hope it might be something else.

"I'm referring to the untimely demise of Jimmy Earl Clayton," said Jekyl. "My phone's been ringing off the hook. As you know, I'm doing the decorations for the Pluvius Ball next Tuesday night." He paused dramatically. "And now there's a slight rumble the ball may be canceled altogether."

"Out of respect for poor Jimmy Earl?" asked Carmela.

"I suppose that would be the general idea," said Jekyl. "Although, from what I've heard about Jimmy Earl, the man didn't garner all that much respect when he was alive." Jekyl Hardy cackled wickedly, pleased with his offbeat brand of gallows humor. "But, Carmela, this nasty innuendo about your ex," Jekyl continued. "Very, very bad. Word on the street is that Shamus is suspect numero uno, the odds-on favorite for the moment."

"Not *my* favorite," replied Carmela.

"I admit it's all circumstantial," said Jekyl. "On the other hand, Shamus does posses a fairly famous temper and has been known to dip his beak in the demon rum. It's a fairly damning combination. I mean, *I* was running around like a chicken with its head cut off last night, trying to get the damn floats out the door, and I *still* noticed Shamus staggering around, sucking down hurricanes like they were Pepsi Colas."

"Shamus always does that at Mardi Gras," said Carmela. "Hell, Jekyl, the whole of New Orleans does."

"Point well taken," agreed Jekyl. "The question is, what's to be done now? What kind of damage control can you engineer?"

"There's nothing to do," said Carmela. "Except let the police do their job. I'm sure they'll blow off all the nasty rumors and innuendos soon enough and get on with their job."

"Which is?" said Jekyl.

"Figuring out who *really* did away with poor Jimmy Earl Clayton," responded Carmela. "Or, rather, I should say determine how he died. Since nothing's really been proven yet."

"Carmela," gushed Jekyl Hardy, "you're such a linear thinker. I absolutely *adore* that aspect of your brain. Me, I'm far too right brain. Just not enough balance between the cerebrum and the cerebellum, I guess. Or does it all take place in the cerebral cortex? I can't remember. Anyway, next question. What lucky gent is squiring you to the Marseilles Ball this evening?"

"No one," said Carmela. "I'm not going."

"But, darlin', you have your beauteous costume all figured out!" protested Jekyl.

Carmela grinned. To pass up a Mardi Gras ball was heresy for a Mardi Gras fanatic like Jekyl Hardy.

"Well," blustered Jekyl, "you most definitely *are* going, and don't bother trying to weasel your way out of it. You'll go with me."

"I don't think so—" protested Carmela.

"Mm-mn, case closed," declared Jekyl over her protests. "I'll meet you in the lobby of the Hotel Babbit at eight o'clock sharp. Okay?"

"Okay," sighed Carmela.

"And you *are* wearing that delightful black-and-gold creation, correct?"

Carmela sighed again. "If you say so." She wasn't sure she wanted to go flouncing into one of the biggest Mardi Gras parties of the year with her décolletage in plain sight while her soon-to-be-ex-husband was being speculated on so freely. On the other hand . . . what could she do? Shamus was surely innocent, right?

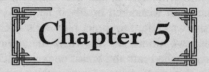

Chapter 5

GRANGER Rathbone paused on the sidewalk outside Memory Mine and narrowed his eyes as he stared in the store's front window. Gazing past his own reflection of a lanky, long-jawed man with an unruly shock of gray brown hair, he could see a young woman standing at the counter. She seemed to be arranging various sheets of paper into some kind of display. Handling them with great care, as though the darn things were terribly fragile or expensive or something.

Granger Rathbone spat on the pavement, ran his rough knuckles across the lower half of his pockmarked face. *Women's stuff.* He snorted to himself. *Frilly, silly, women's stuff.* He glanced at the old-fashioned sign that read *Memory Mine, Scrapbooking Shop.* And underneath in smaller type, *Where Memories Are Made.*

Yeah, right, he thought, *memories.* He had a head full of memories, didn't he? Memories of a childhood spent up on the Saint Louis River. Gettin' the tar whupped out of him by his pa. His ma running off and leaving him and his squalling little sister behind.

Ain't got no time for memories like that, Granger Rathbone told himself. *Or for women who think such things are important.*

Gabby smiled sweetly at the man entering the scrapbooking shop and wondered briefly if he might be lost.

In fact, she was about to direct him to the CC Jazz and Social Club two doors down, when the rather rough-looking man reached into the breast pocket of his rumpled brown sport coat, pulled out a leather wallet, and snapped it open in her face.

"Detective Rathbone here to see Carmela Bertrand," he said with a curl of his lip. "You her?"

"No . . . no, I'm not," stammered Gabby. She was dismayed to see that Detective Rathbone seemed to take great enjoyment in the fact that he'd deliberately flustered her. "Carmela," Gabby called out.

Bent over the craft table in back, Carmela looked up expectantly. In an instant she caught the look of intimidation on Gabby's face, the smug look on the face of the man who had just entered her store. And she knew in a heartbeat that something was up. *Who is this person?* she wondered. *Cop? Private investigator?*

Carmela sauntered to the front counter slowly, taking careful stock of the man who gazed at her with such guarded interest as well as bold-faced arrogance. A cool smile settled across her face as she made up her mind to deal with this better than she'd dealt with Officers Robineau and Reagan last night. "I'm Carmela Bertrand, the owner," she said. "May I help you?"

"Damn right you can," replied the man. "Name's Granger Rathbone. I'm with Homicide. Need to ask you some questions."

"Concerning what?" Carmela said pleasantly. Now that she'd had some time to get used to the idea of Shamus being branded a murder suspect, she wasn't quite as spooked as she had been last evening. Besides, she knew that the charge or rumor or whatever it was, was entirely without basis.

"You know darn well why I'm here," spoke Granger Rathbone. "You husband—"

"Ex-husband," said Carmela.

"I've got it on good authority you're still married to Mr. Shamus Allan Meechum," said Granger Rathbone. "In the eyes of the law that makes him your old man."

"That makes him nobody's old man," Carmela replied breezily. "Case in point, Shamus is a relatively *young* man. Chronologically he's thirty-four. Although, as far as maturity level goes, one might peg him at around sixteen."

There was a titter from the back room. Tandy.

Granger Rathbone narrowed his eyes at Carmela. He'd dealt with smart-ass women like this before. Women you couldn't intimidate, couldn't seem to ruffle. *That's just fine,* he thought, *she'll whistle a different tune when her old man's hauled in and put behind bars and she has to scramble to make bail. She'll be sobbin' her heart out then.*

Granger Rathbone struck a casual pose and pulled out a black leather notebook.

"Shamus much of a drinker?" he asked.

"He likes his bourbon now and then." Carmela paused, managed an innocent smile. "I'll bet you do, too."

"You're just full of answers, aren't you, lady?" snarled Rathbone. "How about drugs. Does your husband do drugs?"

"Hardly," replied Carmela, determined not to let herself be outwardly intimidated by this thug. Gabby, on the other hand, was fairly trembling as she hovered nearby.

"Know if Mr. Meechum ever *deals* drugs?" asked Rathbone.

Carmela let a long beat go by before she said anything. Then she looked carefully down at her watch and gave Granger Rathbone a reproachful look. "Gosh," she said,

"I'd really love to help with this thing, but I've got a scrapbooking class starting in about two minutes."

"We can do this another time," Granger Rathbone said as he fixed her with a hard-eyed gaze.

"Better phone ahead," suggested Carmela with as much sincerity as she could muster. "Things tend to get a little crazy around here." She turned to leave him, then hesitated. "Oh," she said, as though the thought had just popped into her head. "Next time, instead of stalking in here, trying to intimidate everyone in sight, why don't you call Seth Barstow's office first. Perhaps you've heard of his law firm, Leonard, Barstow and Streeter? Well, the thing of it is, Seth is my attorney. And if you have any more questions, I'm sure Seth can arrange a time and proper place when we can all sit down together and talk."

His black notebook snapped closed like an angry alligator as Granger Rathbone leaned forward, his pebbly cheeks flaring with color. "Think you're pretty hot stuff, don't ya, lady? Think you can outsmart me." He shook his head from side to side, curling his lip in disdain. "We'll just see about that." With that, Rathbone stalked out of her store.

"Whew," breathed Gabby after the door had slammed behind him. "I can't believe you handled him the way you did. "You didn't even seem like you were a bit . . . *Carmela?*"

Gabby watched with surprise as Carmela staggered around to the back of the counter and eased herself down onto a wooden stool. Her face was white, and she looked about ready to faint.

"Don't tell me that was all an act," sputtered Gabby, a slow smile beginning to spread across her face.

Carmela bobbed her head, seemed to be having trouble catching her breath.

"Honey . . ." she grasped for Gabby's hand, "I haven't done that much playacting since sixth grade when

I was sadly miscast for the part of Lisle in the *Sound of Music*."

"You mean Seth Barstow *isn't* your attorney?" asked Gabby.

Carmela's face assumed a thoughtful look. "Well, I've certainly *met* the man before. So he could probably *be* my attorney if I paid him a handsome retainer."

Peals of laughter erupted from the back of the room. Baby and Dawn had left an hour ago to attend a luncheon, but Tandy had stuck around.

"Hooray for Carmela," chuckled Tandy as she waved a clenched fist in the air. "That Granger Rathbone is a real rotten egg. He was suspended from the police force last year for roughing up a prisoner he was transporting. I can't imagine how the man ever got his job back. He must have had a stroke of luck and nabbed some poor city official on a drunk driving charge. Applied some not-so-subtle pressure."

"Good lord," said Gabby, "it's beginning to sound like Shamus might really be in trouble."

Carmela nodded her head thoughtfully, and a look of concern stole across her face. "Although I'd probably be the first to proclaim his innocence, it feels like there aren't a lot of people rushing to be in his corner."

Tandy and Gabby exchanged meaningful glances. They were slowly coming to the same conclusion.

"He'll be okay, Carmela, I know he will," Gabby assured her. "You both will."

"I sincerely hope so," said Carmela as the front door to her shop flew open and three of her scrapbooking students eagerly pushed their way in.

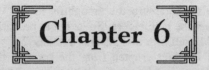

Chapter 6

TUCKED between Richaud's Jazz Club and Toulouse's Live Seafood Bar, the Hotel Babbit wasn't a five star, but it certainly gave an impression of genteel elegance and respectability. To the busloads of tourists who wandered the French Quarter, shooting endless rolls of Kodachrome, the Hotel Babbit was roundly regarded as elegant. Its bright red carpet was appropriately plush, the velvet couches in its lobby, rendered in a sturdy, commercial bastardization of Louis XVI, appeared fairly sumptuous. And palmettos, graceful though slightly dusty, framed the lobby's battered wood reception desk, completing the illusion of a grand hotel. Though it had slipped a bit from grace, the Hotel Babbit was still highly regarded as having one of the best ballrooms.

Jekyl Hardy was five minutes early. In any other hotel in any other city, a man dressed in a red sequined Mephistopheles suit; complete with a tail and carrying a matching pitchfork, would be regarded as highly suspect. In New Orleans it was de rigueur.

Carmela bounded up the stairs of the Hotel Babbit, her black-and-gold dress trailing in bountiful swirls behind her. Costumed as a French courtesan this evening, Carmela's low-cut dress of panne velvet was cinched with a wide-laced corset, and her face was concealed by a gold lamé bird mask with a four-inch beak that Ava Grieux had custom designed for her.

Jekyl Hardy grasped Carmela's hands and kissed her chastely on the cheek. "Careful with that beak, my dear," he warned. "It could be classified as a lethal weapon."

In the Cotillion Ballroom, the Marseilles Ball was in full swing. The ballroom was packed with costumed revelers as a thirty-piece band blared out jazz standards. People danced, cavorted, drank, and screamed in amusement at each other's costumes. Purple, green, and gold bunting was strung across the ceiling in a wonderfully tangled web. Gigantic gold coins, some ten feet across, decorated the walls and served as a historic testament to the various krewes that made Mardi Gras such a delightful spectacle. The Bachus, Proteus, Endemion, Zulu, and Rex krewes were internationally known. These were the big krewes, the high-profile krewes, that had no trouble attracting Hollywood celebrities as their grand marshals. These were the krewes that drew over five million free-spending tourists to the city of New Orleans year after year to partake in the excitement of Mardi Gras.

Ava Grieux came flying across the dance floor toward Carmela and Jekyl. Dressed in an angel costume, complete with wings and a sparkling halo that bobbed provocatively above her head, Ava had a date in tow who was dressed head to toe in a furry costume.

Is he a Wookiee from Star Wars? Carmela wondered. *Or maybe he's just supposed to be an oversized dormouse from* Alice in Wonderland. *It really is a coin toss.*

"I heard you had some trouble at the shop today," Ava said as she grabbed Carmela's arm.

Jekyl Hardy was immediately concerned. His black, greasepaint-enhanced eyebrows shot skyward. "Trouble? Tell us what happened, Carmela? Fess up!"

Carmela rolled her eyes. "It was nothing, really. A detective by the name of Granger Rathbone stopped by to ask a couple questions about Shamus."

"Hey, girl," said Ava, "this is starting to get *serious*." Her halo bobbed wildly. The look on her face said she was clearly concerned.

."No, it's not," protested Carmela. "Because Shamus didn't *do* anything. This is all going to blow over; I guarantee it."

Ava suddenly turned to her escort, the Wookiee-dormouse. "Honey, could you run get us a couple drinks?" Then, remembering her manners, Ava made hasty introductions. "Ricky DeMott, these are my dear friends, Carmela Bertrand and Jekyl Hardy."

There were quick nods of acknowledgment among the group.

"Nice costume," said Jekyl Hardly, running his hand appraisingly down the arm of the Wookie-dormouse's costume. "What is that? Washable acrylic?"

"I think so," said Ricky. "My sister made it. Oh, hey, you're the float guy," he suddenly exclaimed. "The designer who masterminds all those great floats. I recognized you from an article in the paper. Cool. Wait till I tell my friends I met you."

"The drinks, sweetie," Ava reminded him gently.

"Sure thing," said Ricky as he scampered off.

"That Granger Rathbone is a paid thug," said Jekyl, shaking his head. "You watch your step around him," he admonished Carmela. "Tell Shamus to be careful, too. This Jimmy Earl Clayton thing is far from over."

"I haven't really spoken with Shamus in weeks," said Carmela, then suddenly remembered that wasn't true at all. Shamus had called her just this very morning. How strange, she thought, that already their conversation seemed so distant. Just like their marriage.

"The best thing you can do is stay away from him," advised Jekyl. "Until this thing settles down."

"Right," agreed Carmela, wondering if that really was the best thing to do. Then, for her own peace of mind, Carmela decided to put all thoughts of Shamus and Jimmy Earl Clayton out of her head.

Got to concentrate on having a good time, she told herself. *Isn't that why I came tonight? For a little dancing and flirting? Got to get back into circulation. Life goes on . . . or at least I hope it does.*

The band, feeding off the frenzy of the crowd, was dishing up a wild rendition of Professor Longhair's "Go to the Mardi Gras." Carmela danced with a man in a purple Barney costume, was cut in on by a pirate who had a live parrot perched on his shoulder. Then, as she joined a snaking conga dance line, Carmela found herself behind a very brawny man decked out in full Scotsman's tartans, clutching at his exceedingly short kilt.

As interesting as the prospect appeared, she decided it might be more prudent to sit this one out. Time to head for the bar.

Of course the bar was five deep in people. Everyone was waving money in the air, vying for the attention of the two overworked bartenders. All had the same goal, to wrap their hands around a hurricane, mint julep, daiquiri, or even a cosmopolitan.

When Carmela finally jockeyed to the front of the pack, she ordered a soft drink. Weary and warm from the night's revelry, she was, most of all, just plain thirsty.

As Carmela sipped her cola and stuffed a couple dollars in the tip jar, a familiar face caught her eye.

"Dace?" she said, sidling over to the man on her left. "Dace Wilcox?"

A tall, lean man with ginger-colored hair and soft

brown eyes turned his attention toward her. He was dressed in a skeleton costume but had his mask, a black plumed affair, dangling from one arm.

"Yes ma'am?" he said cordially.

Carmela slid her gold mask up. "It's Carmela Bertrand. We were on a Concert in the Parks committee together a couple years ago." She remembered Dace Wilcox as being a conscientious and concerned committee member, one who was zealous in marshaling funds and mindful of dollars being spent.

As recognition dawned, Dace Wilcox flashed her a friendly grin and touched a finger to his forehead in a salute. "Of course. Nice to see you again, Miss Bertrand."

Carmela suddenly realized that Dace probably didn't know she'd been married. Or realize that she was now separated. But, surely, Dace must know Shamus, Carmela decided. Because she was almost certain that Dace Wilcox was also a member of the Pluvius krewe.

"You used to be in the Pluvius krewe, right?" said Carmela.

"Still am," said Dace as he downed the last of his drink.

"Then you must know Shamus Meechum," she said. "He's my—"

Dace fixed his gaze on a point slightly higher than Carmela's head. "No," he said, cutting her off. "Can't say as I do."

"Shamus Meechum of the Crescent City Bank Meechums?" Carmela continued. "Surely you—"

"Nope, sorry," said Dace. His voice was friendly enough, but his eyes slid away, seeking out someone in the crowd.

Carmela had the distinct feeling that Dace Wilcox was definitely not telling the truth. *The man has to know Shamus, right? So what's going on here?* Then she shrugged to herself as Dace melted into the crowd.

Maybe she was wrong. Maybe Dace Wilcox really

didn't know Shamus. No point in browbeating the man. If he said he didn't know Shamus, she ought to take him at face value.

SOME FORTY MINUTES LATER, CARMELA AND Jekyl Hardy were seated at a table in the Praline Queen, a colorful neighborhood restaurant and bar located in Jekyl's beloved Bywater District. Because the Praline Queen was notorious for its jumbo stuffed artichokes, spicy gumbos, and sinfully rich praline pie, it drew customers from all over the city. From the French Quarter, Warehouse District, Garden District, even folks who lived across the river in Metairie.

Tonight was no exception. The open kitchen revealed a frenzied knot of white-coated chefs working at breakneck speed to keep pace with orders. Flames danced above the grill as great slabs of barbecue ribs were slathered with mind-bending sauces and fillets of catfish and skewers of gulf shrimp were plopped on the grill to sizzle and hiss.

Carmela and Jekyl shared a stuffed artichoke, dipping each tender morsel in the zesty lemon and garlic remoulade that accompanied it. Now Carmela was enjoying a bowl of oyster stew while Jekyl dug into a heaping mound of boiled crawfish.

"I'm about ready to go insane," declared Jekyl. "The floats for the Nepthys krewe *still* aren't finished for Saturday night, and I'm supposed to conduct a connoisseurship class that morning. How everything got mishmashed on top of one another *I'll* never know."

Carmela smiled. Jekyl was notorious for taking on ten projects at once, then flipping out from the stress of it all. Then again, there seemed to be a lot of stressed-out folks these days. Didn't everybody have a scrip for Prozac? Wasn't Valium making a big comeback?

"What are you going to cover in your connoisseurship class?" Carmela asked him.

"Oh . . . restorations, fakes and frauds, periods and styles," answered Jekyl. "Same old same old, except for the fact that the ladies still lap it up."

Carmela nodded. Jekyl Hardy had been blessed with an unerring eye for quality and a gift for imparting his knowledge in a nonthreatening, easy-to-digest sound-bite manner. He was expert in discussing oil paintings, old silver, porcelain, and even furniture.

"I take it this is your usual audience?" asked Carmela. Jekyl was wildly popular among the ladies who resided in the immense homes in New Orleans's famed Garden District. Where *she* had lived not that many months ago.

"The usual," agreed Jekyl. "Although most of them have major parties cooking over the next few days, so I don't know how *they're* going to find time, either. But I talked with Ruby Dumaine this afternoon," he said, "and she assured me there's still going to be at least a half-dozen ladies in attendance."

Carmela suddenly perked up her ears. Ruby Dumaine was the wife of Jack Dumaine, the remaining senior partner in Clayton Crown Securities, now that Jimmy Earl Clayton was dead.

"Ruby mentioned that her husband, Jack, is going to deliver the eulogy tomorrow morning at Jimmy Earl's funeral," said Jekyl. He gave a practiced twist of his wrist and snapped the head off another crawfish. "Do *you*, by any chance, have plans to don a black shawl and be in attendance at Jimmy Earl's funeral?" he asked.

Carmela tossed a handful of oyster crackers into her stew. "You know," she mused, "I hadn't really thought about it." Truth be known, she *had* pondered the idea, she just didn't care to admit her rather morbid curiosity to Jekyl.

"For the time being, your life seems to be inexplicably

woven into this Jimmy Earl thing," said Jekyl. "So I figured you'd want to be present for the final disposition." His voice betrayed a somewhat sly tone.

This is the man who advised me to stay under the radar until everything blows over. Oh well, Jekyl likes his fun.

Carmela gazed at Jekyl's purposely bland expression across the table from her. *Attend Jimmy Earl's funeral. Interesting idea.*

Carmela tested the notion in her mind.

The service will be held at the Clayton family crypt in Saint Cyril's Cemetery, of course. Which is the very same cemetery I've been asked to create the scrapbook for. So . . . I could probably finesse my appearance at Jimmy Earl Clayton's memorial service. People wouldn't consider my attendance all that strange.

There was another reason Carmela was suddenly liking this idea quite a bit. Someone had brazenly offed poor Jimmy Earl Clayton the night of his big Mardi Gras parade. And though it was fairly doubtful the culprit had been Shamus, her ex-husband extraordinaire, it surely *had* to be someone fairly close to Jimmy Earl. Didn't it?

Would the culprit, the murderer, dare to show his face at Jimmy Earl's funeral? And if so, will I be able to figure out who it is?

Perhaps the perpetrator of the deadly deed would conduct himself in a highly suspicious manner. Or throw himself on poor Jimmy Earl's coffin out of guilt or remorse. Carmela considered this for a scant moment.

Hardly. Times are tough. And guilty consciences are in exceedingly short supply these days.

Twenty minutes later, Carmela and Jekyl stood in line at the cash register to settle their tab. As she studied the collection of Mardi Gras paraphernalia that hung on the wall behind the cash register, Carmela heard her name called. A long, low, teasing call.

"*Car-mellll-a.*"

She whirled about, looking to see who had spoken. Searching the faces crowded around the various tables, she saw no one gazing in her direction. In fact, everyone seemed immersed in their own conversations or focused intently on chowing down. Frowning slightly, Carmela scanned the crowd again. Nope. Not a soul she recognized.

Turning back to Jekyl Hardy, accepting the couple dollars in change he stuffed in her hand, Carmela once again heard someone call to her.

Only this time it was a teasing, slightly more menacing threat.

"Your old man's gonna be in the paper tomorrow, Carmela."

Jekyl Hardy heard it, too, furrowed his brow. "Let it go," he advised as he took Carmela's elbow and steered her out the door. There was a sudden burst of laughter behind them and a loud hiss just as the door slammed shut.

"Neanderthals," grumped Jekyl.

That's it, Carmela decided. *Pencil me in for that funeral tomorrow. In fact, I'm gonna try to get a front-row seat for Jimmy Earl's big send-off!*

Chapter 7

A jumble of white, sun-bleached aboveground tombs stretched as far as the eye could see. Some were simple rounded tombs that contained a single casket; others were elaborate mausoleums adorned with crosses, statues of saints, and wrought-iron embellishments, built to hold the remains of entire families. One of the strangest features of many of these older, ornate tombs was the one-way trap door built into the floor of the tomb. After a body had laid in state for a decent interval of time, that trap door could be flipped open, and the bones of the deceased could be discreetly disposed down a chute, where they would mingle with all the former relations who'd been buried there.

A block away, at the far end of Saint Cyril's Cemetery, a jazz combo played a mournful tune, while a tight clutch of mourners swayed rhythmically. Such was the business of funerals and burials in New Orleans's old cemeteries.

"Get up here," whispered Tandy. Dressed in a black suit with a vintage black pillbox hat perched atop her tight curls, Tandy had been discreetly worming her way to the front of the group, with Carmela in tow, for the past twenty minutes.

A minister had opened the services for Jimmy Earl with somber prayers and a rousing oratory. Now he had succeeded in coaxing most of the mourners into joining him in a fairly dismal and off-key rendition of *"Nearer My God to Thee,"* the song most noted for having been played by the *Titanic*'s shipboard orchestra as the ill-fated luxury liner headed for the briny depths of the Atlantic.

Carmela tuned out the awful singing and turned her thoughts to the vicious innuendos that had appeared in this morning's *Times-Picayune*.

True to the anonymous heckler's promise of last evening, Shamus had indeed been mentioned.

Not by name, of course. Bufford Maple, the opinionated boor of a columnist who had penned the piece, was much too smart for that. Bufford Maple had been a columnist at the *Picayune* for as long as anyone could remember, although calling him a columnist was putting a pretty glossy spin on things. Rather, Bufford Maple was a nasty viper who liked nothing better than to pontificate, spout off, and launch personal attacks against selected targets.

It had also been suggested more than once that an under-the-table agreement could often be struck with Bufford Maple whereby, for the right amount of money, he would launch an all-out public attack on one's enemy.

When Bufford Maple penned this morning's vitriolic piece, he must have been as elated as a pig in mud.

While not naming names per se, Bufford Maple had managed to insinuate and imply that a certain *"banker turned swamp rat"* had a very nasty bone to pick with a certain *"well-heeled businessman."* Bufford Maple went on to write that this *"cowardly swamp rat"* had plotted and schemed and finally brought about this *"poor busi-nessman's death."*

The rest of the column had been a diatribe about *"swift apprehension"* and *"just punishment."*

Even though Carmela was still hopping mad at Shamus, she had been stung mightily by the nasty innuendos that Bufford Maple had flung. As she glanced about the group of at least a hundred mourners, she wondered if they had all read the article, too. And judging by the pairs of eyes that had flicked across at her, then looked quickly away, she guessed most of them had.

THE OFF-KEY HYMN DREW TO A CONCLUSION, and Jack Dumaine, Jimmy Earl Clayton's business part-ner, proceeded to take his place front and center of the group. Gazing tearfully down at Jimmy Earl's deluxe ma-hogany coffin, Jack Dumaine let fly with his eulogy.

Tuning out Jack Dumaine's quavering voice as it seemed to rise and fall like a politician's speech, Carmela focused her gaze squarely on Jimmy Earl's coffin. With the morning sun glinting off its shined-up facade, it looked a bit like an old Lincoln Continental that had been tricked out with all the options money could buy. Ivory handles, engraved brass name plate, carved geegaws and knobs. She guessed that no expense had been spared for Jimmy Earl's final send-off.

Fixing her gaze on Jack Dumaine, Carmela decided he looked exactly like the exceedingly prosperous business-man that he was. Jack Dumaine's stomach protruded like a dirigible from between the lapels of his sedate black suit coat. His pants seemed to be held up by industrial-strength suspenders. Jack Dumaine was obviously a man who loved New Orleans and indulged freely in its rich bounty. He was a hale-and-hearty good old boy and a world-class gourmand.

Jack's trio of chins wobbled, and his head seesawed like a bobble-head doll as he addressed the group of mourners.

"Jimmy Earl was my best friend," Jack declared with heartfelt zeal, his voice climbing with trembling fervor. Reverently, he placed his chubby right hand over the broad expanse of his chest to emphasize this point. "In the sixteen years we-all were together in business at Clayton Crown, Jack and I might have had ourselves a few rough moments, but we never disagreed on the fine points."

"Like making a shitload of money," Tandy whispered in Carmela's ear. Carmela had to agree with her. Ensconced in huge Garden District mansions, the Claytons and the Dumaines had never seemed to want for anything.

Jack Dumaine continued with his eulogy. "Jimmy Earl was an entrepreneur and a community benefactor," he intoned as he grabbed his lapels and scanned the faces in the crowd. "He was a good father, beloved husband, and a damn fine bass fisherman."

Standing at her husband's side, Ruby Dumaine nodded her punctuation at the tail end of every line Jack Dumaine delivered. Ruby was fifty-something, with a mass of reddish blond curls pulled into a flouncy pompadour atop her head. Poured into a black jersey wrap dress, Ruby didn't look all that bad from a distance. It was only up close and personal that you noticed the slightly wonky eye job.

Easing her digital camera out of her purse, Carmela snapped a couple shots of Jack Dumaine in all his oratorical splendor. Then Carmela aimed her little camera at the crowd that spread out on either side of Jack and clicked off a few more shots. Glancing at the digital counter, she saw that her memory card would easily hold another forty or so shots. Gabby had obviously not taken all that many shots the other night when she borrowed the camera.

As Carmela continued to shoot, ostensibly for a *Funerals Then and Now* section in the Saint Cyril's scrapbook, nobody seemed to notice, since the camera was far smaller in size than her usual Leica. Or better yet, nobody seemed to care.

Of course, funerals in New Orleans were unlike funerals anywhere else. Carmela knew that you could probably haul a Hollywood movie crew in and film the whole shebang for posterity, and nobody would seriously bat an eyelash. Plus, New Orleans funerals were notoriously quirky. Dogs, cats, horses, mistresses, illegitimate children, obscure heirs—you name it—he/she/it had all been in attendance at various New Orleans funerals.

As Carmela continued taking pictures with her digital camera, she scanned the crowd. Mostly Garden District folk, businessmen and their wives. The Taylors, the Coulters, the Reads. Baby was there, too, looking very cool and blond, a little Grace Kellyish, on the arm of her swarthy husband, Del. Two rumpled-looking men who looked like they might be reporters, perhaps sent by Bufford Maple, hung out on the sidelines.

Sitting at the head of the casket, perched on black metal folding chairs, were Rhonda Lee, Jimmy Earl's widow, and her daughter, Shelby.

Carmela's heart especially went out to the girl. Shelby was a beautiful young woman: tall, coltish, with beautiful olive skin and long, tawny blond hair. She was perhaps eighteen at best, a freshman at Tulane. Carmela knew it wasn't easy to lose your father at such a young age. God knows, she'd lost her dad when she was just ten.

A couple days ago, Baby had informed them all that Shelby was one of the finalists for queen of the Pluvius Ball. In light of all that had happened, Carmela wondered if Jimmy Earl's only daughter would still grace the lineup of queen candidates next Tuesday. She thought probably not.

As Carmela continued to gaze at Shelby, Rhonda Lee suddenly shifted her gaze toward Carmela. Rhonda Lee Clayton was short, puffy-faced, with a sleek helmet of brown hair. Hate filled her eyes.

Stung for a moment by the overt hostility she saw there, Carmela quickly lowered her camera and looked away.

Was it possible Rhonda Lee actually *believed* the terrible rumors that seemed to be circulating? That Rhonda Lee actually thought Shamus had been responsible for her husband's death? Carmela sighed. Of course, it was possible. Anything was possible.

SURPRISINGLY, AT THE CONCLUSION OF THE graveside service, Jack Dumaine and his wife Ruby came crunching across the gravel to speak with Carmela and Tandy. Carmela had met the Dumaines over the last couple years at various social and business functions that Shamus had dragged her to. And, of course, they were members of the Pluvius krewe. A somewhat enigmatic couple, they had a peculiar tendency to jump in and finish each other's sentences.

"A lovely tribute," said Tandy, grasping Jack's hand in a goodwill gesture.

"This is the saddest day of my life," declared Jack tearfully. "Jimmy Earl was like . . ." He hesitated.

"Like a brother to him," filled in Ruby Dumaine. "And, don't you know, our dear girls practically grew up together."

Ruby Dumaine was referring to their daughter, Swan, who was standing some twenty feet away, looking morose and talking with Shelby Clayton and several other young women.

"When Jimmy Earl collapsed on that float . . . it was like a member of my family died," said Jack tearfully.

"You were riding on the sea serpent float together?" said Carmela.

Jack nodded sadly, then unfurled a large, white handkerchief, held it to his nose, and blew loudly. "It's a bad business about Shamus," he rumbled solemnly, directing his gaze at Carmela. His eyes, buried in the massive flesh of his face, looked like glinting little pig eyes. Blowing his nose again, hitting yet a higher octave, Jack shook his giant head regretfully. "A real bad business."

"Bad business," echoed Ruby as the two of them slid off into the crowd.

Carmela watched Jack Dumaine lumber off toward the minister and wondered, *What exactly did Jack Dumaine mean by that remark? And whose corner is he in, anyway? Does Jack think Shamus is guilty? Or innocent?*

"I thought I'd find you here," murmured a clipped, slightly menacing voice at Carmela's elbow. "Catch the paper this morning?" Granger Rathbone's eyes glinted like an alley cat who'd just spied a cowering mouse.

"Granger Rathbone," Carmela muttered as she turned to face him. "Tandy, have you met the illustrious Mr. Rathbone?"

Tandy fixed Granger with a hostile gaze. "You were in such a rush yesterday, I'm afraid we didn't have the pleasure of a formal introduction. Such a pity."

Carmela smiled at Tandy. For someone who weighed barely a hundred pounds soaking wet, this gal was certainly blessed with *beaucoup* guts.

"Tell Shamus to call me," snarled Granger as he moved off. "I've got more questions."

"Tell him yourself," snapped Carmela.

Tandy gave Carmela a playful punch on the arm. "You go, girl! Don't let that little dog turd push you around."

Then, when Granger Rathbone was out of earshot, Tandy asked in a somewhat more worried tone of voice,

"Have you talked with Shamus, honey? 'Cause things really *are* getting weird."

"I guess you saw this morning's newspaper?"

"Honey, I guarantee that, right after checking out Jeane Dixon and Dear Abby, *everybody* read Bufford Maple's column. Heck, the darn thing's probably on the Internet by now, whirling around out there in cyberspace."

"It's drivel," said Carmela.

"Of course, it's drivel," said Tandy. "But it's drivel people are starting to pay attention to." She squeezed Carmela's hand, then added, "Girl, you have to *do* something."

Somewhat unnerved by Tandy's words, Carmela turned to gaze toward the crowd that lingered, seemingly reluctant to disperse.

Last night she'd almost convinced herself that the real culprit might show up here today. *Had he? Well, if he had, there'd been no dramatic graveside confession, no bolt of lightning that had shot from the sky and singled him out. There had only been more heavy-handed insinuations against Shamus.*

Are witnesses being interviewed? Carmela wondered. *And if so, who? And, if things continue to go against Shamus, will formal charges be filed?*

Oh lord, thought Carmela. Why couldn't Shamus have kept his size-eleven Thom McCanns parked safely under his desk at the Crescent City Bank? Why couldn't he have gone on doing his mortgage banking thing during the day and plunking his banjo while relaxing on the side portico at night? Better yet, why hadn't their life just gone on and on and on instead of him acting like such a dunce? And why was Shamus suddenly in this terrible fix?

As Carmela and Tandy wound their way through the tangle of tombstones and graves, they could see the very proud Ruby Dumaine dragging her daughter, Swan, over to a cluster of women. Even from forty feet away, they could hear Ruby's high-pitched bray.

"Swan's going to be Pluvius queen this year!" bragged Ruby. "Just look at her, isn't my girl absolutely *gorgeous?*"

Swan, who was indeed very pretty, squirmed uncomfortably under the heavy-handedness of her mother's words.

"This will be a year to remember for all of us," continued Ruby Dumaine. "Swan's official coming out as a New Orleans debutante *and* the beginning of her reign as Pluvius queen. Don't you know, her poppa and I are *soooo* proud."

"Does she know something we don't?" asked Tandy out of the corner of her mouth. "Swan has to get *elected* first, doesn't she?"

Carmela, again wondering whether poor Shelby Clayton had, in fact, formally withdrawn from the queen contest, shook her head in disgust at Ruby Dumaine's braggadocio manner. "Poor girl," she said, "to have such an overbearing momma."

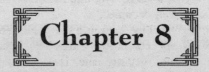

Chapter 8

"HAVE you seen this?" asked Gabby, not long after Carmela returned to the store. She hesitantly held up a copy of the *New Orleans Times-Picayune*.

"Yes," Carmela sighed, "I read it first thing this morning."

"And you *still* went to Jimmy Earl's funeral?" asked Gabby, surprised.

"I'm afraid so. I thought maybe I'd be able to—" Carmela stopped in midsentence. *She'd be able to what? Figure out what really happened? Yeah, right. Lotsa luck, kiddo.*

"I thought I'd shoot some current photos of Saint Cyril's for the scrapbook," Carmela told Gabby instead.

Gabby seemed to accept that as a plausible answer. "Oh, right. I can see where you might want to do that," she said.

Fifty minutes later, Baby pushed her way through the front door of Memory Mine.

"Carmela, honey, I'm *really* sorry I didn't get a chance

to talk to you at Jimmy Earl's funeral. Del wanted to leave immediately so he could get back to his office." Del was a hotshot attorney.

Carmela waved a hand. "Not a problem. As it was, my time was fairly well occupied."

Baby blinked her blue eyes in a quizzical gesture.

"Oh my, yes," continued Carmela. "Fending off Granger Rathbone, getting hate looks from Rhonda Lee . . ."

"Say, Rhonda Lee *was* in a fairly foul mood, wasn't she?" gushed Baby as she shifted her scrapbooking bag off her shoulder to the front counter. "Of course, the poor woman was burying her husband. I suppose you wouldn't classify that as a major social event where you were obligated to appear totally hidebound and *proper*."

"Ruby Dumaine would have," said Tandy as the front door closed behind her and she hastened to join in the conversation. "She was all gussied up, with her hair in those weird little wiener rolls."

Gabby put a hand to her face and laughed, despite herself. "Oh no!"

"My gosh," said Baby, "did you get a load of that wrap dress Ruby was wearing! Did that look go out in the seventies, or did I miss something?"

"Maybe she just dresses vintage," suggested Gabby. "There are lots of stores where you can get stuff like that today."

"Vintage shmintage," hooted Tandy, "Ruby just pulled it from the back of her closet. That old gal is so tight with her money she doesn't throw a thing away!" This produced absolute howls from the women, including Gabby, who normally refrained from gossiping and cracking jokes at the expense of others.

"Say now," said Baby, delicately wiping tears from her eyes. "Carmela mentioned something last week about making keepsake boxes. What say we press her into action and have her deliver a quick lesson?"

"Carmela?" said Tandy eagerly. "Would you?"

Carmela nodded. *Why not? The store isn't particularly busy today. My two best customers are here. And keepsake boxes really are a terrific project.*

"Say," said Tandy suddenly. "You're open tomorrow, right?"

"Right," said Carmela, reaching under the counter for her stash of brown kraft paper boxes.

"Well, CeCe Goodwin is planning to stop by," said Tandy.

"For heaven's sake," exclaimed Baby as they all walked back to the craft table. "You don't mean Darwin's sister-in-law, do you?"

"The one who's a nurse?" asked Gabby, suddenly interested.

Tandy nodded. "Yup. CeCe's off for the rest of the week now, and she wants to work on some scrapbook pages. Remember, Carmela, CeCe was in a few months ago?"

"She worked on her vacation pictures," said Carmela as she set an array of small cardboard boxes, some square, some round, and some octagonal, in the middle of the table. "From when she went to Saint Barth. That's great, it'll be nice to have her back again.

And nice to perhaps get a firsthand account of Jimmy Earl's demise, Carmela thought to herself. For CeCe, who was a nurse at Saint Ignatius Hospital, had been on duty the night Jimmy Earl had been lifted down from his float and rushed to the emergency room.

"Okay," said Carmela, holding up one of the cardboard boxes, "they're rather lowly looking boxes right now, but once you get going, I guarantee they'll be reincarnated in some very marvelous ways. Gabby, if you could get my plastic box . . . the one filled with rubber stamps and stamp pads . . ."

"Sure thing," said Gabby, hopping up.

"And a few sheets of pale yellow parchment paper," added Carmela. "I'll grab a couple bottles of paint . . . let's see, probably the gold, the bronze, and the almond . . . and some brushes."

"I love this already," declared Baby as Gabby and Carmela pulled craft supplies out of the various cabinets and scattered them in the middle of the table.

"Start with your sheet of parchment paper," instructed Carmela. "Then use one of these stiff brushes to stipple on a couple layers of paint. You can work light to dark or dark to light, it doesn't matter, but strive for a nice *aged* look. Think of how the gilt frame on an antique mirror looks. Or maybe an old hand-painted music box. Then, once you've built up your layers of color and your ink has dried, you'll start rubber stamping some of these flower motifs." Carmela held up a tray that held a selection of rubber stamps. "Be sure to trade off on different floral designs, though, and vary the sizes. Use black ink or sepia for stamping the flower outlines." Carmela placed the rubber stamps in the center of the table. "Once your flowers are stamped on in a pattern you like, we'll color them in using varying hues of yellow, gold, and bronze. That will give your sheet an amazing variety of gold tones and mottled hues."

"This is great!" declared Tandy as she grabbed a brush, gingerly dabbed it into one of the dishes of paint Gabby had poured out, then began carefully stippling her parchment.

"Once you get your sheet of parchment painted and stamped exactly the way you want it," continued Carmela, "you'll decoupage that sheet onto your cardboard box. From there, it's simply a matter of adding extra touches."

"Like what kind of touches?" asked Gabby, fascinated by this new dimension to crafting.

"Charms threaded on gauzy ribbons, Roman numerals, even tiny photos," said Carmela. "You could even add a string of antique beads, little gold keys, old coins, you name it."

For the next twenty minutes, heads were bent diligently over their sheets of parchment, as Baby, Tandy, and Gabby transformed their paper into gilded sheets that carried an old world, hand-rubbed look.

As they worked, Carmela gazed around her shop happily. *This is what it's all about,* she decided. *Everyone absorbed by the activity of their craft, excited over creating something that's both beautiful and one of a kind.*

And, since the women were all working diligently on their keepsake boxes, Carmela decided this was the perfect time to finish up the place cards she'd begun for the Claiborne Club.

The Claiborne Club was a private club over on Esplanade Avenue that had been in existence since the mid-1800s. Housed in an Italianate mansion with Greek columns, stained-glass windows, and dark woodwork, and surrounded by an ornate wrought-iron fence, the Claiborne Club had once been the cloistered sanctuary of New Orleans's power elite. It was where men had finalized business deals over lunch, smoked cigars till the air turned blue and, in general, gotten away from it all. As a final testament to an earlier, male-dominated era, brass spittoons had ringed the Claiborne Club's mahogany bar.

But that had all changed. In the mid-'70s, the businessmen's wives decided to claim it as their own. Out went the old mahogany bar and the brass spittoons that had ringed it; in came a silver tea service, Spode dinnerware, and Chippendale furniture. Bathrooms were enlarged, urinals yanked out of the walls, and counter space and pink lightbulbs installed.

A few weeks ago, Alyse Eskew, the Claiborne Club's event coordinator, had asked Carmela to create a couple dozen place cards for a special brunch that was being held at the Claiborne Club on Lundi Gras, this coming Monday.

For these place cards, Carmela had, in turn, asked Ava Grieux to design a plaster mold of a miniature carnival mask. Once that mold had hardened, Carmela had soaked two dozen sheets of thick, handmade paper in water, then pressed each sheet over the mold to create an individual paper mask. When each sheet of paper had dried and formed in the exact shape of the mask mold, Carmela had trimmed and gently rounded the bottom part of each paper mask. Top edges were cut and crimped to create the look of cascading hair.

Now, as Carmela sat at the craft table surrounded by Baby, Tandy, and Gabby, she took a soft piece of cloth, dipped it into a puddle of purple pearlescent paint, and dabbed it gently across the cheeks of each paper mask. She repeated that process using green paint for the hair and luminous bronze paint over the eyes and nose. After a good hour of painting, Carmela had two dozen colorful, gilded mask faces. Once the paint was dry, she would attach a purple tassel to the right side of the mask and a gold name tag strung on tiny pearls to the other side.

"My gosh, Carmela," said Tandy as she squinted over her glasses. "Those little masks are wonderful! I can't believe all the crafts that seem to spin off from scrapbooking and your collection of wonderful papers!"

Tandy was right. Scrapbooking was only the tip of the iceberg. The same techniques used for scrapbooking could be employed to create beautiful journals as well as family history books. And the fabulous arsenal of paper she had amassed was perfect for creating invitations, tags, cards, and even picture frames. Likewise, the rubber stamps the ladies were using to emboss their keepsake boxes could just as easily be creatively employed to decorate scrapbook pages.

Laying in a more substantial supply of rubber stamps and inks would probably be her next big investment, Carmela had decided. Why, you could do incredible things using rubber stamps! You could even use them to apply the most marvelous designs to flowerpots, jars, velvet pillows, and even evening bags!

IT WAS QUARTER TO ONE, AND NOBODY WAS showing signs of quitting or even a slowdown in enthusiasm. So Gabby was tasked with running down the block to the Orleans Market to bring back a sack full of po'boys and a couple pints of coleslaw.

Po'boys were the quintessential New Orleans sandwich. They usually consisted of a long French roll stuffed with fried shrimp, fried oysters, or meatballs. Of course, po'boys could also veer toward being highly creative, with fillings of crab, roast beef, deli cheeses, or ham, usually slathered with Creole mustard or *mynaz*, which is what everyone in New Orleans called mayonnaise.

"Byrle!" called Tandy, who was in the middle of biting into her very squishy po'boy sandwich. "You made it!"

Byrle Coopersmith, whose first experience at Memory Mine had been this past Tuesday, came hurtling toward the craft table.

"Do you think I could get out of my house today?" Byrle exclaimed loudly. Then, without waiting for an answer, declared, "Of course not. The Wicked Witch of the West called to request a recipe for pickled okra that I *know* I've already given her a zillion times."

"Who's the Wicked Witch of the West?" asked Gabby.

"Zelda Coopersmith," answered Tandy. "Byrle's mother-in-law and queen bee of the New Orleans Garden Club." Tandy paused, an impish grin dancing on her face.

"I prefer to address *my* mother-in-law as Mum-zilla."

"And my kids . . ." continued Byrle as she shook her head in mock despair. "Sometimes I want to string the little darlings up by their thumbs." Byrle swiveled her head and flashed a quick smile at Carmela, who was quietly listening as she worked. "Hello again," said Byrle pleasantly. "Could you please tell me what those delightful little masks are all about?"

"Carmela's doing place cards for a luncheon at the Claiborne Club," volunteered Tandy. "Aren't they adorable?"

"Too cute," said Byrle as she hoisted a floral duffel bag into a clear spot on the craft table. "And look at those little boxes. What do you call those?"

"Keepsake boxes," said Baby. "Don't you just love them?"

"I do," declared Byrle. "Gonna have to make me one of those, once I finish up my scrapbook."

Carmela smiled over at Byrle. "Before you get started, can I interest you in half a sandwich? We've got lots."

Byrle waved a hand. "Thanks, but I just choked down a candy bar on my way over."

"A woman after my own heart," murmured Baby, who was notorious for her passion for chocolate and her firm belief that chocolate should definitely be acknowledged as one of the four major food groups.

CARMELA TOUCHED THE TIP OF HER INDEX FINger to the face on one of the masks. It came away clean, which meant the paint had dried.

Good, decided Carmela. *While Byrle works on her scrapbook and Tandy, Baby, and Gabby finish their keepsake boxes, I'll letter names onto these tags to finish them off.*

She pulled out the luncheon list Alyse had faxed her a

couple weeks ago, counted the names again just to make sure, then laid out two dozen gold tags. With a ruler and a pen filled with special disappearing ink, Carmela drew a quick guideline across the lower length of each tag. Then, using a calligraphy pen, she meticulously hand-lettered each name onto the tag. By the time Carmela finished hand-lettering the final name, the guidelines she'd drawn on the first few tags had begun to disappear. Gradually, all the lines would disappear. Using this disappearing ink was a technique Carmela often employed in scrapbooking. It was perfect when you wanted to add a bit of text under a picture or write a poem or fun phrase on a page.

Next, Carmela dabbed a cloth in gold paint, then buffed the gold around the edges of each tag to give it a soft, rich look. Then she attached each of the finished name tags to the finished masks. Leaning back, she admired her handiwork.

"Those are spectacular," commented Byrle.

"I wish I would've asked you to do the invitations for my party," lamented Baby. "Then they really would've been special."

Baby and her husband, Del, were having their traditional Mardi Gras party this Saturday night at their large Garden District home. This year Baby had mailed out invitations in little silver picture frames, which were just as spectacular in their own right.

Tandy stood up to stretch. Her keepsake box was looking good, she decided. That brass dragonfly charm she'd added to the top of it looked really fun. Now she was debating about adding a ribbon edging around the bottom of the box. It had definitely progressed from a little box made of kraft paper to something that looked like a gilded treasure from the turn of the century. "My gosh," Tandy exclaimed, suddenly glancing at her watch. "It's almost three o'clock. We've been at this for *hours*."

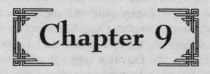

Chapter 9

THE infamous streetcar named *Desire* had been retired way back in 1948. And, while the Regional Transit Authority has memorialized the name by emblazoning it on a city bus that dutifully chugged along New Orleans city streets, something seemed forever lost in the translation.

But the St. Charles Avenue streetcar was still very much alive and operating.

Hopping on at Canal Street and Carondolet in the French Quarter, a rider could travel on the old-fashioned trolley through some of New Orleans's most historic and picturesque neighborhoods for the bargain price of one dollar each way.

Rather than pull her vintage Caddy, Samantha, out of her carefully guarded parking space, Carmela had opted to pack up her finished place cards and ride the trolley to the Claiborne Club to deliver her handiwork.

Bells clanged, metal wheels clicked steadily, and passengers shouted with glee as the old green trolley zoomed down St. Charles Avenue past LaFayette Square, around Lee Circle, and through the bustling CBD, or central business district.

As the trolley approached the fashionable Garden District, noses were suddenly pressed to windows, the better to catch a glimpse of the elegant old mansions, stately live oaks draped in Spanish moss, and Gothic-looking wrought-iron fences. For here was antebellum Louisiana at its finest. Novelist Truman Capote and French Impressionist Edgar Degas had both called the Garden District home for a short while. Jefferson Davis, president of the Confederate States of America, had died here. And though many of the old homes now exuded a patina of age, they were still quite spectacular.

Carefully gathering up her package, Carmela hopped off the trolley at Fourth Street and walked a block over to Prytania. As she strode down Prytania, just blocks from where she had lived not so long ago with Shamus, she could see a spill of women on the steps of the Claiborne Club. Probably, they'd just emerged from one of their afternoon teas and were hanging around to chitchat and speculate whose daughter or granddaughter would be chosen as reigning queen this year by the various Mardi Gras krewes.

As she approached the front door, the gossip and chatter suddenly died out, and Carmela found herself edging her way past a half-dozen women who stood on the front steps eyeing her cautiously.

"Afternoon," she said, smiling and nodding, determined to maintain her poise.

"Afternoon," came cool replies back as heads nodded imperceptibly.

Good lord, thought Carmela as she pushed her way through the ornately carved doors of the old mansion into what was now the lobby and reception area. *What's going on here? The sins, or in this case, alleged sins, of the husband are suddenly (and rather rudely!) being heaped on the head of the soon-to-be ex-wife? Talk about jumping to conclusions and being utterly unfair.*

"Hey there, Carmela," called Alyse Eskew as she spotted Carmela from her office. "I was just about ready to take off."

Carmela walked into Alyse's office, set her box down on top of Alyse's rather disorganized-looking desk. "Special delivery," she said.

"You finished the place cards!" exclaimed Alyse. "Ooh, I can't wait to take a peek." She popped up from her chair and wrestled the top off the box. Then, upon seeing the finished place cards, Alyse's face lit up with joy. "Oh, my gosh," she marveled. Then, carefully lifting one of the masks out, she cradled it in her hand. "These are beautiful," she crooned. "You've absolutely outdone yourself, Carmela. I know everyone is going to be extremely pleased with these. In fact, I'd say they're probably going to be viewed as Mardi Gras collectibles."

"Great," said Carmela, pleased at the thought. "It was a fun project to do."

Alyse grabbed the box and moved it over to an equally crowded credenza that sat against a wall in her office. "I'm going to put these over here for safekeeping, since we don't need them until next Tuesday."

"I take it they're going to be used for a luncheon?"

"That's right," said Alyse. Her thin shoulders rose in a shrug; her face assumed a harried look. "And I don't mind saying we've been absolutely *inundated* lately. We're catering luncheons, morning cream teas, afternoon high teas, receptions, you name it. It seems that the wives and daughters of almost every Mardi Gras krewe want to hold some special event. Of course, most of the events have to do with queen candidates and such." Alyse focused weary eyes on Carmela. "And since we're smack-dab in the middle of Mardi Gras, there doesn't even seem time to breathe. But I imagine you know what that's like," said Alyse. "Your shop must be busy, too."

"Fairly busy," said Carmela. "Although the brunt of our business will come right *after* Mardi Gras, when people are most eager to incorporate their recent photos and mementos into scrapbooks."

"Good for you," said Alyse as she walked Carmela out.

Gazing about at the lovely interior of the Claiborne Club, Carmela remarked casually, "You know, I've been asked to join the Claiborne Club a number of times. Next time around, I think I just might seriously consider it."

The smile froze on Alyse's face.

Oh, no, thought Carmela. *Not you, too.* "Is there a problem?" Carmela asked innocently.

Alyse fumbled to cover her faux pas. "It's just that . . . well, the club is not actually *accepting* new members at the moment. And you understand, of course, that if one is fortunate enough to be nominated, that nomination has to be *seconded* by at least three long-standing members. . . ."

"Of course," said Carmela. Looking down, she saw that her hand was gripping the doorknob so hard her knuckles had turned white. "I understand completely."

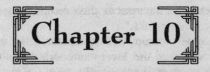

Chapter 10

MILD temperatures and a mass of warm air billowing up from the Gulf of Mexico had rushed smack-dab into a degenerating yet static cool front. And now fog, a vaporous haze that cast a scrim over the entire French Quarter and put everything into soft focus, had seeped in. In this strange atmosphere flickering gas lamps looked even more romantic. Old weathered wooden buildings, painted shades of bottle green and indigo blue like so many Caribbean cottages, took on a misty feel. Curlicued wrought-iron balustrades that topped the second stories of so many French Quarter buildings virtually disappeared. Even the clip-clop of the horse's hooves that pulled the jitneys filled with tourists down Bourbon Street sounded muffled tonight. Redolent with atmosphere, the area suddenly felt very much like the Vieux Carré, or French Quarter, of a century ago.

As Carmela turned down the arched walkway that led to her courtyard apartment, she could hear Boo's insistent, high-pitched bark.

"What's going on?" she asked the little dog as she stuck her key in the rusty old gate that cordoned her courtyard off from the walkway.

Boo's inquisitive little shar-pei face pushed up at her. Carmela could see a torrent of shredded paper in the dog's wake.

At the same moment Carmela entered her courtyard, Ava Grieux peeked out the French double doors at the back of her voodoo shop and gestured at Carmela through the glass. Holding up one finger, she mouthed, *Be right there.* Then, moments later, Ava shut off her shop lights and let herself out the back door.

"How long has she been outside?" Carmela asked, surveying the damage.

"I let her out maybe ten minutes ago," said Ava. "Fifteen at the most." She grinned and shook her head at Boo. "Amazing, isn't it? You'd swear a team from the FBI had swooped in here and gone through your garbage."

"Maybe they did," said Carmela. "Or at least a few spies from the New Orleans Police Department."

"Uh-oh," said Ava, "have you been having problems with Granger Rathbone again?"

"You might call it that," replied Carmela. "The little slug accosted me at Jimmy Earl Clayton's funeral this morning."

Ava fixed Carmela with a level stare. "You showed your sweet little innocent face at Jimmy Earl's final send-off? Girl, you are seriously endowed with chutzpah."

Carmela tried to gather up the worst of the shredded paper while Boo followed behind her at a safe distance. The little dog was looking decidedly guilty. A shred of green plastic clung to her lower lip, snippets of newspaper were caught between her toes.

"That little dog works so fast I bet she could get a job shredding documents at a Swiss bank," volunteered Ava, determined to cheer Carmela up.

Carmela didn't answer.

"Look," said Ava, snatching up some of the shredded paper, "I think Boo might have even torn up Bufford Maple's column." Ava put her hand atop Boo's furry brow and petted her gently. "Good girl, you still love your daddy lots, don't you?"

"Don't," Carmela warned.

"Carmela," said Ava, finally, "you need to seriously chill out. Stay home, put your feet up, have a glass of wine. *Good* wine. Maybe even get a little snockered if you feel like it. And try to forget about all this stuff, because it's not worth worrying your head over. You know as well as I do that excessive worry only leads to crow's-feet. And you are far too young to begin a costly and somewhat tedious regimen of Botox or laser resurfacing."

"Ava," said Carmela, turning to face her. "I'm at the point where I'm not so sure Shamus is innocent anymore." There was a note of desperation in her voice. "I want to *believe* he is, but there is some very negative energy swirling around."

"Mn-hm," agreed Ava. "That there is. And you are certainly in need of a walloping dose of *gris gris*." *Gris gris* was the term for good luck. "But I don't think white candles and herbs in velvet bags are gonna do it, *chérie*."

"Neither do I," said Carmela. She paused dejectedly and thought for a moment. "Ava, you know as well as I do that Shamus is hotheaded as all get out. And he was seen arguing with Jimmy Earl Clayton. Seen, apparently, by a lot of people. What would that suggest to you?"

"That Shamus is hotheaded and ill-tempered?" said Ava. She sauntered over to the trash can, lifted the lid, and stuffed a glut of papers inside. "No surprises there. You *knew* all that when you married the man, right? Now what you *really* got to figure out is *why* somebody wanted Jimmy Earl Clayton out of the way. You've got to look for motive." Ava paused. "Did Shamus have motive?"

Carmela gave serious consideration to Ava's question. "I really don't think so."

Ava threw her hands in the air. "There you go. Then he's probably innocent."

"Right," said Carmela, grabbing Boo's collar and giving her a tug. "But who's the nasty fruitcake who did away with Jimmy Earl?"

"That, my dear," said Ava, "is the sixty-four-thousand-dollar question."

ONE OF THE MOST POPULAR THEORIES HOLDS that Jambalaya is directly descended from the rice dish, *paella*, which was brought to New Orleans by the Spanish. Over the years, Cajuns, Creoles, African Americans, Haitians, French, and just about everyone else in and around New Orleans fell in love with and adopted that steamy, spicy rice dish. They improved it, fiddled with it, and created endless varieties of rice until it finally evolved into the unique delta staple that's known today as jambalaya.

As a rule, jambalaya contains a savory mixture of andouille sausage, crawfish, shrimp, and chicken. But jambalaya can actually be made from any combination of the aforementioned ingredients. What's *really* indispensable, of course, are spices. Tabasco sauce, pepper, garlic, fresh parsley, thyme, and chili powder are *de rigueur*, with liberal amounts of onions and bell peppers tossed in as well.

For the last forty minutes Carmela had been dancing around her kitchen, chopping, blanching, peeling, coring, seeding, and dicing. She was bound and determined to give her mind a rest from the debacle of Jimmy Earl Clayton's murder and the nasty accusations that seemed to be piling up against Shamus. Cooking seemed as good a refuge as any.

Now she was ready to simmer most of her ingredients atop the stove in a large pan for an hour or so. Then, once everything was tender and aromatic, she'd toss in the sea-food and sausage and finish the whole dish off for another thirty minutes. And, per her momma's stern advice, she would scrupulously avoid *stirring* the rice dish toward the end of the cooking process so it for sure wouldn't lump up.

As the big blue enamel kettle hissed and burped atop the stove, Carmela *did* help herself to a glass of wine. She yanked the cork from a nice crisp bottle of Chardonnay she'd lifted from Shamus's private stash before she left.

Grasping her glass of wine, Carmela poured out a cup of dry dog food for Boo, topped it with a dollop of cottage cheese, then finally settled into her wicker easy chair. Even though she'd vowed not to let herself get over-wrought about this whole mess, she found her thoughts once again turning toward the man who had once made her life seem joyful and rich, then had haphazardly turned everything ass over teakettle: Shamus Allan Meechum.

Good lord but the man was maddening! And to skip out on her as he had. What had been his plan, anyway? Keep your fingers crossed behind your back when you mumble the old marriage vows, then hit the fast forward button? Hold everything, whatever happened to the pause button?

Maybe she should be glad Shamus was up to his arm-pits in trouble. Glad he was getting some form of come-uppance for his reckless ways.

Am I glad?

No, not really.

And did she honestly believe that Shamus was involved in Jimmy Earl Clayton's demise? Well, she'd be the first to admit it didn't look good. Shamus *did* have a famously hot temper, that was for sure. And certain events in his life *had* proved that Shamus wasn't always a colossally clear-headed thinker or was immune from acting the fool.

There had been that silly business about stashing a goat in the dean's office when he was a senior at Tulane. In addition to consuming a perfectly good leather couch, the goat had committed a nasty indiscretion on the dean's Aubusson carpet. Besides rating a couple inches in the newspaper, that goat incident had almost kept Shamus from being admitted to graduate school. But then his family had stepped in. God forbid the pride of the Meechum clan didn't continue on and earn his MBA.

There had also been some problem with a belly dancer from Meterie that Shamus had hired for Joe Bud Kerney's bachelor party. Besides her penchant for Casbah-style dancing, Miss Meterie also had a nasty little habit of picking pockets. So, while she'd been charming her audience with the dance of the seven veils, she'd also been pocketing Rolexes and pinching Diners Club cards.

Shamus had also been involved in something a few months ago, just before he'd walked out on her. Carmela recalled hearing Shamus on the telephone, angry and insistent, telling Seth Barstow, one of Crescent City Bank's corporate lawyers, to *handle it. It* being something that had to do with construction loans and land zoning. She'd asked Shamus what the heck was going on, but he'd never made her privy to any of the details. Again, his family had swooped in and supposedly taken care of things. The big fix, as he always called it.

Will they be able to fix things this time? Carmela wondered.

That would remain to be seen.

THUMBING THROUGH A CATALOG OF RUBBER stamp art, enjoying her steaming bowl of jambalaya, Carmela had finally been able to calm down. In fact, she was determined to look ahead and plan for the future, especially when it came to her little store, Memory Mine. She was particularly excited by the variety of decorative rubber stamps that were available: fanciful stamps depicting trailing vines, elegant picture frames, fans, filmy summer dresses blowing on hangers, tiny ballet slippers, filigree designs, and teacups.

All would lend delightful extra touches to wedding and anniversary scrapbooks and would also be perfect should her customers decide to create invitations for engagement parties, baby showers, and such.

Just as Carmela was imagining how a pair of doves would work on a sheet of soft blue-flecked paper with a deckled edge, the phone rang.

She kicked the footstool out of the way, hoping for a telemarketer to take her excess energy out on.

"Carmela," came a rough purr.

Oh shit. It's Shamus.

"Where are you?" asked Carmela.

"Can't say, darlin'."

"You mean you *can't* say because you've somehow lost your memory and are wandering around the parishes of Louisiana in a delirium, or you *won't* say?"

There was quiet laughter. "Your phone could be tapped."

Darn Shamus, Carmela thought to herself, *why does he have to go and act all spooky and mysterious? Like he's playing Mission Impossible or something.*

"This isn't a game, Shamus. And my phone isn't tapped. Where are you?"

"Why do you want to know?"

"Why?" said Carmela, feeling her blood pressure begin to inch up. "Because I just won the lottery, Shamus. A hundred million dollars. And I want to give you half. *Helloooo.* Why do you *think* I want to know?" Carmela hissed. "Because last time I looked, I was still your *wife,* that's why. Even though half of my queen-sized bed is decidedly unoccupied." She paused. "And because, Shamus, whether you want to admit it or not, you're in deep doo-doo."

"I know, darlin', that's why I called. I don't want you to worry."

"Worry?" said Carmela. She suddenly shifted the tone of her voice. "Why would I worry?"

"Because you worry about everything," laughed Shamus.

"I do not," said Carmela, indignant now.

"Of course you do. You used to worry about the baby birds that fell out of their nests in the oak tree out back. I came home once and you were using this teeny tiny little eyedropper to—"

"That's different," said Carmela. "Those were creatures."

"Listen, honey," said Shamus. "If you need to get in touch with me, you just get a message to a guy named Ned Toler. He owns a boat place out in the Barataria Bayou, in a little village called Baptiste Creek. If you bring him a six-pack of Dixie Beer, he'll know it's really you."

"Where are you going to be?" asked Carmela.

"Around," said Shamus. "But don't worry." There was a sharp *click*, and the line went dead.

Damn. He hung up on me again.

Sprinting across the room, Carmela grabbed for her purse, then threw herself back in her easy chair. She dug for her address book, fumbled for the phone number of his family's camp house, then punched the number into the phone, determined to call him back, *finish* this conversation once and for all.

But the phone out there just rang and rang. She could picture it, an old black enamel wall phone, hanging on the wooden wall of the two-room camp house that sat on stilts above sluggish brown green water.

Probably Shamus wasn't staying there anymore, Carmela decided.

Then where is he? And why has he gone into hiding?
Because he's guilty?
Oh please. Say it ain't so.

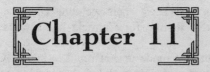

Chapter 11

GLORY Meechum was a woman who still put a great deal of faith in girdles. Nice, durable, reinforced panty girdles designed to smooth out unsightly blips and bulges and carefully encase both thighs.

Glory Meechum also had a penchant for floral-print dresses. Not demure daisies or elegant roses but big, splotchy prints of indeterminate floral and fauna origin. Certainly not as nature had intended.

When Carmela looked out the window Friday morning and saw Glory Meechum steamrolling down Governor Nicholls Street, headed straight for Memory Mine, her first thought was that Shamus's older sister looked like an overstuffed parlor chair.

Then the door flew open, and Glory Meechum exploded inward. Plunking her sturdy black leather Queen-of-England-style purse on the front counter, Glory planted chubby hands on Lycra-encased hips.

"You've got to help me!" she wailed loudly at Carmela. Keenly aware that both Baby and Tandy were sitting at the back table and that Gabby was close by in the storeroom, Carmela willed herself to stifle any unseemly urge to giggle. The idea of Glory Meechum coming to *her* for help was over-the-top ridiculous. Glory had barely even been present at their wedding ceremony and her thinly veiled dislike for Carmela had always hung between them.

Carmela also made up her mind to handle Glory with a fair amount of decorum and try her very best to forestall any shouting match that might threaten to erupt. On Glory's part, not hers.

"Glory, what's wrong?" Carmela asked with as much civility as she could muster.

Glory fixed beady, bright eyes on Carmela. "That nasty little Granger Rathbone came looking for Shamus yesterday. Poking his nose into things over at the house."

The *house* Glory was referring to was one of three elegant manses in the Garden District that were owned by the Meechum family. According to the Meechum family's whims, these houses were allowed to be occupied by whomever was most recently married in the family or needed a place to live. Not necessarily in that order and certainly not a family dictum that had ever applied to Carmela.

"Well, have you seen him?" Glory demanded.

Carmela shook her head regretfully. "No. Sorry."

"Have you *talked* to him?"

Carmela hesitated. "No," she said finally. *If Shamus wants to talk to his sister, he'll call her, right?*

Glory Meechum threw her hands up in the air, exhaled a gush of air through her nostrils. Her sigh emerged as a distinct snort. "Then, where in heaven's name *is* he?" Glory demanded.

"Glory, I don't know," said Carmela. "Shamus left me, remember?"

Glory Meechum flashed Carmela an exasperated look,

a look that said *Oh, give me a break.* "Yes, yes, of course," said Glory hastily, "but I thought for sure you two would keep *in touch.* That your little spat would eventually blow over."

If you thought we just had a little spat, then why was I asked to vacate the house?

But Carmela held her tongue. She simply replied, "Sorry I can't help you, Glory." *Gosh,* she thought, *I wish my momma hadn't instilled so much civility in me. This really could have been fun. Sport, actually.*

There was a scrape of chair legs against the wooden floor as Tandy slid her chair back a few inches, jockeying for a better position from which to observe Glory Meechum's rantings.

"Don't get me wrong," thundered Glory as she snatched up her purse and hung it possesively in the crook of her hefty arm. "It's not Granger Rathbone who concerns me. He's not nearly smart enough. What worries me is who Granger might be working for." With that, Glory Meechum spun on her sensible low heels and darted out the door.

"Who was *that?*" asked Gabby. She emerged from the storeroom with an armful of paper and a startled look on her normally placid face.

"That, my dear girl, was Glory Meechum, Shamus's big sister," answered Tandy, obviously relishing the heated exchange she'd just witnessed. "Isn't she a doozy? The old gal really fancies herself the matriarch of the family."

Gabby put a hand to her heart. "I don't mind telling you, that lady frightened me to death. I found the stencils and paisley paper I was looking for five minutes ago, but I was afraid to come out. I thought she might take off on *me!*"

Baby waved a manicured hand dismissively. "Glory barks like a rabid Rottweiler, but I doubt there's much real bite in her." Baby, who owned four Catahoula hounds, adored making dog analogies. There had even been Mardi Gras queen candidates who, over the years, had been referenced as poodles, poms, and pugs.

"Here's that picture frame stencil you wanted," said Gabby, passing the stencil, along with a stack of mauve cardstock, to Baby.

"Thank you, dear," said Baby, who was bound and determined to finish off her daughter's album of wedding reception pictures with a real flourish.

"If you slide the stencil right to the edge," suggested Gabby, "I think you can cut two frames from one—" The ringing of the telephone interrupted her.

"Memory Mine," answered Gabby as she snatched up the phone. Listening for a second, she nodded. "Yes, she's here. Hang on, please." Gabby punched the hold button, then turned toward Carmela. "It's for you. Something about your lease?"

"My gosh, don't tell me you've been here a full year already!" exclaimed Tandy. "*Tempus fugit,* how time *does* fly."

Carmela picked up the phone. "This is Carmela."

The crackly voice of Hop Pennington from Trident Property Management greeted her on the other end of the line.

"Carmela," he said cheerfully. "I might have a spot of bad news for you. That nice fellow who has the space next door to you . . ."

"The art dealer?" said Carmela. "Bartholomew Hayward?" Barty Hayward was a self-styled antique impresario with delusions of grandeur. Carmela saw the delivery trucks pulling up at the back door of Barty Hayward's store. She knew most of his antiques were really replicas and reproductions, and that Barty carefully and surreptitiously aged and distressed them in the workroom behind his store.

"That's the fellow," chirped Hop. "He might need your space."

Hold everything, thought Carmela, *just what the heck is going on here?*

"What if I need *his* space?" replied Carmela, thinking quickly.

"What?" sputtered Hop. From the surprise in his voice, Carmela knew he obviously hadn't considered *that* scenario. "What are you talking about?" asked Hop.

"Does Bartholomew Hayward have an option on my space?" asked Carmela. She knew that in order for someone to *really* force her out of her retail space, they had to have some kind of option clause written into their lease. And probably hers, too. And she didn't recall seeing anything like that.

"Well, he doesn't have an option per se," Hop replied slowly. "It's more like a gentleman's agreement. Should Mr. Hayward wish to—"

"Tell Mr. Hayward that you're terribly sorry, but my space simply isn't available. In fact, I'm probably going to want to sign a five-year lease this time around. Business is booming. And I like it here."

"Carmela . . ." wheedled Hop Pennington, "it doesn't work that way."

"Sure it does," said Carmela. "In fact, I bet this whole thing will work out just fine if we're all decent and honest and civilized about it."

"You know, sugar," said Hop Pennington, "I don't *own* the building. I just work for the management company. I'm really just the hired help."

Like that makes everything all right? thought Carmela.

"I understand," said Carmela. "I meant nothing personal. By the way, Hop, who *does* own the building?"

"Investors," replied Hop vaguely.

"Which ones?"

"Ah . . . private ones."

Carmela hung up the phone, more than a little miffed, verging on cold fury. *Is this another subtle pressure being exerted from somewhere? And if so, who was doing the exerting?*

"CeCe!" called Tandy, who was right in the middle of cutting a group of so-so color photos into small slivers with the idea of piecing them together to form a collage. "I'm so glad you could make it." CeCe Goodwin, a petite woman with green eyes and a modified shag haircut, strode through the shop and back to the craft table.

"Hello there," she said to Carmela, sticking her hand out in a friendly, forthright gesture. "It's great to see you again." CeCe hoisted a plastic shopping bag into a clear spot on the craft table. "As you-all can probably see, I'm in photo hell right now. I *love* taking pictures, but my hours at Saint Ignatius are crazy, and I am definitely *not* making time for myself." CeCe paused, looking around the table at all the friendly, welcoming faces. "You know . . . not enough bubble baths, candlelit dinners with my hubby, flower arranging, or scrapbooking. Boo-hoo," she finished with a goofy smile.

"Let's see what you've got there," said Carmela as CeCe dug into her shopping bag and began scooping out piles of loose color photos.

"CeCe," exclaimed Tandy as she watched Carmela and CeCe lay stacks of pictures out on the table, "you've got as many pictures of your dogs as you do of your kids."

"Smart woman," noted Baby. "See, she *does* have her priorities straight after all. What are their names?"

"Andrew and Livia," said CeCe.

"She meant the dogs," said Tandy.

"Oh," said CeCe. "Coco and Sam Henry."

"They sound like people names," observed Gabby.

"Well, dogs are people, too," said CeCe as she dug into her pile of photos. She turned toward Carmela with an imploring look. "Can you help me, or am I totally beyond redemption?"

Carmela had to laugh. CeCe was turning out to be a real card. In fact, after the earlier antics of Glory Meechum and the sleazy tactics of Hop Pennington, CeCe Goodwin was a welcome breath of fresh air.

"Why don't we start by organizing your photos," suggested Carmela. She reached behind her, pulled a handful of oversized, clear plastic envelopes off the shelf. "Let's put dogs in one, kids in another," said Carmela. "Vacation photos, relatives, whatever, in the rest."

"Got tons of husband stuff, too," said CeCe.

"Fine," laughed Carmela. "We're an equal-opportunity scrapbooking store. We'll allot your husband an envelope as well." She smiled down at CeCe. "Want a cup of tea or bottle of juice?"

CeCe shook her head. "No thanks. Don't want to get my hands sticky."

"How are the arrangements going for your party tomorrow night?" Gabby asked Baby as she continued to cut out a series of ornate frames.

Baby looked over at Gabby and grinned, her pixie face suddenly all aglow.

"Fantastic! You-all know I'm using that new caterer, Signature & Saffron, over on Magazine Street?"

"Mmn," said Tandy squinting, "I've heard wonderful things about them. They're very avant-garde and *chichi*. Or at least that's what I read in that fancy magazine, *New Orleans Today*. So what delightful little tidbits are in store for us, if I may be so bold as to inquire?"

Delighted that she'd finally been asked, Baby's face lit up with anticipation. "For appetizers they're doing miniature crawfish cakes, andouille sausage bites, and scallop ceviche. Doesn't that all sound dreamy?"

"Are you serving the little crawfish cakes with remou-

lade sauce like Liddy Bosco did a couple weeks ago?"
asked Tandy.

"No, honey, if I remember correctly, that was a *Creole*
remoulade that Liddy served," Baby pointed out. "Signature & Saffron is doing a *French* remoulade."

"What's the difference?" asked Gabby.

"Oh, the French remoulade has capers and anchovies
but is *sans* tomato sauce," said Baby conspiratorially.
"And it's got a much lighter touch. Effortless, one might
say."

"Especially effortless if one is having the entire gala
affair catered," said Tandy with a wry grin. She reached
over and patted Baby's wrist just to let her know she was
kidding, not criticizing. "Then what about your main entrées, honey?" Tandy asked. "What'cha gonna serve for
that?"

Baby leaned back, clearly in heaven. "Tiny roasted
squab, sweet potato galette, pumpkin risotto, creamy coleslaw of cabbage and jicama . . ."

The women all groaned in anticipation as Baby ticked
off her rather fantastic menu.

"I can't *wait*, declared Gabby. "Everything sounds simply divine."

"Divine," echoed Tandy, nodding her approval.

"ISN'T THIS A COZY LITTLE GROUP," PRO-
nounced the rather shrill voice of Ruby Dumaine.

"Hello there, Ruby," called Baby, looking up from the
scrapbook album she was putting together for her daughter. "Long time no see." Since she had just seen Ruby
Dumaine at Jimmy Earl Clayton's funeral yesterday
morning, her comment was obviously intended to be humorous.

But Ruby Dumaine wasn't laughing. Dressed in a suit
that could only be called crustacean coral, her face was

set in a grim mask that would have given even the statues on Easter Island pause.

"Carmela," Ruby called out in her loud bray, "I have a serious emergency, and I need your help *tout de suite.*"

Carmela scrambled to the front of her store to see what she could do for Ruby.

"I am in dire need of a guest book," said Ruby, rolling her eyes as though it was the most important thing in the world. "Specifically for use by my dear daughter, Swan. Don't you know, so many folks will be dropping by our home over the next couple days to congratulate her. In fact, we're having a group of people in tonight, then again on Sunday night after the big Bachus parade."

Carmela nodded, even as she grabbed four albums off the shelf to show Ruby.

"And, of course," continued Ruby, "we'll be doing a fancy barbecue Monday night, after everyone returns from watching the Proteus parade. And then there's the Pluvius queen candidate luncheon on Tuesday." She threw up her hands as though it was all too much for her, though the smile of self-satisfaction on her face said she was relishing every single moment.

"Of course," said Carmela. She especially knew about the Pluvius queen candidate luncheon. She'd designed the place cards, after all.

"Any one of these albums should work beautifully for you," said Carmela as she laid them out carefully on the counter.

Ruby Dumaine fingered the smaller of the four albums, one with a brilliant purple satin cover and creamy pages rimmed with a fine gold line. "This is nice . . ." she began.

The satin cover was a bright royal purple, the purple of kings and queens and royal heraldic banners. Carmela had chosen it specifically for Mardi Gras, since purple, green, and gold were the official Mardi Gras colors. Purple for justice, green for faith, and gold for power.

"This must be a very exciting time for Swan," offered Carmela as she watched Ruby deliberate.

Ruby turned wide eyes on her. "Exciting?" she trumpeted as though Carmela had dared to trivialize the events she'd just spoken of. "This is the most *important* thing that's ever *happened* to us!"

"I'll bet it is," said Gabby pleasantly as she brought two more albums to the front of the store for Ruby's perusal.

But Ruby Dumaine had already made up her mind. She abruptly thrust the purple album into Carmela's hands. "I'll take this one," she said. "It should do very nicely."

"What's got into her?" asked Gabby as the door closed behind Ruby Dumaine.

Carmela gave a quizzical smile. "Mother-of-the-queen-candidate jitters?" She was amused to observe that Ruby had also been wearing squatty little low-heeled shoes that must have been dyed to perfectly match her suit. And that the leather on one heel had split.

Gabby nodded knowingly. "You're right. Must be jitters. Wonder if I'll be that nuts when I have a daughter?"

"You'll probably keep the poor girl under lock and key," came Tandy's voice from the back.

"No," said Gabby, "but I know Stuart will."

"I guess Shelby Clayton has dropped out as Pluvius queen candidate," said Tandy as she pushed her cropped photos around, trying out different arrangements.

Baby slid one of the frames she'd punched out on top of a photo and positioned it on a sheet of creamy paper that had a background of tiny silver wedding bells. "It should be a shoo-in for Ruby's daughter then," she murmured. "Oh well . . ."

"Carmela," said Tandy suddenly, "are you *ever* going to show us what you're working on for Saint Cyril's?"

*　　　*　　　*

BABY TOOK OFF AT NOON TO HAVE A FINAL powwow with her florist, but CeCe and Tandy stayed at the store. Gabby fired up the toaster oven in the back room and toasted bagels for everyone, while Carmela broke out a batch of sour cherry cream cheese spread she'd whipped up a couple days ago.

After the women had munched their bagels, they went back to their scrapbooking projects. CeCe continued to doggedly organize her photos while Tandy worked on her own album even as she paid rapt attention to Carmela's efforts on the Saint Cyril's scrapbook.

"I'm going to create an art montage for the introduction page of the scrapbook," Carmela explained to them. "A kind of establishing visual that will set the tone all the way through." She fingered a nubby piece of paper. "I'll start with this five-by-seven-inch piece of beige paper, then stamp it in brown sepia using this oversized rubber stamp that depicts an architectural rendering."

"Looks like the doorway to an Italian villa," said Tandy, peering over her glasses.

"Or a home in the Garden District," suggested Gabby enthusiastically. She had a serious case of I-want-to-live-there.

"Actually, the design is taken from the front of a Roman tomb," said Carmela. "I'm hoping it will pass for one of the family crypts in Saint Cyril's."

"Perfect," breathed CeCe. "You could have fooled me."

"Okay," said Carmela, "so first I stamp the architectural rendering using brown ink so it looks like sepia. Then I'm going to write over it using a copper ink."

"What are you writing, honey?" asked Tandy, as Carmela began writing in a flowing longhand.

"It's a French inscription I found on one of the old tombs at Saint Cyril's," said Carmela.

"Neat," allowed Tandy. "What does it say?"

"Something about peace and eternal rest," said Carmela.

"Then what?" asked Gabby, fascinated.

"Now I take these dried acanthus leaves and tie them at the top of the page with some metallic copper ribbon," said Carmela, as she punched two holes, then threaded the ribbon through.

"Wow," enthused Gabby, "the folks at Saint Cyril's are going to love this."

"You think?" said Carmela. "But wait, I'm not done yet."

"What else?" asked Tandy.

"This finished piece gets mounted on this dark reddish brown paper, which is just slightly larger. You see," said Carmela, "it gives it a sort of floating mat look. Then I paste *that* onto a slightly larger ivory sheet of paper with a deckled edge."

"Wow," said Tandy, impressed.

"It's elegant and somber," said Gabby, eyeing it carefully, "but very scrapbooky." She sounded slightly envious that Carmela was able to put together such a pretty art montage with seemingly little effort.

"Hey, everybody," CeCe exclaimed suddenly, "I think I've finally got my photos organized!"

Tandy stood up and arched her back in a leisurely stretch. Her collage had actually worked out far better than she'd hoped. Once she'd trimmed away the uninteresting backgrounds and pieced together the shards of what was left, she got a pattern going that was not unlike a stained-glass window. In fact, there was real charm to the jumbled image.

"Isn't this interesting," commented Tandy as she picked up one of the envelopes that CeCe had sorted photos into and riffled through it.

"Those pictures are all from Bobby's Tulane days," pointed out CeCe. "His birthday is in a couple weeks, so

I thought I'd pull together a bunch of mementos and stuff and make him a little memory book. Bobby pretends to bc so tough, but he's really sentimental as hell. You should see him . . . blubbering away at weddings, funerals, football games . . . that sort of thing."

CeCe had, indeed, pulled together a great many photos of her husband, Bobby. Plus she'd thrown in clippings that related to his fraternity days, an old homecoming button, and a frayed blue ribbon he'd won at a state track meet.

"Darwin's a big softy, too," said Tandy, referring to her own husband. "When he participates in those catch-and-release fishing tournaments, he gets *so* upset if he can't get the hook out clean," said Tandy as she continued to peer into the envelope. "If some poor fish gets a torn lip or starts gasping and goes belly up, Darwin really feels bad."

"The strong but sensitive type," grinned CeCe. "I know what you mean."

"You're right about a memory book being a good birthday present for him," continued Tandy, "and what great stuff you have to work with. Carmela, do you still have those brown leather-looking photo corners?"

Carmela nodded as she worked. "I'm pretty sure we do."

"They'd look nice and masculine with all this stuff," said Tandy.

"I agree," said Carmela. "Especially if CeCe chose one of the old-fashioned photo albums with the black pages."

"Oh, my gosh, would you look at this!" said Tandy as she held up a photo and stared pointedly at it.

"Oh, that's just one of Bobby's old fraternity pictures," remarked CeCe. "Wasn't he adorable? Wasn't he young?"

"Wasn't Shamus in Phi Kappa Sigma?" asked Tandy suddenly.

Carmela's head spun around like a gopher popping up

out of a hole. "Yes, he was," she replied as she paused in her careful application of gold paint to the deckled edges of her montage.

"Lord honey," exclaimed Tandy excitedly, "I think this fellow in the picture *is* Shamus. Come over here and look for yourself."

Frowning slightly, Carmela stood up and made her way around the table.

"Right here," said Tandy, pointing with a carefully manicured index finger. "See the fellow with the silly grin, standing behind the beer keg?"

Carmela peered at an old color Polaroid that was starting to go orange with age. It *was* Shamus. But seeing Shamus in the old photo didn't surprise her half as much as recognizing the young man who was posed next to him. Because it was none other than Dace Wilcox!

The same Dace Wilcox who'd claimed he didn't know Shamus. Or even remember Shamus from the Pluvius krewe!

Why had Dace lied? Carmela wondered. *Was he trying to hide something, or had he simply forgotten?*

Gabby," said Carmela suddenly. "You were at the Pluvius den the other night. Do you remember seeing this man, Dace Wilcox?"

Gabby came around the table and studied the picture, cocking her head to one side. She nodded. "Yes, I know Dace Wilcox. Or at least I've *met* him. And he was there."

"Talking to Shamus?"

Gabby thought for a moment. "Don't think so."

There followed a long moment so pregnant with silence you could've heard a pin drop.

"Was he talking with Jimmy Earl?" asked Carmela.

Gabby continued to study the old Polaroid of Shamus and Dace, taken at the Phi Kappa Sigma fraternity at Tulane.

"I *think* I might have seen the two of them talking," said Gabby finally.

"Just so we're absolutely clear on this, Gabby, you saw Dace Wilcox talking with Jimmy Earl Clayton," said Carmela.

Gabby nodded her head again. "I'm pretty sure I saw 'em together." Her brows knit together as she suddenly realized what she'd just said. Then she added, "Just before the floats rolled out of the den."

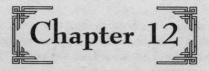

Chapter 12

AT twenty to five, the store was deserted, all the papers, stencils, and fancy-edged scissors put away in
drawers and cupboards for the weekend. Still, Carmela
was reluctant to leave. She wandered about the store,
snapping out display lights and fretting about the strange
events of the day.

Seeing Dace Wilcox's picture next to Shamus's had
been a stunner. And learning that Dace might have been
talking to Jimmy Earl Clayton right before he died was
downright eerie.

Was it possible Dace Wilcox was not what he appeared
to be? That he'd had some sort of bone to pick with
Jimmy Earl Clayton? If Dace had somehow engineered a
nasty "accident" using a lethal dose of ketamine, how con-
venient to help steer the rumors and innuendoes to point
toward Shamus.

The call she'd received earlier from Hop Pennington
didn't help things either. In fact, it had left her feeling
terribly unsettled. Carmela loved her retail space and

dearly wanted to remain there. *Had* to remain there, really, if she had any notion of supporting herself as she continued to grow her fledgling business.

Is the landlord trying to ease me out? Or is Hop Pennington just trying to cut a better deal so he can garner a fatter commission check? And who the heck is the property owner anyway?

Now that Carmela thought about it, she realized she didn't have a clue. Of course, there was a legitimate reason for that. When she was setting up the store a year ago, Shamus had volunteered to handle that aspect of the business. She had located the empty space on Governor Nicholls Street, but Shamus had volunteered to negotiate the lease for her.

Curious now and hungry for information, Carmela wandered back to her office, plunked herself down behind the tiny desk that was wedged between a counter that held a paper cutter and one of the flat files where their expensive handmade papers were stored.

Reaching down and pulling open a file drawer, Carmela's fingers flipped across the hanging files with their hand-lettered labels. Way in the back was a file marked *Lease*. After she'd signed the lease, she'd stuck the document in there without really reading it or giving it a second thought. She'd just assumed Shamus would deal with the lease again when it was time to renew.

And wasn't that a nice assumption. Welcome to never-never land, dear girl.

Carmela pulled the lease out and studied the first page. It was printed on company letterhead and listed Trident Property Management at the top of the page. Their address, phone number, and fax number were printed below.

Carmela dialed the phone number listed on the lease. It was doubtful anyone would still be in the Trident offices. Still . . . she could try.

"Hello," said a voice on the other end of the phone. It

was a woman's voice. Probably a secretary or the front desk person. At least it wasn't Hop Pennington who answered.

"I'm glad I caught you," said Carmela, with a friendly greeting. "I didn't know if anyone would still be there."

"Well, I'm the last one here," said the woman, a touch of impatience in her voice. "I was just about to lock up and make my escape."

"Listen," said Carmela, thinking quickly. "My boss wanted me to call and get some numbers."

The woman on the other end of the line sighed heavily. "Now? Late Friday afternoon?" Clearly this was an imposition.

"Yeah," said Carmela, trying to match her tone. "I was trying to get out of here myself. Don't you just love bosses and their last-minute requests?"

"Tell me about it," said the woman, warming up to Carmela now. "What property was your boss interested in?"

Carmela racked her brain, wondering exactly how to play this out. She'd seen the blue and green Trident Property Management signs all over town. They were a fairly big outfit. They handled leasing and the management of lots of different commercial properties.

Carmela took a stab at it. "Trident has some property for lease down on Bienville, right?"

"You mean the new Rampart Building?"

"That's it," said Carmela. She held her breath as she heard papers rustling. "My boss talked to someone about square footage and lease rates for the second and third floors."

"Gosh," said the woman. "I don't have that kind of information. That building's so new it's not even handled by property management yet. It's still in the initial leasing stage, so everything is being handled out of the executive office."

Bingo, thought Carmela. *Now we're getting somewhere.*

Who should I ask for at the executive office?" asked Carmela.

"I suppose you'd want to chat with one of the partners," said the woman. "Although I seriously doubt they're still there. Anyway, tell your boss to get in touch with Mr. Michael Theriot. He's the managing partner. He handles day-to-day operations and works up lease proposals, that sort of thing."

"And the other partner?" asked Carmela.

"That would be Mr. Maple," said the woman. "You want the number?"

Carmela was suddenly stunned beyond belief. "Mr. Maple?" she asked in a hoarse voice. "Would that be Mr. Bufford Maple, the newspaper columnist?"

"Yes," said the woman pleasantly. "Would you like his number?"

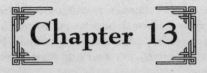

Chapter 13

THE gold statue of Hermes, winged courier and mes-
senger of the Greek gods, cut through the night like
the illuminated prow of a ship. Horsemen in flowing gold
robes clattered down the street, flanking the gleaming
Hermes float on either side. Costumed jesters in billowing
purple and gold silks accompanied the contingent as they
strutted along, balanced on six-foot-high stilts.

Brass bands blared, the flambeaus twirled their torches
and handfuls of shimmering blue, purple, and pink doubloons were flung into the crowds.

And even though the entire Vieux Carré seemed caught
up in the grip of Mardi Gras madness, Carmela wasn't.
Heresy as it might be for a native New Orleanian, her
heart simply wasn't in it.

She had allowed herself to be dragged along tonight by
Ava Grieux on the pretext (Ava's) that it would be *good*
for her.

It wasn't.

Try as she might, Carmela just couldn't seem to make

walk-around drinks and catching beads and shiny candy-colored souvenir doubloons her A-number-one priority. And when Ava confided to her that she had a serious *in* with one of the bar owners who could get them *upstairs* to one of the coveted second-floor wrought-iron balconies, that was the final straw. Because cavorting on a wrought-iron balcony, being urged on by hundreds of leering, drunken men on the street below to *pleeease* waggle her bare ta-tas just wasn't the kind of evening she had in mind.

No, while everyone around her carried on with wild abandon, Carmela's mind was running through the *other* things she could be doing if she'd stayed home tonight. Like defrosting her refrigerator. Hemming that silk skirt she'd bought on sale last fall. Wrestling Boo into a half nelson and trying to clip her pointy little toenails (what Baby would no doubt call a *pet*icure). Maybe even phoning that dirtbag Granger Rathbone and telling him to back off, to take a hard look at a couple of *other* suspects.

Like the illustrious newspaper columnist Bufford Maple, who just *happened* to be the owner of her building. And who might be, for whatever reason, trying to ease her out even as he used his newspaper column to cast nasty suspicions upon her soon-to-be ex.

Or how about the standoffish Mr. Dace Wilcox? Dace had just happened to conveniently forget that he and Shamus had been in the Pluvius krewe together. And Dace had been seen talking with Jimmy Earl Clayton just before Jimmy Earl gasped out his final breath. She had it on good authority from Gabby.

Carmela grabbed Ava's arm as they pushed their way through the crowd inside the Blind Tiger. "Ava, I'm going to duck out," she told her friend.

Ava stopped in her tracks to stare blandly at her. A waiter with a tray of drinks held over his head had to quickly divert with a minimum of rum and bourbon sloshing. "Please tell me you're leaving me because you've got a hot date," pleaded Ava.

"I am," said Carmela. "I have."

"Liar," snorted Ava. "You're just pooping out on me." But when she saw the look of real worry on Carmela's face, she immediately relented. "All right, you're excused for tonight. Go directly home, do not pass go, do not collect two hundred dollars."

"I am going home," said Carmela.

"It's probably a good thing," said Ava. "I don't mind telling you, you're not exactly a barrel of belly laughs tonight." She put her arms around Carmela, pulling her into a gentle hug. "Poor girl, feelin' so sad."

"I've got to figure a couple things out," said Carmela. She had to shout at the top of her voice to make herself heard in the noisy bar.

"I know you do," said Ava, shouting back. "Be careful, though. Play it safe, okay?"

Carmela nodded, then headed out the door. Once she found herself on Bourbon Street, it was a palpable relief, even though the crowds that milled about were still over-whelming. Strangely enough, Bourbon Street had been named for the French family of Bourbons and not the drink itself, like most people assumed.

When Carmela was finally a good five blocks away from all the pandemonium, she ducked into a little neigh-borhood grocery store.

"Going to the parade?" the man behind the counter asked her. He was dressed in a Robin Hood costume, complete with tunic, loden green tights, and a jaunty cap with a pheasant feather stuck in it.

"Eventually," she told him, dumping her groceries on the counter.

"Party hearty," was Robin's parting shot as she pushed her way out the door.

When Carmela got to Governor Nicholls Street, she

saw that Ava Grieux had wisely covered her store windows with a grid of chicken wire. She'd done the same thing at Memory Mine a couple days ago. Neither of their shops were on the parade route per se, but that didn't mean that Mardi Gras revelers were immune from flinging the occasional liquor bottle or getting into skirmishes and shoving each other around. It happened, and it happened with regularity in the French Quarter.

Arriving home, Carmela snapped the leash on Boo, the leash she'd bought at the Coach store back when she'd had money. Then she took the little dog for a brisk walk around the block. Boo, with her canine sensitivity, must have picked up on the Mardi Gras mood because, much to Carmela's consternation, Boo seemed to make a huge production out of staring pointedly at every costumed person who walked by.

Finally arriving back home, Carmela got around to putting her groceries away, then slumped into her wicker chaise.

Walking Boo hadn't really cleared her head at all. In fact, it had just served to make her feel more nervous and apprehensive. On the other hand, one thing *had* crystallized in her mind. And that was that maybe the police should be hassling Dace Wilcox instead of Shamus.

Should she call Granger Rathbone? He probably wasn't in his office this time of night, but she could leave a message on his voice mail or something. *Hey Granger, why don't you take a good hard look at Dace Wilcox while you're at it.*

Would that be way too forward? Naaah.

Because the thing of it was, old Dace Wilcox *had* been hanging around Jimmy Earl Clayton the other night. And even though this fact was predicated on Gabby's recollection being correct, Carmela knew that Gabby rarely misspoke. If Gabby said Dace was there, Dace had surely been there.

So now we've put Dace Wilcox in the immediate vicinity of Jimmy Earl Clayton right before the sea serpent float rolled out the door. Right before Jimmy Earl cacked on his lethal drink of rum and ketamine.

That could mean that, hopefully, Shamus *was* innocent. And that maybe, just maybe, if Dace *hadn't* had a hand in offing Jimmy Earl, he still might know considerably more than he let on.

Carmela looked up the central number for the New Orleans Police Department. She punched in the digits, then asked to be connected with Homicide. When a very bored, gum-snapping secretary came on the line, Carmela asked for Granger Rathbone and got his voice mail instead.

That's okay. It's what you expected.

When the beep sounded, Carmela mustered up all her courage and outrage and left a message that, to the best of her recollection, went something like, "Hey Granger, you sack of shit. Why don't you take a look at Dace Wilcox while you're at it."

While it probably wasn't the most friendly or eloquent of messages, Carmela figured it would do the trick in at least garnering Granger Rathbone's attention. *And that was the whole point, wasn't it?*

Now, what was she going to do about Bufford Maple? *Is he a member of the Pluvius krewe?* That she'd have to find out. *And is Bufford Maple trying to ease me out of the building he owns?*

Good question. For now she didn't have an answer. But she'd find one. Sooner or later, she'd find one.

Shucking out of her blue jeans and poppy red cashmere sweater, Carmela pulled on a comfy oversized sweatshirt that came down to her knees. The front of the voluminous shirt proclaimed *Voulez Bon Ton Roulez.* Let the Good Times Roll.

That's right, she thought. And that was exactly what she was going to do tomorrow. Roll. She'd fire up her

'88 Cadillac Eldorado and blow out the carbon as she barreled down Highway 23 to the Barataria Bayou.

She'd tote along that six-pack of Dixie Beer she'd bought at the little grocery store tonight, then stashed in her refrigerator to chill. She'd see what she could find out from Shamus. And try to hold his feet to the fire so she could get some real answers to her questions.

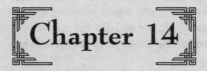

Chapter 14

IN the murky depths of the Barataria Bayou, saltwater intrusion from the Gulf of Mexico has created a primordial tangle that yields a frightening but amazing habitat for animal and plant life. Among lurking, waterlogged trees, alligator, opossum, and nutria flourish. So do the dreaded cottonmouth and water moccasin.

But the Barataria Bayou is also a fisherman's paradise. Redfish, black drum, sheepshead, speckled trout, and black bass are easily caught here. No wonder herons with six-foot wingspans, Mississippi kites, and magnificent bald eagles wheel casually overhead, scanning the brackish waters intently.

Shamus was ostensibly holed up in or near his family's old camp house at the far end of the Barataria Bayou just east of Baptiste Creek. So, early this morning, Carmela had loaded Boo and her cooler into her trusty Cadillac, Samantha, stoked up with Premium at Langley's Superette, then pointed the broad nose of her gas guzzler southwest down Highway 23. Passing through the towns of

Port Nickel, Jesuit Bend, and Naomi, Carmela continued on down some sixty miles or so to Myrtle Grove. From there she maneuvered her way over fifteen twisting miles of seashell roads through dank swampland and the occasional dark piney forest until she arrived at the tiny village of Baptiste Creek.

Truth be known, *village* might have been putting it kindly, for the term conjured up romantic images of quaint shops and picturesque vistas.

Baptiste Creek was more on the order of a rough-and-tumble fish camp. Rough because most of the inhabitants were fishermen and trappers by trade. Tumble because that's what a lot of the buildings seemed to be in the process of doing.

Carmela didn't have any trouble locating Toler Boat and Bait. Their international headquarters consisted of a ramshackle, once-canary-yellow building that was now weathered mostly silver gray and featured a motley collection of old fish nets, alligator hides, and antique tin signs nailed to its roof and outside walls. It was what an avant-garde installation artist might call an architectural *objet trouvé*, a treasure trove of found objects.

From the rear of Toler Boat and Bait, a rickety dock extended out into a dank slough. Roped to this dock were a half-dozen boats that creaked and rocked as they tugged gently at their moorings.

On one side of the shack, a skinny man wearing overalls, a blue T-shirt, and a straw hat was painting foul-looking brown stuff onto the bottom of a boat that had been hoisted up onto two sawhorses. Carmela saw immediately that the boat was a pirogue, a shallow, flat-bottomed boat used for travel in the bayou. In fact, before the advent of fiberglass and aluminum, Cajuns had traditionally hollowed out pirogues from cypress logs.

"Ned Toler?" Carmela called.

The man stuck his brush in the can of brown goo and

gave her an appraising glance. Brown as a nut, his face careworn and lined from a life spent outdoors, Ned Toler appeared to be in his early sixties. Interestingly enough, Ned Toler also had one brown eye and one blue eye. A half-dozen spotted hounds lay snoozing on the ground around him.

Carmela hoisted her six-pack of Dixie Beer and dangled it provocatively in front of him.

A wide smile suddenly creased the man's face, revealing a glint of white teeth. "Carmela?"

She nodded.

Ned Toler's big paw swiped at the six-pack. It was, Carmela thought to herself, much like a brown bear effortlessly grabbing a jar filled with honey.

"Thought you might show up," Ned Toler told her as he cranked the cap off one of the long necks. The *whoosh* of the twist top coming off was followed by an appreciative *"Aaah"* from Ned as he tilted the amber bottle back and let malty brew roll down his throat.

When he had drained half the bottle, Ned wiped at his mouth and flashed Carmela a contented smile. "He ain't here."

"Do you know where he is?" asked Carmela, her hopes of finding Shamus and really talking to him suddenly dashed.

"Nope." Ned Toler glanced over at her car. She'd pulled it off the gravel road and parked it halfway in the weeds. "Nice car." He squinted at it again. "Eighty-seven?"

"Eighty-eight."

"That your dog inside?" Boo was jumping about excitedly, lathering up the rear windows and making a general mess.

Carmela nodded. "Yes."

"What the hell kind of dog is it?"

"She's a Chinese shar-pei," said Carmela.

"You don't say," said Ned, starting toward the car. "Exotic breed, huh? Looks a little like a crissy-cross between a boxer and a basset hound. You know, 'cause of all that wrinkly skin."

Carmela walked over to the car and opened the rear door so Boo could jump out. She immediately gave Ned Toler a tentative slobber, then turned her attention to the pack of leggy brown-spotted hounds that were edging toward her.

"Play nice," Ned admonished his motley band of dogs. "She's a little lady from the city."

Boo, who was suddenly in seventh heaven to be cavorting with a passel of other dogs, bounded off energetically with her newfound friends.

Ned Toler wandered back to the boat and the six-pack. Picking up his brush, he resumed his painting or waterproofing or whatever it was he was doing.

"I'd still like to go out to the camp house anyway," Carmela told him.

Ned Toler bit his lower lip as he worked. "It's your choice. Boat rental's five dollars an hour."

Carmela considered the twisting maze of swamp, the purple water hyacinth that was so rampant it often choked off entire channels, and the towering stands of bald cypress that enveloped Baptiste Creek and stretched beyond it for many dark miles. The journey to the camp house could be a daunting one. And then, of course, one could always run into *el lagarto*. Literally translated as "the lizard," it was what early Spanish sailors had called the alligator.

"What if I get lost?" Carmela ventured.

"Cost you more then," responded Ned. "All that wasted time spent wandering around in the swamp, tryin' to find your way back."

"And if I hired a guide . . . ?" Carmela slipped out of the cardigan she'd thrown on earlier. The sun was shining down, and the air was redolent with humidity and the sweet smell of water lilies and wild camellias. She'd forgotten just how truly lovely it could be out here.

Ned Toler sucked air through his front teeth. "I'm pretty busy right now."

"I can see that," said Carmela. She paused. "I'd certainly make it worth your while."

Ned pulled the battered straw hat from his head and scratched his lined forehead thoughtfully. "Twenty dollars says I can run you out there right now." He checked his watch, an old Timex stretched around his wrist on what looked to be a snakeskin band. "But we gotta be back by two."

"What happens at two?" asked Carmela.

"Gotta get ready for my date," Ned Toler said with relish. "Takin' the widow Marigny to a *fais-dodo* at the church over in Taminy Parish."

A *fais-dodo* was a Cajun shindig. A big party with lots of food and dancing.

"They gonna have a crawfish boil and cook up some gumbo and frog's legs, too," continued Ned Toler. "Plus they got a pretty good zydeco band that cranks up early."

"Okay," said Carmela, who didn't have a lot of trouble conjuring up a vision of Ned Toler doing the Cajun two-step with the widow Marigny. "Deal." She looked around for Boo but didn't see her.

"Don't you worry none about your little dog," Ned Toler assured her. "She won't go nowhere. My hounds stick closer to home than a wood tick on a possum. They'll take good care of her." Ned Toler snatched up the remaining beers and headed for the dock. "Come on then."

Carmela pulled a pair of sunglasses from her bag and slid them on. Following Ned Toler onto the rickety dock, she was surprised at how lighthearted and at home she suddenly felt out here.

Cajun country. That had to be it.

Her momma had grown up not far from here, in a little shrimping village over on Delacroix Island. She herself had never lived out here, of course, had only really lived in Chalmette and, more recently, in New Orleans proper. But she'd visited out here plenty of times. Had enjoyed some weeklong stays with her cousins during the summer when she was young. The mists that crept in at twilight, the cry of screech owls, and the sharp, hoarse bark of the alligator raised goose bumps on a lot of people who ventured out this way. Sent them scurrying right back to the apparent safety of the city. But not Carmela. She liked the wildness of the bayou, the abiding sense of being surrounded by raw nature. It was somehow very comforting. And peaceful, too.

Isn't it funny, Carmela thought to herself, *that Shamus grew up in relative luxury in the Garden District but chose this as a place to hide out. To try to find himself.*

Had something of her rubbed off on him? Hmm. Now there was a weird thought.

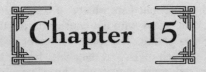

Chapter 15

THE Meechum family's camp house, located at a promontory point at the far end of the Barataria Bayou, had been constructed some eighty years ago. Each one of the cypress and cedar boards had been split, sawed, planed, and nailed in place by hand.

Viewing the camp house from a distance as Carmela was now, coming up the river in Ned Toler's sputtering motorboat, the structure appeared fairly substantial. Built on stilts and hunkered into a grove of saw palmetto and tupelo gum trees, it looked impervious to the occasional hurricane that lashed its way in from the Gulf of Mexico. Windows that were hinged on top and opened outward to allow breezes to sift through could be battened down in a heartbeat. The steeply pitched roof shed water easily. The cypress and cedar boards were thick and sturdy. An open-air porch wrapped around the front and sides.

As Ned's boat puttered up to the small dock, he reached over and handily tossed a rope around one of the wood pilings. Then Ned snugged his watercraft up close, allowing Carmela to jump out.

She'd been here twice before, always with Shamus. The first time had been when they'd returned from their honeymoon in Paris, and Shamus still had a couple days before he had to get back to his job at the bank. That had been a wonderful couple of days. Evenings they snuggled together in the double bed upstairs in the loft and talked about their future. Mornings Carmela had struggled good-naturedly to cook bacon and grits on the old-fashioned wood-fired stove.

Carmela's second visit to the camp house had been last spring. Shamus had wanted to come out here and take photographs of the azaleas and water hyacinths that were in bloom. Back then he'd been mumbling and grumbling about how much happier he'd be if he were a photographer instead of a banker. About how much happier he'd be if he could work outdoors. Of course, back then she hadn't really *heard* what he was saying.

Skipping lightly up a path of crushed oyster shells, Carmela climbed the steep, sturdy stairs and found herself on the wide porch that spanned the camp house on three sides. With its roof of pressed tin, she could imagine sitting out here in a storm. You could put your feet up on the railing, watch the bursts of heat lightning. Or listen to the beat of the rain, cozied up under a homemade quilt in one of the old cane chairs.

Carmela could hear the jangle of keys as Ned Toler came up the stairs behind her, pulling a heroic ring of keys from his pocket.

But the door to the camp house stood wide open.

Frowning, Carmela stepped over the threshold into the camp house.

The place looked like a hurricane had whipped through.

"Oh no!" exclaimed Carmela. Someone had obviously ransacked the entire place. What had been a fairly utilitarian and orderly little home was now an utter mess.

Carmela stared in dismay at the jumble of papers,

dishes, knickknacks, and utensils that littered the planked wooden floors. The simple wooden chairs, so spare in their design, were overturned and strewn everywhere. One of the chairs had been completely smashed.

Ned Toler pushed in behind her. He held up a hand, indicating she should remain quiet. He stood, head cocked, listening for anything or anybody that might still be around, but the intruders seemed to be long gone.

"Damn," he said. "I was just out here day before yesterday, and everything was fine."

"Was Shamus here then?" asked Carmela.

"Yeah," said Ned Toler. Striding around, with his brow furrowed, his face displayed a fair amount of displeasure. "What a mess," he snorted as he grabbed a cane chair and set it upright.

"Who would do this?" said Carmela.

"Who's ever got it in for Shamus, I s'pose," barked Ned.

The main floor of the house was a combination living room–kitchen area with a small partitioned-off storage room. Upstairs was the bedroom loft.

Ned clumped up the narrow flight of steps that led to the loft. "It's all catawampus up here, too," he called down to Carmela. "Damn."

"How else would somebody get out here if they didn't come through Baptiste Creek village?" Carmela called to him.

Ned Toler came clumping back down the stairs, looking grim. "Lots of ways, really. There's fishermen and sightseers that come through here all the time. That's why I make it a point to check out here every few days. No tellin' when somebody decides to play squatter." Ned shook his head angrily again. "We've had people camp out here and help themselves to firewood and such, but nobody ever broke in and *trashed* the place before."

"What now?" said Carmela, looking around at the devastation and noting that a venerable old cypress table now had a broken leg.

"Now I better get back quick and grab a couple new locks." Ned Toler frowned at his wristwatch. "Then I'll run back out and install 'em. Tomorrow, I'll come back and sort things out as best I can."

Carmela nodded. There was nothing to be done here.

What had the intruder been looking for? she wondered. *Clues as to Shamus's whereabouts? Or something else?*

She shrugged, puzzled, and followed Ned back to the boat. *Have to think about it later. Like Ned Toler said, he wants to get back quickly.*

Back at the village of Baptiste Creek, Carmela thanked Ned Toler for his trouble, then headed off to round up Boo. She found the little dog snoozing in the sun with Ned Toler's hounds. Clipping a leash to Boo's collar, Carmela pulled her away from her hound dog friends and started for her car. Then, at the last minute, she decided to investigate a little food stand that had seemingly sprung up like a mushroom in her absence. Somewhat lifted out of her low mood by the dazzling array of fresh produce and home-canned goods, Carmela bought a dozen fresh brown eggs from the old woman who was manning the stand, then added a loaf of prune bread and a couple jars of homemade pepper jelly to her order. The boudin sausage, a Cajun sausage of pork and rice, looked wonderful, but Carmela passed. Just way too many calories.

"Lagniappe," said the old woman with a shy smile as she pressed a little package of bourbon balls wrapped in cellophane into Carmela's hand as she handed over her change. Lagniappe was a word that meant "a little extra." It was a charming custom that still flourished in many parts of Louisiana. Grocers giving a little extra to a customer's order, restaurants adding a little something on the plate of a favored patron, ordinary folks sharing the bounty of their garden with their neighbors.

*   *   *

IT WASN'T UNTIL CARMELA WAS DRIVING BACK
to New Orleans, with a dozen or so miles racked up on
the odometer, that she slowly became aware of the blue
car behind her.

She studied the innocuous-looking dark blue sedan in
her rearview mirror. *Am I being followed?* she wondered.
And, if so, what the heck is this all about?

Carmela speeded up. The blue car behind her immediately sped up. She eased off the gas a bit. So did the
blue car.

Okay, genius, she told herself. *You're being followed.
You figured that out all right. Now what would old Kojak
do?*

In the next half mile, Carmela got her big chance. Just
past an old gray clapboard church with a flickering blue
neon sign out front that proclaimed *Jesus Saves*, she
swerved off the main highway onto a narrow little trail
marked Two Holes Swamp Road. It was a dirt road she'd
traveled a few times before. It was also one that wound
circuitously through a generous portion of the Barataria
Bayou, then eventually snaked back and hit Highway 23—
if you knew exactly where to turn. The operative word
being *if*, since Two Holes Swamp Road had more darn
spur roads and offshoots than a tangle of wild grapevine.

Right now, Carmela's Cadillac, Samantha, was bump-
ing along, kicking up a voluminous trail of dust. She figured it had to be completely obscuring the vision of the
driver behind her. *Piece of cake,* she thought. *I ought to
lose this joker in a matter of minutes.*

Carmela narrowed her eyes and pushed her foot down
hard on the accelerator as she spun down the narrow dirt
road. Dear Samantha, always hungry for a hit of high
octane, guzzled deeply and responded with another appreciative burst of speed. But the driver in the blue car,

seemingly unfazed by the dust she'd been kicking up, stuck tenaciously behind her like a burr.

Now what? she wondered.

With a flash of inspiration, Carmela cranked open her sun roof, then dug her right hand into the sack of eggs that rested precariously on the seat beside her. She waited until the car pursuing her was lined up directly behind her, then eased the little brown egg onto the roof and let it roll backward.

The egg skittered and danced along her car's roof like a billiard ball, then slid down the back window and bounced off the trunk like a missile spat from a grenade launcher. Hitting the windshield of the car behind her, the little brown egg landed with a deadly splat, obliterating the vision of the driver.

Rocketing down the dirt road, Carmela wove the Caddy from side to side, kicking up a barrage of dust and debris. Now the windshield of the car behind her, coated with sticky egg yolk, had become a virtual magnet for dirt.

"He goes to get that car cleaned up," Carmela advised Boo, "the seven ninety-nine econo-wash isn't gonna cut it. That boy's gonna have to pop for the fourteen-dollar suds-o-mania with plenty of hot carnuba wax!"

Approaching a Y in the road, Carmela barely hesitated as she navigated toward the right fork. This road was slightly narrower and bumpier, and as the bayou closed in around her, fronds of palmetto swatted at her windshield.

Peering in her rearview mirror, she saw that the driver of the blue car either didn't see her make the cut or chose not to follow.

When Carmela finally passed an old wooden sign that pointed toward a dilapidated boat launch, she knew the next left turn would loop her back to the highway.

Hah! It would almost be worth it to double back and see where that blue car ended up!

But Carmela didn't. She was anxious to get on back to
New Orleans. To get home. After all, like Cinderella
who'd bumped about in the dust all day, she had to get
all cleaned up and pretty for a very fancy party tonight at
Baby Fontaine's.

Chapter 16

THE hot, needlelike spray from the shower pinged against Carmela's back and shoulders. After rattling around Jefferson Parish for the better part of the day hunting for Shamus and eluding whatever obnoxious oaf had been tailing her, Carmela was anxious to shrug off any dust and residual bad karma she might have picked up and start the evening in splendiferous freshness.

Which meant emerging from her shower all pink and wet like a freshly netted gulf shrimp, then slathering on her favorite shea butter lotion. Once said lotion had been absorbed into her skin and her hair had been tousled and finger-combed into a semblance of the choppy do that Mr. Montrose Chineal had perfected at the Looking Glass Salon a scant two weeks ago, Carmela plunked herself down in front of the old vanity her momma had given her to do her makeup.

The vanity was an old-fashioned fifties-style piece of furniture. Big round mirror, sunken table in the center, drawers to either side. Carmela had a clear memory of being maybe six or seven years old and watching her momma get ready to go out with her daddy on Saturday nights. Her mother's *toilette* had always seemed like such an elegant ritual. Makeup dabbed on just so, dark eyeliner applied, fingers dipped into shimmering pots of colorful lip gloss, finishing spritz of floral perfume.

She remembered the look her momma and every other woman had tried to affect some twenty years ago. Big hair, big shoulders, big eyes. A vision that was slightly disco, a little bit *Dallas* TV show, and a little bit New Orleans. Nothing that would qualify as the natural look.

The phone rang, rousing Boo from one of her snory little dog dreams and causing her to utter a high-pitched yip.

"Shush," warned Carmela as she picked up the phone.

"You ready?" came a sharp voice. It was Ava, checking up on her.

"Almost," said Carmela.

"Honey, I've poured myself into my gold silk dress and, I don't mind telling you, it's pure evil. I only hope you can boast the same."

"I didn't know I was vying for runner-up in the Miss Slinky Tits contest."

"Life's a contest," shot back Ava.

Still holding the phone, Carmela studied her image in the mirror. *Hmm, not bad.* "I'll try not to disappoint you, Ava," she told her friend.

"Try not to disappoint faster. This girl is ready to party."

"Five minutes," said Carmela. "I'm heading down the home stretch even as we speak."

"Hey, did you see him?" asked Ava.

"Nope," replied Carmela. "Nobody home out there."

Carmela dropped the phone in its cradle and finished dabbing on her makeup, using a light touch with the eyeliner and mascara, preferring to adapt a softer, more natural look.

Thank goodness Baby's party hadn't been designated a costume ball, she thought to herself. There were *so* many costume parties during Mardi Gras. And by last count, she'd already attended four. Instead, Baby had carefully specified on her invitation that the evening would be *"black tie or suitably elegant attire."* Which was just hunky-dory with Carmela, since it offered the pluperfect opportunity to wear the black slit skirt and matching camisole bodice she'd bought in a wild fit of madcap spending right after the holidays.

Zipping the pencil-thin skirt, pulling the laces of the bodice tight, Carmela marveled to herself how she wouldn't have dreamed of wearing an outfit like this a year ago. Back then, life with Shamus had always seemed like it should be fairly proper and filled with decorum. He'd been a banker, she a banker's wife.

On the other hand, dressing like this was decidedly fun. She was young and attractive and, when she wasn't mooning about Shamus, could almost manage vivacious. So why on earth shouldn't she dress the part? Besides, Ava Grieux had threatened to put a curse on her head if she didn't start getting her head in the game.

Ava Grieux would have also whispered in her ear, *"If you've got it, flaunt it, kiddo."* But then again, Ava had long legs, a mass of curly auburn hair, and a body with seriously dangerous curves. In other words, an awful lot to flaunt.

Pulling open the closet door, Carmela searched for her shoes. Ah, there they were. Black suede, very strappy and sexy. Perfect. She studied her toenails for a moment, glanced at the clock. She had one minute before she was supposed to meet Ava. Carmela grabbed for her nail buffer and gave them a quick shine. There. She straightened

up, stared at herself in the mirror, decided she was pleased
with the pretty lady who smiled back. She hadn't quite
achieved drop-dead vamp. No, that role still belonged to
Ava for now. But still . . . she was looking mighty fine.

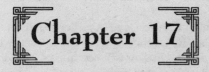

Chapter 17

MARK Twain once wrote, "There is no architecture in New Orleans, except in the cemeteries." But anyone who has actually wandered the tree-bowered lanes of the elegant Garden District might hasten to take exception to Mr. Twain's somewhat flippant remark. For here are huge, elegant homes that resonate with history, with architectural symbolism, and with such pure Southern style that you feel like you've slipped back a hundred genteel years in time.

Just as the French Quarter is revered for its bawdy clubs, posh shops, cutting-edge restaurants, and picturesque architecture, the Garden District is the *pièce de résistance* of residential bliss. Once the sight of the great Livaudais plantation, the Garden District is now a grand dowager neighborhood filled with Victorian, Italianate, and Greek Revival homes that stand shoulder to elegant shoulder alongside each other. And just as its name implies, the Garden District delivers gardens galore. Gardens awash with camellias, azaleas, and crape myrtle. Gardens that echo with pattering fountains, chirping birds, and the quiet crunch of footsteps on pebbled walkways. Even private, hidden gardens enhanced with crumbling Roman-style columns, cascading vines, and greenery-shrouded loggias.

Tonight, as Carmela and Ava hopped from Carmela's car, the Garden District seemed to resonate with excitement. Up and down Third Street, homes were ablaze with lights, and stretch limousines rolled up, one after the other, to drop off elegantly attired couples. Strains of music from the hired jazz trios, bands, and combos echoed throughout the neighborhood.

"Don't you just love the smell of money?" exclaimed Ava as she adjusted a shimmery little shawl about her bare shoulders.

"What does money smell like?" Carmela asked with amusement.

Ava scrunched up her shoulders in a gesture that was pure Marilyn Monroe. "Like this!"

As Carmela and Ava hastened down the sidewalk, drawn like moths to the light, it seemed that *everybody* in the Garden District was throwing a party tonight. But on this sparkling evening, with lights blazing from every window and tiny garden lights dotting the path to her door, none of the houses seemed so grand as Baby Fontaine's.

Baby stood in the entry of her Italianate home, looking cool and pixieish in a shimmery emerald-green strapless gown. Her husband, Del, who was her physical opposite, swarthy and dark, wide-shouldered and tall, held court next to her.

"Carmela! Ava!" cried Baby as two maids, specially employed for this grand evening, ushered the two women through the wrought-iron and glass double doors. Rushing to embrace them, Baby bestowed enormous air kisses which, of course, were eagerly returned.

"Gosh, this is absolutely stupendous," said Ava, dropping her shawl a little lower to show off her spectacular décolletage and gazing about at the interior of Baby's house. The walls of the front entry were covered with pale pink silk fabric. Ornate plasterwork and carved cypress moldings crowned the room, an enormous crystal chandelier dangled overhead, a huge circular staircase curled upward.

Peering down the center hallway, Ava could see a grand living room furnished with Louis XVI furniture and hung with original oil paintings to her right, a spectacular library with floor-to-ceiling bookshelves on her left.

"Baby, I really love your house," gushed Ava.

Baby waved a hand in a dismissive gesture. "Oh, it's just home," she said. "Casa Fontaine."

But Ava was still very impressed. "I do believe this is even nicer than Anne Rice's behemoth over on First Street." Ava had once peeked inside when she delivered some of her voodoo trinkets for use as favors at a Halloween party.

"Well, *we* certainly think so," allowed Baby. "And thank heavens we're located over here on Third Street. We don't get quite the hordes of sightseers that First Street or Washington Avenue or some of the other streets in the Garden District do."

"Lafayette Cemetery and Commander's Palace *are* awfully big draws," allowed Ava, referring to City of Lafayette Cemetery No. 1, a historic cemetery crowded with family tombs and wall vaults that abutted the Garden District, and Commander's Palace, the famed restaurant from whence Emeril Lagasse got his start.

Del put an arm around Baby. "If we start drawing crowds, honey, we'll just go on ahead and charge admission," he said in a leisurely drawl.

Baby batted her blue eyes at her husband. "Trust Del to find a way to turn a profit! Now, you two girls run along and kindly enjoy yourselves," she urged Carmela and Ava. "Gabby and Stuart are already in there somewhere, cooing like lovebirds and acting like the newlyweds they are. Say, that Stuart *is* a handsome devil, isn't he? And Tandy and Darwin are here, too. Although I think Darwin is huddled in the library with a bunch of menfolk, puffing on one of those awful cigars that Edgar Langley imports illegally from Cuba. I don't understand *what* the fascination is, those things stink to high heaven. We're probably going to have to air the place out for at least a week!"

"Is Jekyl Hardy here?" asked Carmela.

"He's here somewhere," said Baby. "And he was so worried about finishing up some of his floats. But then he got one of his assistants to oversee the final preparations, and he made it here just the same." She smiled, pleased. "*Everyone's* here tonight."

Del put a hand on his wife's bare shoulder. "Course they are, darlin.' Nobody in their right mind would miss one of *your* parties."

"My gosh," exclaimed Ava as Carmela propelled her toward the bar. "Baby's husband seems like he might be from one of those old Southern aristocrat families whose ancestors fought with Andrew Jackson."

"Actually," said Carmela, "I think Del's great-great-grandfather *did* fight with Andrew Jackson."

"Cool," exclaimed Ava. "Very cool."

THE PARTY WAS, AS AVA PUT IT, A BLAST. BEAUtifully dressed women and elegantly attired gentlemen rubbed shoulders and exchanged outrageous compliments and pleasantries. Crystal tumblers and champagne flutes were filled and refilled, and melodious strains from a string quartet drifted gently from room to opulent room.

Carmela drifted from room to room, too. Ava had disappeared almost immediately in a flurry of golden silk, having laid eyes on two thirty-something men she deemed "extremely interesting." In Ava-speak it meant the two men were bachelors whom she was itching to subject to her rigorous yet surreptitious questioning. For when it came to determining a man's merit as a "likely prospect," Ava was definitely an analytical left-brain type. And her scrutiny rivaled the process used for admitting prospects to the FBI Academy. Carmela had even kidded her about being a "profiler."

"Carmela," squealed Gabby as she waved from across Baby's glittering living room. "Come say hello to Stuart. He's absolutely *dying* to see you again."

Carmela threaded her way through a sea of silk-covered sofas and ottomans, noting that Stuart Mercer-Morris looked nowhere near dying to see anyone. Rather, his youthful face bore a somewhat bored, been-there done-that look. It was, Carmela figured, the jaded countenance of a young man who was raised with money, lived with money, would always have a plenitude of money.

"Carmela darlin'." Stuart greeted her with a chaste peck on the cheek and a hearty handshake. Carmela noted it was not the limp-rag grasp that many New Orleans males reserved for the fairer sex. Then again, Stuart had gone to an East Coast school. Princeton. Or maybe it had been Harvard. Carmela couldn't recall exactly which one, except that it was one of those stalwart, preppy institutions where women were refreshingly considered the intellectual equal of men. Quite unlike little Clarkston College over in Algiers, where she'd attended school. There, they still elected a Crawfish Queen, Cotton Blossom Queen, and Sternwheeler Queen. Or course, there was never a crawfish, cotton blossom, or sternwheeler *king*. Gosh, life just wasn't fair.

"Gabby is always regaling me with the most marvelous stories about the things that go on in your shop," said

Stuart pleasantly. "It would seem the problems of the world get sorted out there. Or at least the social peccadilloes of greater New Orleans."

"I've always thought we'd make a good premise for one of those reality TV shows," said Carmela. "Just prop a camera in the corner and see what goes on when you get a pack of Southern women together."

"What would you call it?" asked Gabby, clapping her hands together, caught up in the fun of the moment.

Carmela thought for a moment. " 'Cotton Mouths'?"

"Ah, very good," said Stuart with a somewhat forced smile on his face. He snaked one arm about Gabby's waist possessively. "And how is your husband, Shamus?"

Carmela kept her smile plastered on her face, maintained her voice at an even pitch. "Gone," she said. She hoped it sounded like a casual, offhand remark.

"But not forgotten," added Gabby, who suddenly looked a trifle nervous at the turn the conversation had taken.

"Shamus had such a promising career," continued Stuart. "I was so sorry to hear he'd left his position at the bank."

"And so was his family," said Ava, joining the conversation as she slipped in next to Carmela. "They probably haven't had a Meechum go rogue on them in the entire history of the family. Honey," Ava said, focusing her big, brown eyes directly on Carmela. "You have *got* to pay a visit to the buffet table. The food those caterers laid out is simply out of this world."

"Thanks for the save," Carmela whispered to Ava as they pushed their way through the crowd and headed for the buffet table in Baby's enormous dining room. "Stuart and Gabby are *so* hung up on my separation, it's beginning to get out of hand. I was afraid Stuart was going to start reciting pithy little quotes about Mars versus Venus."

"Oh, honey," said Ava as she fluffed back her hair and

reached for a bone china buffet plate, "don't you know that touchy-feely caring-sharing thing is just a clever ruse with Stuart? The man owns car dealerships, for goodness sakes. He was just trying to soften you up so he could move in for the kill and sell you a nice big Toyota."

"You think Stuart knows what I drive?" grinned Carmela as she grabbed a gleaming white plate bordered by pink roses.

"*Everybody* knows what you drive," quipped Ava.

Baby's description of the menu a few days earlier had been vastly underplayed. For here was a buffet that was truly sumptuous. Enormous silver chafing dishes offered up their bounty of Oysters Bienville, crawfish cakes with red bean relish, and cunning little eggplant pirouges, tiny little eggplants that had been hollowed out and stuffed with crabmeat and melted cheese.

The overhead lights in the dining room had been purposely dimmed and giant candelabras with sputtering pink candles placed strategically on the table to lend a warm, mellow glow.

Truly, Baby's new caterers, Signature & Saffron, had come through like troopers. And they were even handling food for three other major parties taking place in the Garden District this evening.

Carmela dug an enormous silver serving spoon into an ocean of okra gumbo and transferred a helping to her plate. At the next chafing dish she reached for the fried plantains and succeeded in covering up part of the pink rose border on her plate. She cast an appraising eye down the table at the dishes she *hadn't* tried yet, and decided she could probably cantilever a tiny sliver of duck au jus on top of her pork roulade.

"You're going for the double-decker," said Ava, impressed. She never knew Carmela could eat so much.

"Tonight I am," said Carmela as they moved down the line.

"If I eat too much, I'm for sure going to bust the seams of this dress," declared Ava. But Carmela noticed that didn't stop her from helping herself to a little of everything.

Carmela was munching a crawfish cake and balancing a ramos fizz when Jekyl Hardy came rushing up to her some ten minutes later.

"Car-*mel*-a!" he exclaimed, planting a giant kiss on her cheek.

"Jekyl, hi," she said. "Have you tried the food yet?"

Jekyl rolled his eyes. "Let's not go into that right now. Suffice it to say I *stormed* the table with Tandy." He grabbed her arm. "But right now, my dear, you are going to have your fortune told!"

"What are you talking about?" asked Carmela as Jekyl pulled her along with him and she practically had to toss her empty plate, Frisbee-style, to one of the tuxedo-clad waiters who was clearing away dishes and wineglasses.

"I'm referring to Madame Roux or Lou or whatever her name is," said Jekyl. "Baby hired a fortune-teller for the evening. Isn't that an absolute kick?"

Ensconced in Baby's solarium on a Chinese-style settee, Madame Roux wasn't so much a fortune-teller as she was a reader of tarot cards.

"See," said Jekyl proudly as he prodded Carmela into the solarium ahead of himself, "you've just got to have a go at it."

"Come in," Madame Roux beckoned to Carmela. "Open your heart and mind, and let Madame Roux see what the tarot has divined for you." Clad in a flowing hot-pink robe, armloads of bangle bracelets, and a Dolly Parton wig with a slightly pinkish cast, Madame Roux looked not so much like a fortune-teller as a flamboyant senior citizen dressed for a hot date at the bingo parlor.

"I'm not a big believer in fortune-telling," Carmela confided to Madame Roux as she sat down on the low stool that faced her. "I think people create their own destinies."

Madame Roux shuffled the cards like a practiced blackjack dealer, then fanned them out on the table between them. "I do, too, *chèrie*," she said with a slight French accent. "The cards only point out choices; *you* make the final determination."

"So what do I do?" asked Carmela, feeling kind of silly.

"Choose three cards," Madame Roux instructed. "The first card will reveal your past situation, the second card your present situation, and the third card your future. But . . ." She held up her hand with theatrical flair. "Choose carefully."

Carmela grinned. *Past, present, and future, huh? Okay, this should be interesting.*

She indicated her first card. Past. Madame Roux plucked it from the line of fanned-out cards and turned it over. It was the queen of wands.

Madame Roux crinkled her eyes in a smile. Or as much as one could crinkle when wearing double sets of false eyelashes. "You have always been very sympathetic and friendly," said Madame Roux. "You were brought up to have a kind nature and also to be a good hostess."

Carmela returned Madame Roux's smile politely. "Not as good as Baby Fontaine is," she quipped.

"Now you must select the card that indicates your *present* situation," continued Madame Roux, unfazed.

Carmela chose a card from the middle.

Madame Roux turned it over, revealing the six of swords. A tiny frown crossed her face. "Difficulties. Anxieties."

Carmela shrugged. "A few, yes." *Well, that was a strange choice of cards. Probably won't come up again in a zillion years, right?*

"And now your future card," urged Madame Roux.

Carmela pointed to the last card on the far right. "That one."

Madame Roux flipped it over. It was the hierophant card. The ancient Greek priest who was the interpreter of mysteries and arcane knowledge.

"What does it mean?" asked Carmela as she studied the card. Her final choice of cards *looked* fairly benign. An ancient priest sitting between two Greek columns with a gold key at his feet. Still, it could probably be interpreted any number of ways.

"The meanings are varied," said Madame Roux. "Mercy, kindness, forgiveness."

"All good things," said Carmela. "And what does the key mean?"

Madame Roux studied the card. "Not completely clear," she said, "but it *should* be revealed soon enough."

Carmela continued to take this experience with a grain of salt. "So this is a short-term reading?" she asked, her bemusement apparent. This was like one of those psychic hot lines on TV, she decided. Got to flash a disclaimer that said, "For entertainment purposes only."

Madame Roux's eyes sparkled darkly as they met hers. But even as her eyes were filled with kindness, they also projected a certain seriousness. "You will know about the key in a matter of days, *madame*," said Madame Roux.

"Well, thank you," said Carmela, standing up. She dug in her evening bag for a tip, but Madame Roux held up her hand.

"Not necessary," Madame Roux told her. "Everything has been taken care of."

There were loud giggles and a shuffle of feet behind Carmela. Obviously other guests were waiting their turn to commune with Madame Roux.

Carmela turned around to leave and almost ran smack-dab into Ruby Dumaine.

"Carmela!" exclaimed Ruby loudly. Her round face was

pink and flushed, her manner bordering on boisterous. A glass of champagne was clutched tightly in one hand. It was obviously not her first.

"Hello, Ruby," said Carmela. She noted that Ruby was dressed not unlike Madame Roux. Lots of flashy jewelry, a hot-pink dress that swirled around her.

Ruby leaned unsteadily in toward Carmela. "A little bird told me someone was *very* mad at you!"

Carmela favored Ruby with a wry smile. Ruby Dumaine was notorious for hinting at little bits of gossip and then dropping nasty clues.

"Let me guess," said Carmela, playing along with Ruby the best she could. "The garden club booted me off their roster for failing to produce a single Provence rose." Carmela moved a few steps away from Ruby, noting that the woman was a notorious space invader.

Ruby Dumaine rolled her eyes in an exaggerated gesture. *"Noooo,"* she said.

"On the other hand, I'm not even *in* the garden club anymore," laughed Carmela. *Have I exchanged enough polite banter with Ruby to pass as being sociable?* she wondered. *Can I please exit stage left now?*

But Ruby was in an ebullient mood. "If I recall, Carmela, when you resided in this rather hoity-toity neighborhood not so very long ago, you managed to coax a fair amount of flowers into bloom."

Carmela heard familiar voices and glanced sideways. Tandy Bliss and Jekyl Hardy were bearing down on her. Bless them. Rescue was in sight.

"Ah, you'll have to take that up with Glory Meechum, matriarch of the Meechum clam," said Carmela to Ruby. "For, alas, I am no longer a resident of this glorified zip code."

"Matriarch," shrieked Jekyl, moving in next to Carmela. "Doesn't that word conjure up images of incredibly stolid-looking women wearing togas and metal helmets?"

"I think you're confusing matriarchal images with opera icons," said Tandy. She smiled perfunctorily at Ruby. "Hello there," she said.

"Oh, but I *adore* opera," protested Jekyl. "It's just those enormous opera singers that put me off. Stampeding across the stage as they do. Opera is so refined, so genteel. The art should reflect that, should it not?"

"But then the singers wouldn't be able to *project*," argued Tandy. She flashed Carmela a look that said, *We'll get you out of here in a minute.*

Jekyl favored Tandy with a sly smile. "But *you* do. You can talk louder than a foghorn in a hurricane when you want to. And you're only . . . what . . . a hundred pounds?"

"Please," said Tandy. "I tip the scales at ninety-eight pounds." In her short black dress with its teeny, tiny spaghetti straps, Tandy looked even skinnier.

Jekyl Hardy gave an elaborate shrug, as though he'd proven his point. "See."

Carmela was pleased to see that her friends were now on either side of her, ready to spirit her away from Ruby.

But Ruby Dumaine wasn't so easily put off. "Carmela," she began again, "you *are* being whispered about. People are saying *terrible* things."

Jekyl Hardy peered at Ruby peevishly. "Who's got their undies in a twist over some insignificant slight on Carmela's part?"

"Wrong," interrupted Tandy. "When Carmela slights someone, *if* she slights someone, it's significant. They *stay* slighted."

"Good girl," laughed Jekyl. "No sense pussyfooting around."

"It's Rhonda Lee," Ruby blurted out loudly. "Rhonda Lee Clayton thinks Shamus is responsible for her husband's death." Ruby's eyes blazed wildly as she stared directly at Carmela. "And she's positive that *you're* covering up for him!"

Carmela was suddenly dumbfounded. "She thinks *I'm* covering up for him?" she said to Ruby. "Does Rhonda Lee know that Shamus and I are separated? That we have been for almost six months now?" Carmela almost reeled from the impact of this nastiness. "Aside from the fact that Shamus had nothing to do with Jimmy Earl's death," she added. *I hope,* said a little voice inside her.

Ruby Dumaine nodded slowly, obviously pleased at the impact her words had on Carmela. "Rhonda Lee has been telling *everyone* that it's all part of your master plan." Ruby smiled, looking decidedly like the cat that just swallowed the canary.

"*My* master plan?" Now Carmela's voice carried real outrage. "The woman is insane."

Tandy rolled her eyes. "Why do I feel like I'm standing in Pee-wee's Playhouse where things are getting crazier by the minute?"

"You're right," said Jekyl. "Time to take our leave."

"Bye-bye, Ruby," said Tandy as they propelled Carmela down the hallway and away from Ruby Dumaine.

"Whew," said Jekyl when they were out of earshot. "What was *that* all about?"

"I think the old bat's been drinking absinthe," said Tandy.

"Actually," said Jekyl, "Ruby was drinking a French fizz. Pernod and champagne."

"A hooker's drink," sniffed Tandy.

"This is such craziness!" said Carmela, still smarting from the nasty gossip Ruby had been so happy to spread. Her angst and frustration were obvious. What started out as a lovely evening had suddenly taken a nasty twist.

"Do you know what?" said Tandy in a low voice. "The insidious thing is that people *do* listen to Rhonda Lee."

Jekyl's face was suddenly lined with concern as he

stared at Carmela. "They do," he said. "Carmela, do you know if Shamus has a lawyer? A good one?"

"I don't know. Probably," said Carmela, recalling Shamus's many phone conversations with the attorneys who were kept on retainer by his family's Crescent City Bank.

Tandy gave a quick look around to make sure no one was listening in on their conversation. "Do you even *know* where Shamus is, Carmela?"

Carmela shook her head. Tears had begun to gather in her eyes and threatened to spill down her cheeks. *Why*, she wondered, *am I getting so damned emotional about this all of a sudden?*

"My God," exclaimed Jekyl, peering at her. "You still love Shamus!"

Carmela shook her head fervently. "I don't. Absolutely not."

"Yes, you do!" Jekyl insisted.

"Leave her alone," hissed Tandy. "Can't you see she's upset?" Tandy slipped a thin arm around Carmela's waist and pulled her close. "Don't you dare make her any more worried than she already is," she sternly admonished Jekyl.

"Sorry," said Jekyl. "Really. I had no intention of . . . ah . . . upsetting Carmela."

"I think the two of us better go outside for a little fresh air," Tandy announced imperiously. She grabbed Carmela's elbow and began to lead her through the crush of people that buzzed about the makeshift bar in Baby's game room. "S'cuse us, s'cuse us," Tandy intoned as they pushed their way through the crowd, heading for the French double doors that led to the patio outside.

JUST AS THEY HAD FOR LAST YEAR'S BIG PARTY, Baby and Del had hired two different musical groups: a string quartet that played in one corner of the living room from seven-thirty until about nine o'clock, and a zydeco band that had as its venue an enormous white tent in the Fontaines' backyard.

Carmela's and Tandy's heels clacked across the bricks of the patio as they crossed toward the tent. They could see that the zydeco musicians were just starting to warm up, and a few couples were already lolling about the dance floor in anticipation of the music. Carmela knew it wouldn't be long before the entire crowd, lured by the rousing music and wildly engaging beat, would thunder outside, lubricated with drink and ready to cut loose. And Carmela also knew that once the really wild music started, the party would go on until God knows when.

"Tandy," said Carmela, "you go on back in. Let me take a breather by myself."

Tandy's pencil-thin eyebrows shot up, and her face suddenly assumed a worried look. "Are you sure, Carmela? Because you seemed awfully upset in there."

Carmela sighed deeply. "Ruby Dumaine just got the best of me for a moment. Plus I went out to Shamus's camp house today and found it totally trashed."

"Oh, no!" exclaimed Tandy. "Who on earth would want to—" She stopped suddenly, bit her lip. Obviously, someone *did* want to discredit Shamus or cause him serious problems.

"I'm pretty sure Shamus *is* in some sort of trouble," confided Carmela. "I just don't know what kind." She was also recalling the blue sedan that had followed her for a while this afternoon. Suddenly her rollicking adventure didn't seem quite so rollicking anymore.

"Jeez," breathed Tandy. "So your ex is seriously on the lam. I didn't know old Shamus had it in him. The Meechums always seemed like such a prim and proper family. The kind of people who are born with the proverbial stick up their butts, if you know what I mean."

Tandy's somewhat unkind characterization of Shamus

and his family brought a wry smile to Carmela's face. "Lots of people think that," she admitted. "But the fact remains, Shamus is an *honest* person, a *good* person." Carmela wanted to add, *Except with me,* but she didn't. Instead she simply added, "I can't believe Shamus was in any way involved in Jimmy Earl's murder."

"Course he wasn't, honey," said Tandy. "Ruby Dumaine is just a big old loudmouth pea hen. She's got nothin' to do all day but fret, bug her daughter Swan to death, and spend Big Jack's money as fast as he makes it. It's a lethal combination. Breeds contempt of others."

"I think you're right," said Carmela.

"I *know* I'm right," responded Tandy. "Now you go on and take a few minutes to pull yourself together, then I want you to march that cute little tush of yours back here. I am hereby issuing strict orders that you're to be on that dance floor shaking your booty in approximately five minutes. Okay?"

She didn't know how much booty shaking she'd be doing, but Carmela decided the easiest thing to do was agree with Tandy. "Okay," she told her.

Tandy leaned forward and gave Carmela a motherly peck on the cheek. "Good girl."

Standing on the side portico, some twenty feet away, Dace Wilcox had just witnessed this exchange between Carmela and Tandy. And, from the depths of the shadows, he was staring at them intently.

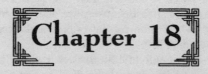

Chapter 18

SLIPPING down a stone walkway into the shrouded depths of Baby Fontaine's backyard garden, Carmela was decidedly glad to have a few moments away from the crush of the party. It had been wonderful to see all her friends, and the food was truly delightful. But why did catty old Ruby Dumaine have to bring everything to such a screeching halt?

Did Rhonda Lee Clayton *really* believe there was some *master plan*? And was Rhonda truly spreading stories about her and Shamus?

And why did I get so teary-eyed just a few moments ago?

As a gust of cool air swept through the sweet olive and boxwood trees, stirring the shrubbery around her, Carmela gave a little shiver. Clutching her arms to her chest, she was still reluctant to go back inside. Like an F5 tornado, the party was swirling at a feverish pitch. Men were drinking, women were flirting outrageously, the zydeco band was about to cut loose big time. But then again, that's what a Mardi Gras party was all about. The word *carnival* was derived from a Latin word meaning "farewell to flesh." And the whole concept of the Mardi Gras *carnival* was to eat, party, drink, live fast and hard, and commit more than a few sins. Because once Ash Wednesday arrived, you had to slam on the brakes and observe forty long days of denial.

A glint of moonlight illuminated a stone bench just ahead of her. Carmela walked over and sat down, still reluctant to return to the party. Out here, she could still *feel* the residual rush of the party and hear the muffled voices and musical strains. But it was removed, filtered, safer.

As Carmela stared into the darkness of the garden around her, she could hear the strains of *"If Ever I Cease To Love."* As the official Rex anthem, it was played constantly during the Rex parades and the Rex krewe's imperial receptions. Today, most of New Orleans viewed the song as the official Mardi Gras ballad.

> *If ever I cease to love*
> *May sheeps' heads grow on apple trees*
> *If ever I cease to love*
> *May the moon be turn'd to green cheese*

Humming along to the haunting tune, Carmela *still* couldn't get Ruby Dumaine out of her head.

What is her problem? thought Carmela. *Why is Ruby so all-fired set on spreading rumors, on promoting Rhonda Lee's paranoia? Is this just sport on her part? Does she just want to see Shamus's ears get nailed to the wall?* Carmela shook her head regretfully. There were a lot of things she was having trouble figuring out. Like why did Bufford Maple, the columnist, seem to have it in for both her and Shamus? And what was Dace Wilcox's connection to all this, if anything?

Carmela stood up, strolled to the back gate, and pushed it open. Now she found herself in the middle of a narrow cobblestone alley that ran between the backyards of a half-dozen enormous houses. A hundred years ago, this had been the carriage lane, the tradesman's and servant's entrance. Now BMWs, Porsches, and Audis were the only vehicles that rumbled down this lane. And tonight, hired car parkers had jammed extra vehicles up and down the length of it, narrowing the roadway even more.

Gingerly, Carmela eased her way past the parked cars. She was beyond the boundaries of Baby's estate now and staring at the back of the house next to them. These neighbors were throwing a party, too, albeit a smaller, more sedate one. If there was such a thing as a sedate Mardi Gras party.

Carmela paused, ready to turn back toward Baby's house, when she was suddenly stopped in her tracks. Parked across the alley from her was a dusty blue car.

Is this the car that followed me today? Parked right here? Whoa, better take a closer look.

Even in the dim light Carmela could see the windshield had streaky smears on it.

Egg yolk? Gotta be.

She blinked, looked around, wondered again whose car this was and did they live around here or had they just popped in for a visit?

Well, the car's parked directly behind this palatial home with the peaky, almost Chinese-like roof. This would be the place to start. So . . . take a look? Not take a look?

Carmela's eyes sought out a glowing window on the second floor. And there, sitting just a few feet from the window, talking on the phone or maybe to somebody else who was in the room, was Swan Dumaine, Ruby and Jack Dumaine's daughter!

How bizarre, thought Carmela. *This is Ruby and Jack Dumaine's home!* And on the heels of that came the thought, *It also feels like a scene out of the movie, Rear Window.*

All her sensibilities told Carmela to just walk away. Yet she was drawn by the thought of the blue car. *Was the driver of the blue car a guest in Jack Dumaine's house? And who exactly was this person who found her trip down to the Baritaria Bayou so all-fired interesting?*

Carmela tiptoed down a gravel path toward the back of the house, acutely aware of rocks crunching underfoot.

Can anyone hear me? Will someone come dashing out of the house? Is anyone even in there besides Swan?

As if in answer to her question, a muffled roar of applause emanated from the tent in Baby's backyard. Then the zydeco band started up with what sounded like a cataclysmic crash.

Carmela put a hand into a clump of bushes and parted it slightly, the better to catch a glimpse of the lower floors.

Is Jack Dumaine home? Or is he down the street, prowling around at Baby's party, too? Spreading the Dumaine good cheer, same as his wife.

Carmela suddenly caught a flicker of movement on the first floor of the house.

Somebody's in there. Somebody's home.

Her curiosity made her bold. Creeping closer to the house, Carmela peered in through draperies that were not fully drawn.

Jack Dumaine was sitting behind a massive wooden desk in what had to be the library. Behind him, bookcases lined the walls, and books with leather bindings gleamed in the low light. A Tiffany lamp with a dragonfly motif sat on Jack's desk. It was one of the old ones, a mosaic of brown and gold glass with a burnished brass lamp base. Surrounded by all that apparent luxury, Jack was smoking a cigar and haranguing an unseen person who seemed to be perched at a right angle to his desk.

Who was Big Jack chewing out, anyway? It couldn't be

Ruby; she was still at the party across the way.

Jack Dumaine was angry, though. Extremely hot under the collar. Red-faced, with thunderclouds for eyebrows, he bounced up and down in his leather chair, speaking with great force and stabbing the air with his cigar, as if to underscore each point he was making. Since Carmela couldn't hear Jack Dumaine's words and could only see his angry expressions, it was like watching the antics of an overwrought mime.

Who are you talking to, Big Jack? What poor soul is sitting in the hot seat across from you getting royally drilled?

Feeling with her toes, which were by now half frozen, Carmela gingerly shuffled her way around the bush. Then she took a deep breath and leaned toward the window, peering between Ruby Dumaine's not-quite-closed curtains of green velvet.

Carmela was rocked by who was sitting across from Big Jack.

Ohmygosh, it's Granger Rathbone!

Granger Rathbone sat in a high-backed chair that was set at an angle to Jack Dumaine. His pockmarked face was set in grim repose, and he looked like a bobble-head doll, as he bobbed his head and nodded while Jack lectured to him.

So what is Granger Rathbone doing in Jack Dumaine's library? wondered Carmela. *Has Jack Dumaine got Granger on his payroll? Did Jack Dumaine kill his business partner, Jimmy Earl Clayton, and now he's enlisted Granger Rathbone to help him cover it all up?*

Maybe, could be were the answers that came back to her.

And on the heels of that happy thought came the grim realization: *They're trying to set Shamus up!*

Suddenly panic-stricken, Carmela tried to halt her runaway thoughts. *Are they? Really?*

She backed slowly away from the window. *Let's just think about this for a minute,* she told herself. *Someone murdered Jimmy Earl Clayton by feeding him a megadose of ketamine. And a lot of people close to Jimmy Earl seemed to be growing increasingly suspicious of Shamus. But nobody had uncovered any hard evidence that linked him to the deed. So far, this whole thing against Shamus was being fueled only by rumors and innuendos.*

The thing she had to decipher was, *who exactly was doing the fueling?* Jack Dumaine and Granger Rathbone? Or were they working on something else?

Could Bufford Maple or Dace Wilcox have a motive as well?

Carmela quietly exited Jack Dumaine's yard, pondering the whole mess. One thing was for sure, Jack Dumaine seemed to have Granger Rathbone in his hip pocket. And that wasn't good. That wasn't good at all. Granger Rathbone was a nasty, vindictive cop of the worst kind. And in New Orleans, cops had power. A lot of power.

As Carmela stood in the alley, she heard the back door open and a low mumble of voices, then footsteps crunch on gravel.

Somebody's coming!

Diving behind a silver BMW, Carmela ducked down and held her breath. As the footsteps passed close by, she allowed herself a quick peek.

It was Granger Rathbone, all right. *What a creep.* Remaining in her hiding spot, Carmela waited until she heard his car door open, then slam shut, hesitated as the engine revved and turned over. Then headlights flared, and Granger's blue car swept noisily down the alley away from her.

So that's who'd been following her today. Quite probably, the old boy had gotten her phone call from the previous night and categorically blown off her suggestion to take a look at Dace Wilcox. But he *had* decided to follow her out to the bayou this afternoon in hopes of finding Shamus.

Finding Shamus for who, though? For the New Orleans PD or for Jack Dumaine?

There was also another possibility that loomed large.

Had Granger Rathbone trashed Shamus's camp house?

Carmela considered the idea for a moment. Somehow, it didn't feel right. Granger Rathbone would have had to sneak out there earlier, then wait around for her.

No, the most plausible explanation was that Granger had followed her, plain and simple. Hoping, of course, that the trail would lead to Shamus.

As Carmela stood behind the silver BMW pondering this new twist, one of the garage doors across the alley suddenly emitted a loud *cha-clunk*, then began to rise. Easing back into the shadows, she watched carefully. And, in the dim light from the overhead bulb that hung in the center of the garage, she recognized the somewhat ample profile of Jack Dumaine.

Jack Dumaine is going somewhere! And he was agitated. In fact, he looked as though he was in a powerful hurry as he tried to insert his bulk into the front seat of his jumbo-sized Chrysler Voyager.

Where's he off to? Carmela wondered. Then just as quickly decided, *There's only one way to find out.*

In a flash, she scampered through the side yard between Baby's house and the neighbor's big money pit of a home. When she hit Third Street, Carmela darted left, sprinted the length of a city block in what had to be record time, then dove into her car.

Raised by a careful Norwegian father who had always worn a belt *and* suspenders, Carmela, too, was a careful, cautious person. She always kept a spare key under the dashboard. She grabbed for it now, jammed it into the ignition, and cranked the engine hard. It was quicker than pawing through her evening bag in the dark.

As the Caddy came to life with a roar, Carmela pulled
out into the street, then experienced a moment of high
anxiety. *Which way is Jack Dumaine headed? Should I
flip a U-turn or continue on straight ahead?*

It was a fifty-fifty proposition, with no time to get over-
ly analytical or toss a coin. *Straight*, Carmela decided.

At the corner of Chestnut she hooked right and was
rewarded with a glimpse of Jack Dumaine's fat-ass Chrysler, just a block ahead of her.

Awright, good call, she told herself.

Carmela settled in behind Jack Dumaine, staying a safe
distance behind him. As they puttered along, Carmela decided that Jack Dumaine drove his car the same way he
walked. Ponderous bordering on lugubrious. Jack's car
seemed to lurch forward slowly as though he kept tapping
the brake every few seconds instead of just proceeding
smoothly.

They bumped down Washington until it turned into Palmetto, then hit the Airline Highway. This was the side of
New Orleans that wasn't so quaint and pretty. Lots of fast-
food franchises, neon lights, tacky rib joints, and drive-
through daiquiri bars.

Jack Dumaine eased his car onto Airline Highway and
headed west. But rather than working up a full head of
steam, he stayed in the right lane, carefully observing the
fifty-five-mile-an-hour speed limit. A mile later, his right-
turn signal pulsed, and Jack turned off. Carmela followed,
again keeping her distance behind him. Driving down a
side street now, Jack wove his way past an all-night rib
joint, a seedy office building, and the Calhoun Motel.

Jack made a slow, wide turn into the motel's parking
lot.

Cutting her headlights, Carmela rolled in behind him.
She stopped her car in a shadowy part of the parking lot
and waited. Watched as Jack Dumaine pulled into a parking space, then eased himself out of his vehicle and

stretched languidly. A sharp *bleep* sounded as Jack Dumaine locked his car with his electronic key. Then Jack
strode confidently toward the door of one of the motel
rooms.

Carmela tried to time her drive-by so she'd be rolling
past the motel room at the exact same moment the door
opened and Jack slipped inside.

It worked like a charm.

Because just as the door opened and light shone out
into the dark parking lot, Carmela was rewarded with the
surprise of her life. Rhonda Lee Clayton, Jimmy Earl's
grieving widow, stood in the doorway to greet Jack, wearing a black-and-gold floor-length caftan and a pussycat
smile on her face.

Chapter 19

*J*ACK *Dumaine and Rhonda Lee Clayton. Rhonda Lee Clayton and Jack Dumaine.* The words played over and over in Carmela's brain like a feverish mantra. What *were* the two of them doing together?

Canoodling, that much was obvious. But what were they *really* doing together?

Had Jack and Jimmy Earl's partnership not been as cozy as Jack had made it out to be? He'd certainly sung Jimmy Earl's praises to high heaven and made their partnership sound like a mutual admiration society when he'd eulogized him at the memorial service a scant two days ago.

Could it be that Rhonda Lee was the *real* partner in the company, the silent partner, and Jimmy Earl had just been a figurehead?

No, that didn't make any sense either, Carmela decided. Jimmy Earl had been quoted frequently in the business pages. And he'd gotten lots of little blurbs written about him in some of the smaller business magazines attesting to the fabulous deals he'd engineered. So Jimmy Earl *had* to have been a real partner in his own right, despite all his pathetic frat boy antics.

So maybe Big Jack had just plain offed Jimmy Earl in a straight-ahead murder?

Yeah, that's gotta be the answer, figured Carmela. *Jack offed his partner to gain control of the company and bed Rhonda Lee.*

On the other hand, that answer seemed far too pat.

For one thing, Rhonda Lee was no great prize.

No, Carmela decided, there was something else going on. Something she hadn't figured out yet.

Turning the key in her lock, Carmela let herself into her apartment. Even before she flipped on the lights, she knew she wasn't alone. Someone was in there with her. Someone who had obviously become a new best friend with Boo. Could it be Granger Rathbone? Maybe. Pity Boo had such poor taste.

"Awright," Carmela called into the darkness with as much bravado as she could muster. "Let's cut the games. I know you're in here."

The cushions in the wicker chair gave a muffled squeak as someone shifted their body weight and reached for the ginger jar lamp that occupied the adjacent table.

There was a bright flash, and then Carmela was staring wide-eyed at her soon-to-be ex-husband. "Shamus!" she exclaimed. This *was* a surprise.

"Howdy, Carmela," he said, returning her greeting.

She stared at him, hating the insolent look he wore on his face. Or maybe it was just his confidence. Shamus had always been a supremely confident being. Even when he played varsity football at Tulane, he was the kind of guy who could drop a pass and still walk off the field looking like a winner.

What the hell, Carmela decided, it didn't matter. What

did matter was that she was getting more and more angry with every second that passed.

"Brushing up on your breaking and entering?" she asked him.

He responded by shifting his long legs off the ottoman and giving it a gentle pat, trying to entice her to come sit down next to him.

She sauntered over carefully, plunked herself down.

"Nice dress," he remarked, reaching for the laces of her camisole.

Carmela held up a cautionary index finger. "That's off limits," she told him sternly.

He pulled his hand back, favored her with a lazy smile. "Still, you're looking quite delicious," he said.

Carmela didn't answer him. What she wanted to say was, *No, you're looking good.* Because damned if he wasn't. Shamus's olive skin, brown eyes, and shaggy, slightly sun-streaked hair were pure eye candy. Very appealing. In fact, he looked happier and healthier than when he'd been living with her. Being on the run seemed to agree with him.

Damn, she thought, *how can it be? It just doesn't make sense. Then again, nothing seems to make sense.*

She also noticed that Shamus hadn't abandoned his Rolex Datejust and his Todd loafers. He may have ditched her, but he'd kept his toys. She guessed the Meechum family trust was still operating in full force.

"I came looking for you today," she told him. "I was out at the camp house."

"Yeah, I heard," said Shamus. Boo came pattering over to him and rested her head on his knee. Shamus reached down and gently kneaded the dog's tiny, flat ears. "Good girl," he cooed to her.

"It's been totally trashed," Carmela told Shamus. She was trying not to let his apparent affection for Boo get under her skin. How could Shamus be so sweet and attentive to a little dog and act like an inconsiderate louse with her?

"I'm not surprised," said Shamus.

"Everybody thinks you're on the lam," Carmela told him.

Shamus gave a disinterested shrug. "If that's what everybody thinks, then I suppose I am," he said.

Carmela was beginning to get very frustrated by his apparent lack of concern for himself. "People are accusing you of murder, Shamus! They're trashing your camp house and saying incredibly nasty things about you. Doesn't that bother you just one teeny tiny bit?"

Shamus turned liquid brown eyes on her. "Should it? Should I really care what vitriolic lies are being spewed out about me?" he asked her.

Carmela was flustered. This was not the hardheaded banker of the notoriously conservative Crescent City Bank that she'd known and loved. "No, but—" she started.

"But what?" he asked. His flashing eyes challenged her.

"But you should at least *defend* yourself," she sputtered. Carmela stopped abruptly, tried to pull herself together. Why did she feel like she was suddenly playing one of the lead roles in a romantic comedy from the '40s? One of those frothy, fast-moving films where the leading man and woman constantly snapped and snarled at each other, yet everyone knew they were madly in love and would end up happily-ever-aftering at the end of the picture.

Will Shamus and I end up back together at the end of the picture? Somehow it doesn't seem like a Hollywood ending is on the horizon.

"I saw Jack Dumaine with Rhonda Lee!" Carmela suddenly blurted out.

"Where?" asked Shamus.

"Tonight. At the Calhoun Motel. A hot sheet joint just off Airline Highway." Burned in Carmela's mind was the vision of Rhonda Lee Clayton in her sixties-style earth mother caftan. It was an image that projected far more than she cared to know about the woman.

"You don't say," said Shamus. "With the grieving widow, no less. I'm amazed Big Jack is still out wolfing around. My hat's off to the old boy."

"Shamus," said Carmela, "I think Big Jack is trying to set you up. In fact, I'm pretty sure he is."

Shamus leaned back and steepled his fingers together, looking as though he was lost in deep, impenetrable thought. Carmela had seen him do this before. It meant Shamus was stalling. Or, worse yet, merely toying with her.

"Let me get this straight," said Shamus. "You think that just because Jack Dumaine decided to have a toss in the hay with Rhonda Lee . . . that he's plotting to set me up? Destroy my career and my good family name?"

"Well, yes. He certainly could be," said Carmela. "Beside the fact that he's sleeping with his dead partner's wife, Jack Dumaine also seems to have Granger Rathbone in his hip pocket."

"Really," said Shamus. "And what do you make of that?"

"Duh," said Carmela. "A setup?" *Jeez*, she thought, *is this boy dense or what? Or just in very serious denial?*

"You're right," Shamus said finally. "It doesn't look good."

Aware that her skirt was beginning to ride up, Carmela shifted about on the ottoman, trying to smooth it down and assume a slightly more decorous pose. Shamus's eyes followed every aspect of her struggle.

"Shamus, tell me something," she said finally. "What words did you have with Jimmy Earl, right before he climbed up on that big green float and took a drink that snuffed out his gray matter?"

"Nothing that would interest you, my dear."

"Try me." Carmela stood up suddenly, placing her

hands on her slim hips and gathering her face into a semblance of a thundercloud.

Shamus flashed a smile at her. "God, you're a pretty thing."

"Shamus . . ." Carmela's voice carried a warning tone.

He threw up his hands in mock defeat. "Okay, okay, you win. If you must know, Jimmy Earl called me an asshole."

"The man *did* have a way of making sense of things," Carmela said with the beginning of a wry smile. She paused, staring into Shamus's intense brown eyes. He didn't seem all that amused by her banter. "Okay, Shamus, I'll bite. Why did Jimmy Earl call you an asshole?"

"For leaving you."

Carmela gave an audible snort. "I don't believe you."

"Honey, you can believe whatever you want, but I swear on a stack of Bibles . . . on my momma's grave, in fact . . . that it's true."

"Where were you today?" Carmela asked him.

Shamus gathered his long legs beneath him and suddenly stood up. He stepped close to Carmela, towering over her. He looked like he was about to wrap his arms around her, then he suddenly seemed to do an about-face. "You came to see me today," said Shamus. "I told you not to."

"You said that if I needed to get hold of you to contact Ned Toler," replied Carmela. "That's exactly what I did. Followed your wishes to the letter of the law, in fact."

Shamus thought for a second. "You're right."

"I'm sorry the camp house got trashed," she told him. He was still standing way too close to her. It angered her and made her feel shivery at the same time. *Oh God*, she asked herself, *why do I suddenly turn into a gelatinous mess when I'm around this man?*

Shamus shook his head sadly. "One of my macro lenses got smashed."

"Where were you?" Carmela asked him. "Where are you hiding out?"

Shamus gazed down at her with a look of complete innocence. "Hiding? I wasn't hiding. In fact, today I was driving up and down the River Road."

Carmela frowned. *He was driving around? Doing what?* "Doing what, I might ask?"

"If you must know," said Shamus, "I was photographing some of the old plantations. The Destrehan, the Laura, the Houmas House," said Shamus, naming some of the more famous plantations that graced the scenic River Road just north of New Orleans. Shamus shrugged his shoulders and rotated his head as though he was trying to work out a few muscle kinks. "You might not believe this, Carmela, but I truly believe I'm finally doing my best work ever."

Carmela regarded him as you would a seriously demented person. "Your best work?" she exclaimed. "Shamus, I hate to be the one to break the news to you, but *you don't work*! You quit your job at the bank to run off and cohabit with alligators and possums. And, in case you're not entirely plugged into reality, might I remind you that your name keeps coming up in connection with a *murder* investigation!"

But Shamus was already moving swiftly across the room, heading for the door.

"Yeah," he muttered with his back to Carmela, "ain't it a bitch." He yanked open the door and slipped out without bothering to say good-bye.

Carmela ran to the door, pulled it open, fully prepared to hurl a nasty invective at him.

But Shamus had already melted into the dark.

From the *click click* of toenails, Carmela knew that Boo had followed her across the room. She slammed the front door shut, fixed the security chain in place, and looked down at Boo. "If that cad comes back here, I want you to bark your head off," she told the dog. "Better yet, you have my permission to bite him in the ass."

Boo gazed placidly at Carmela, then her nose crinkled up in a tired doggy yawn.

"Some help you are," said Carmela with disgust.

It was only after she'd crawled into bed and pummeled her pillow for a while that Carmela realized she'd completely forgotten to ask Shamus about any possible connection he might have to Dace Wilcox or Bufford Maple.

Damn, she thought, *there are still so many loose ends.*

Chapter 20

"WHERE did *you* disappear to last night?" came a shrill voice.

Carmela sat up in bed and rubbed her eyes. *How did I get the phone to my ear, and who is this person shrieking at me and drilling me for answers?*

"Ava?" she said, a giant question mark in her voice.

"Of course, it's Ava," came the reply. "Who were you expecting? Madame L?" Madame L, or Marie Laveau, was an early nineteenth-century folk heroine who was a hairdresser, volunteer nurse, and voodoo queen.

"I had to take off in a hurry. Sorry," said Carmela.

"You should be. I hope it was with a man."

"Actually, it was," said Carmela. Jack Dumaine was nobody's idea of a dream date, but she had, technically, taken off with him. Or at least taken off *after* him. On the other hand, Carmela decided, Jack just might be Rhonda Lee Clayton's idea of a dream date. Truth was indeed stranger than fiction.

"I'm glad to see you're back in the social swing," said

Ava, her voice dripping with praise. "I told you it was like riding a horse. You fall off, you get right back on again."

"I'm not sure that's the best analogy," offered Carmela.

There was silence as Ava took a few moments to contemplate this. "You might be right," she admitted. "Okay, how about this. Men are like shoes. They start to crimp your toes, you toss 'em out and get a new pair."

"I'll go along with that," yawned Carmela.

"Listen," said Ava, "I've got an idea you're really going to adore. How's about you and me meet at Brennan's for brunch. Say about tenish? We can indulge ourselves with praline pancakes dripping with syrup, an order of thick-sliced bacon, and a dollop of bread pudding with brandy sauce. Of course, we might want to indulge in one of their deliciously refreshing hurricanes to wash it all down." For a woman who was worried about busting dress seams last night, Ava certainly seemed to have changed her tune.

Carmela sighed. Brennan's hurricanes were notorious. Triple shots of rum mingled with fresh-squeezed fruit juices, crushed ice, and a floral garnish. You didn't need more than a couple of those to start seeing the world through rose-colored glasses. But instead of saying yes, Carmela flopped back on her pillow and snuggled in. "Ava, I have to take a rain check, okay?" she told her friend.

"You're not alone!" came Ava's delighted shriek. "The fair maiden's bed is finally *ocupado*!"

"No, I'm alone," Carmela hastened to tell her. "But I have some figuring out to do."

"Life-decision figuring out or more mundane stuff like deciding whether to pay the rent or pop for a new cashmere sweater?"

"Both," said Carmela.

"Okay," agreed Ava, "I can see you've got a lot on

your plate—other than praline pancakes, that is. But I'm gonna call you later."

"Do that," said Carmela.

Hanging up the phone, Carmela stared at the white-washed ceiling and the ceiling fan that swished slowly overhead. That was the way her mind felt. Like it was going in endless circles. Trying hard to figure things out but always ending up back where she started. It was frustrating. And downright debilitating in a strange kind of way.

A VACUUM CLEANER HOWLED FROM SOME-where deep within the old house when Carmela banged on Glory Meechum's screen door some fifty minutes later. It felt strange to be back in the Garden District, just a few blocks from where she'd been last night. She wondered vaguely if the big white tent was still flapping in Baby and Del Fontaine's backyard. Or had it been struck down at first light?

"Glory?" Carmela shouted. "It's me. Carmela. Are you home?" Carmela banged on the door again. Nothing. Maybe they couldn't hear her in there.

Wait a minute, what am I thinking? Of course they can't hear me in there. With that vacuum cleaner blasting away, it sounds like the motor pit at the Indy 500.

Frustrated, Carmela reached down to grab the door handle. She was just about to pull it open and step inside when the ample form of Glory Meechum suddenly loomed behind the screen. Off in the distance, but farther away now, as if the vacuum cleaner had moved into another room, the mournful howl continued.

Does Glory make her poor maid clean on Sunday, too? Carmela wondered. Then she decided to shelve that thought. Of course she did. Glory Meechum's behavior often bordered on obsessive-compulsive.

*Is the iron unplugged? Better check it again. Lights off?
Got to make sure. Definitely a touch of the old OCD.*

Shamus had told her it was a harmless little foible. That
Glory was really a sweet and gentle person. Carmela
wasn't so sure. She thought, if probed deeply enough,
Glory Meechum might reveal a fairly dark side, kind of
like that wacko, Annie Wilkes, from the Stephen King
novel, *Misery*.

"What do you want?" demanded Glory Meechum.
She'd opened the screen door, but with her arms folded
across her sizable chest, she still blocked the entrance to
her house.

"Good morning to you, too," said Carmela pleasantly.
"It *is* a gorgeous day, isn't it?" She tried to smile her most
convincing smile. This was, thought Carmela, the same
technique you'd use to handle a large, hostile dog. Stand
your ground, smile, betray not one iota of fear.

Glory Meechum, with her sensible housedress, helmet
of gray hair, and no-makeup complexion, stared at Carmela and her sudden cheeriness as though she were a
strange science project that had been unceremoniously
dumped on her doorstep.

But Carmela's upbeat approach was obviously working,
because Glory seemed to soften just a tad. Her countenance lost its hard, accusing look, and she gazed at the
pecan trees and flowering oleander in her yard as if finally
seeing them for the first time. "Yes," Glory replied
briskly, "it is a very nice day."

"Glory," said Carmela, still on her best behavior, "may
I come in for a moment?"

Glory nodded abruptly and stepped back, admitting
Carmela to her inner sanctum.

Carmela, walking a few steps ahead of Glory, turned
toward the living room.

"No," said Glory hurriedly, grabbing at her arm.

"That's just been freshly cleaned. Let's go sit in the dining room instead."

Glory's dining room was really the old breakfast nook. But it was still big enough to accommodate a rather nice Sheraton table that easily seated twelve. Carmela supposed there might be extra leaves, too, to enlarge the table even more. Although Glory Meechum certainly didn't impress her as an entertaining hostess with the mostest.

Light spilled into the dining room from a trio of windows that overlooked the bucolic and somewhat overgrown backyard. Carmela realized she'd only been in this room once before. That was well over a year ago, when she and Shamus were planning their wedding and Glory had thrown what they'd laughingly referred to as the "grand inquisition dinner." Most of Shamus's family had been in attendance that evening, and it was amazing how prophetic their little nomenclature had turned out to be.

Glory plunked herself down on a dining room chair, causing it to utter a sharp *creak*. "What do you want?" she asked. Clearly, Glory was not a woman who felt she had to ease gracefully into a conversation.

Carmela decided the smartest thing to do was play this by the book.

"Glory," she began, "when you paid a visit to my scrapbooking shop the other day, you were awfully upset."

Glory's full lower lip seemed to protrude a tad more than was normal. "Still am," she told Carmela with all the aplomb of a petulant five-year-old.

"And you asked me to help you," said Carmela.

Glory Meechum sat there like a lump, surrounded by an uncomfortable silence.

Wow, thought Carmela, *Glory must have colossally lost it the other day. Is that regret showing through right now or just stubborn reluctance?*

"I think we could help each other," prompted Carmela. This whole conversation was proceeding with a lot more difficulty than she'd thought it would. In fact, trying to get a response from Glory was like trying to yank out teeth.

Glory folded her flabby arms across her chest in one of her favorite poses. "How so?" she demanded.

Carmela took a deep breath and began. "I think we both know that Shamus is in some kind of trouble," she said. "What the exact nature of it is, I have no idea. But, what I *am* proposing is that we pool our resources in an effort to unearth a clue or two."

"And how would we go about that?" asked Glory Meechum in her flat tone.

"Shamus still has his office at the Crescent City Bank, does he not?" asked Carmela. Carmela knew for a fact that he did. In fact, Glory probably kept Shamus's office looking like a shrine, the way some parents do with their children's rooms, even though the little darlings have long since departed the old homestead.

What did they call that? Carmela wondered. *Probably Whatever Happened to Baby Jane syndrome.*

"Yes," said Glory somewhat reluctantly. "Shamus *does* still have his office at the bank." She paused. "We're *holding* it for him." Disappointment and disapproval were evident in her voice.

"Then I'd propose we start there," said Carmela.

"At the bank," said Glory. "Going through confidential records." Glory Meechum had stonewall in her voice.

Uh-oh, thought Carmela. She shifted in her chair, bent forward, and tried to project what she hoped was a kinder, gentler sort of conspiracy. "Not snooping," she told Glory. "Sifting through *information*. Information that might give us a clue as to what's going on."

Glory continued to stare at her with reluctant, hooded eyes.

"You saw the column Bufford Maple wrote," prompted

Carmela. "That had to sting. And you've no doubt heard the innuendos."

Glory's head nodded ever so slightly.

Did the other guy just blink? wondered Carmela. *Am I starting to actually get somewhere?*

"And, of course, Granger Rathbone stopped by here the other day," continued Carmela. "I'm sure his little invasion of privacy angered you. In fact, I *know* it did." *That's right*, Carmela told herself, *play on the woman's paranoia.*

"Granger Rathbone is a very hostile person," spat Glory.

Touché, thought Carmela. *The pot calling the kettle black.*

But Carmela's words were working on Glory. Because Glory was beginning to get wound up, actually seemed to be seriously considering the need for taking action. Glory's eyes shone brighter, and her hands began to clench ever so slightly. A good case of outrage was starting to smolder deep within.

"Okay, then," said Carmela. "For sure we can't just stand idly by. We've got to take a proactive stance."

The spark inside Glory Meechum suddenly ignited into a white-hot flame. "If Shamus won't lift a hand to clear his good name, then we'll do it for him," proclaimed Glory. "If not for your own family, then who else? Am I right?"

"You are *so* right," declared Carmela fervently as the whine of the vacuum cleaner suddenly sounded nearby. She wanted to leap up on the table and declare *Liberté, Égalité, Fraternité*, even as she wondered to herself, *Does that family thing still include me? Am I still technically part of the Meechum clan?*

Chapter 21

THEY'D been at it for well over an hour. Bent over stacks of files that had been pulled from Shamus's desk drawers in his office at the Crescent City Bank.

Glory Meechum had produced a giant ring of keys that had admitted them into the bank lobby, taken them beyond the teller cages, and finally into the inner sanctum of executive offices. As a senior vice president herself, Glory had punched in the code numbers on the various keypads at the different checkpoints to alert the security company that she was in the bank but that everything was just fine.

Strangely enough, Glory had left Carmela alone for most of the time. She had hung around for the first twenty minutes, while Carmela went through Shamus's appointment book and desk drawers, then poked through a few piles of paper that sat on his credenza. But then Glory had drifted down to her own office, and now Carmela could hear the faint strains of a radio playing. Well, that was just fine with her. It was easier to work alone than under Glory Meechum's stolid gaze.

Carmela sighed and gazed around Shamus's office. It was just as she'd suspected it would be. Like a scene out of *The Day the Earth Stood Still.*

Shamus's calendar was still turned to the day he'd walked out, some six months ago. His pen lay where he'd set it down. A letter was waiting to be signed. Carmela glanced at it, hoping it wasn't an important letter, that some poor soul hadn't put his entire life on hold while waiting to hear if his mortgage application had been approved.

But, no, it was just something about interest rates. Besides, Shamus hadn't handled residential loans, he'd only worked on commercial loans. *What did they call that again?* Carmela wondered. *Oh, yeah, mortgage banking.* She guessed that telling people you were a mortgage banker sounded a whole lot fancier than just saying you were a loan officer. People who worked in banks were funny that way. They always had to have a fancy title.

She'd also learned long ago that, in a bank, everybody and his brother-in-law was a vice president. Those titles were handed out like candy to kindergarten kids. Apparently, customers felt much happier and more secure when they knew they were dealing with a vice president. Of course, they probably still got the same crappy service, but since it was coming from a vice president, there was justification for it, right? After all, vice presidents were busy people! Vice presidents had a lot on their plate! Vice presidents were . . . *vice presidents!*

Carmela snorted. *Hah! Right. Just like Shamus and Glory and the rest of the Meechum family.* Their big break had really come from having a great-great-granddaddy who'd had the cold cash and the good foresight to start a bank. Then, all the following generations of Meechums really had to do was tread carefully in the proverbial family footsteps. If the bank's interest rates on savings accounts and CDs weren't too high, and if the bank was prudent when extending loans, then the business would essentially be self-perpetuating.

Carmela had even learned early on from Shamus how exceedingly simple it was to start a bank. All you needed was about a hundred thousand dollars in your hot little hand, and you could go ahead and apply for that all-important charter from the federal government. A hundred thousand dollars—that was all it took! Far less than most people paid for a house these days!

Then again, Carmela had decided that a lot of things in business didn't make sense. How could a giant accounting firm with everything to lose cover up for an unscrupulous utility? How could major corporations suddenly go bankrupt? Who was the genius who thought they could sell fifty-pound bags of dog food via the Internet? Wasn't anybody thinking? Wasn't anybody looking ahead? Wasn't anyone minding the store?

Kneeling down in front of a squat, silver filing cabinet, Carmela pulled out the top drawer. Running her fingers across the plastic file tabs, she skimmed the labels. Delphi Corp., deYoung & Company, Crowell Ltd., Theriot & Partners. Everything very neat and businesslike.

Wait a minute. Theriot? Why did that name sound so darned familiar?

Carmela racked her brain.

Oh no! Theriot. Isn't that the name of Bufford Maple's partner? Sure it is. Theriot is one of the men who owns Trident Realty!

Carmela ripped the file folder from the cabinet, eager to see what was inside.

The top sheet was an application for a bridge construction loan, whatever that was. An application that had been turned down. By Shamus.

That's it? Shamus turned Theriot and maybe Bufford Maple down for a loan? A bridge loan? That's why they're trying to set him up?

Carmela frowned, slumped down into a sitting position, cross-legged on the carpet.

It doesn't seem earth-shattering enough, it doesn't make sense, and it for sure doesn't seem related to Jimmy Earl Clayton's death.

Also, what about Big Jack Dumaine? I thought he was the guy trying to set Shamus up to take the fall?

Carmela skimmed through every paper contained in the folder. There were about ten pages. Nowhere did she find a mention of Jack Dumaine. Or even Jimmy Earl Clayton.

How strange, thought Carmela. *Here I thought I was on to something big, and everything I've found so far has just made things even more confusing and tangled.*

"Carmela!" Glory Meechum's shrill voice roused Carmela from her jumble of thoughts.

"I'm almost done, Glory," Carmela called back. She grabbed the Theriot file, hesitated a split second, then folded it in half and jammed it in her handbag.

Have to give this a little more thought, she decided with a slight twinge of guilt. At the very least she could possibly bring it up to Shamus. That is, if the old boy came skulking by her apartment for another nocturnal visit.

Carmela sprang up from her cross-legged position on the floor and yanked open the office door. "Hey there," she said to Glory, who stared in at her with suspicious eyes.

"You find anything?" demanded Glory.

Carmela assumed a wistful expression and shook her head sadly. "No, not really." She hoped she projected total innocence and guile.

"Hmph," said Glory. "Chased all the way down here on Sunday for naught."

Carmela smiled ruefully. *I'm back to being the family dingbat again*, she decided. *I was Glory's big ally for a few short moments, but now I'm relegated to dingbat*

*status once again. Well, at least it's a role I've had some
experience with.*

IT WAS STILL EARLY, JUST TWO IN THE AFTER-
noon. So Carmela popped back to her apartment, changed
into jeans and a yellow Spiderman T-shirt that Ava had
talked her into buying, then hustled Boo into the backseat
of her car. For the past couple years, she'd been serving
as a volunteer for the Children's Art Association. Started
by a community-minded group of artists and craftspeople,
the Children's Art Association taught drawing, painting,
and crafts to kids between the ages of eight and fifteen at
various neighborhood centers around the city.

Today, Carmela was headed for the Chamberlain Center out near Audubon Park. If memory served her correctly, Jekyl Hardy should be there, teaching the kids the
fundamentals of still life drawing.

He was there, all right, along with a couple other vol-
unteers. They were warning a group of squirming kids to
*"Please do not eat the apples, oranges, grapes, and pears.
Please do not eat any of the props!"*

Carmela saw that, like kids everywhere, they were
steadfastly ignoring the volunteer artists' pleadings. Orange peels littered the floor as the rowdy children feasted
mightily on the forbidden fruit and drew on each other's
faces with paint.

"Carmela!" exclaimed Jekyl Hardy when he saw her.
"Come over here and help me! These little darlings are
completely out of control."

He good-naturedly snatched a pear from the sticky
hands of a beautiful little African American girl. "Ar-
iella," he warned. "You've already eaten two apples.
These are to paint!" She giggled and proceeded to mix
her yellow with her blue to produce a luminous pool of
green.

"Good," Jekyl told her as she made an artful brush-stroke across her canvas, "that's a very auspicious start. Oh, you brought your dog," he exclaimed to Carmela. "She's very cute." Jekyl knelt down and faced Boo. "Can you shake?" he asked her. "Can you shake hands?"

Boo, an old pro at shaking hands, promptly sat on her butt and stuck her right paw in the air. "Good girl," said Jekyl. He took her paw, pumped it gently, then released it. Boo, loving the attention, promptly stuck her left paw out at him.

"Oh, I see she's ambidextrous," laughed Jekyl, patting her. "That talent can come in handy."

"She's a show-off," said Carmela. "And don't let that sweet little face fool you. She'll steal one of those oranges if you don't watch out. Toss it around like a tennis ball and then eviscerate it."

Jekyl Hardy threw up his hands. "So what else is new? Oh, honey," he said, clasping Carmela's arm tightly. "I am *sooo* sorry about last night. I didn't mean to get you all upset. And I really didn't foresee the bizarre antics of Ruby Dumaine. I think Tandy was right, she must have been sipping absinthe."

"I believe it," said Carmela. "That woman packs a lot of punch when she sets her mind to it."

"But hey," said Jekyl. "What's with you? Where did you sneak off to last night? Did you go out chasing leads in the great Shamus mystery? Or were you just chasing around?"

"Jekyl, you have no idea," sighed Carmela. "This whole thing just gets stranger and stranger."

"Do tell," said Jekyl. He turned to the little boy at the table next to him. "Carlyle, I love that arrangement. So unconventional. Now don't be afraid to add in some high-lights. Red on top of purple is *good*."

As she was watching Jekyl interact with the kids, Car-mela felt a tug on the back of her T-shirt. "Can we take your dog outside and play with him?" asked a little boy.

"Her name is Boo, and she's a she," said Carmela. "And yes, you certainly may. But please lead her out this side door here so you'll be in the fenced-in play area, okay?"

Two more kids put their hands gently on Boo's shoulders and marched out to the playground with her. *Gosh,* thought Carmela, *this is nice. This is so sane after hanging out with the likes of Glory Meechum this morning.*

Jekyl Hardy turned back to Carmela with a smile. "Now, what were you saying?"

"Jekyl, you did the floats for the Pluvius krewe. . . ." said Carmela.

"Indeed I did," declared Jekyl. "Twenty magnificent oceania-themed beauties. Some of my finest work, I might add."

"Do you know a Pluvius krewe member by the name of Theriot?

Jekyl Hardy rolled his eyes upward, thinking. "Theriot . . . Theriot . . . *Michael* Theriot? Yes, I think I might have bumped shoulders with him. Is he a somewhat portly fellow?"

"I have no idea," said Carmela. "I've never met him."

"You know who's probably more plugged in?" said Jekyl. "My assistant, Thomas Waite." Jekyl pulled a tomato-red StarTac from his pocket and promptly hit the speed dial. "Thomas knows *everyone,*" Jekyl assured Carmela. "And he keeps lists of all the Pluvius committees."

"Thomas?" said Jekyl when his call was finally answered. "Yes, it's Jekyl here. Say, a dear friend of mine is trying to glean some information on one of the Pluvius krewe members. A Mr. Michael Theriot. Do you know him?"

Jekyl winked at Carmela and gave an exaggerated nod as he listened to Thomas on the other end of the line. Finally, Jekyl thanked his assistant and hung up.

"Here's the scoop," said Jekyl in a conspiratorial tone. "Michael Theriot is one of the newer Pluvius members. And by that I mean maybe two or three years with the krewe, since some of the other fellows have been with it for just eons. It seems this Theriot is some kind of real estate mover and shaker, or *claims* he is, anyway. Of course, you never know for sure with these business types. I say give me an artsy type any day. They may be poor as church mice, but they're generally a lot more honest. Anyway," continued Jekyl, "this Theriot has a reputation as a real gung-ho volunteer. He was on the parade route committee, the marching band committee, and the refreshment committee."

Carmela stared at Jekyl. "The refreshment committee," she repeated.

"Yes," said Jekyl. "And Thomas says that—oh, my God!" Jekyl suddenly clapped a hand over his mouth. "You don't suppose . . ." His eyes widened; his mouth fell open. "I mean, are you thinking what *I'm* thinking?" he sputtered. "That horrible thing with Jimmy Earl? Wow . . . I wonder if the police took a hard look at who was serving drinks that night. Or who *mixed* the drinks."

"I always assumed they did," said Carmela. "Now I'm not so sure."

THE CHOKING SOUNDS COMING FROM THE backseat of Carmela's car weren't good. Gazing in her rearview mirror to make sure she wouldn't sideswipe anyone, Carmela swerved over to the curb. She was just in time to see a spurt of yellow foam issue from Boo's gaping mouth.

"No you don't!" Carmela was out of her car in a split second. "Not on Samantha's backseat!" She yanked open the rear door and grabbed the terry cloth towel she kept stashed back there for just such occasions. She positioned it under Boo's chin in anticipation of a second outpouring. Annoyed, Boo promptly jerked her head away and gave a violent shake. Tendrils of yellow gunk flew everywhere, decorating the interior of Carmela's car.

"Boo, we talked about this," said Carmela firmly. "No oranges and no spinning on the merry-go-round. Evidently you once again flung caution to the wind and did both." Carmela mopped gingerly at the backseat of the car. Boo, who seemed to have made a speedy recovery, now licked her paws happily with that amazing nonchalance dogs often have. *Sick? Who me? Nah. Never happened.*

As Carmela pulled into her parking space in the alley behind her apartment, Ava was just returning from a trip to the market. "Hey," she called to Ava, "you ever make it to Brennan's?"

Ava shifted her grocery bag from one arm to the other. "No. I ended up at Cardamom's with some other friends. Obviously not you."

Carmela jumped from her car, hauled Boo out of the back.

"What's that awful smell?" asked Ava, wrinkling her nose.

"Air freshener," said Carmela. "That car wash down on Marais Street is letting me try out some new chemicals they developed. Smells real bad at first, but then the interior of your car reverts to that pleasant new car smell."

Ava narrowed her eyes. "Well, it smells like dog puke, if you ask me. In fact, it's amazing what companies will try to foist on an unsuspecting public."

"Hey," said Carmela. "Why don't you come over for dinner tonight. I made jambalaya the other night, and I've still got gallons."

"Why don't you come to the Bachus parade with me?" asked Ava. "I'm supposed to meet Smoochy Peabody and some of his friends over at Tipitina's."

"To tell you the truth, Ava, I'm kind of paraded out," admitted Carmela. In the final twelve days of Mardi Gras there were something like fifty different parades. The whole thing could really set your head to spinning.

Ava brushed back a mass of auburn hair and rocked back on the heels of her espadrilles. "You want to talk, huh?"

"Kind of," admitted Carmela.

"You found something out today?" inquired Ava.

"I did," said Carmela, "but I'm not exactly sure what it means."

Ava put a hand to the side of her face to shade it from the late-afternoon sun. "To tell you the truth," she said, "I'm a little bit paraded out myself. What say I drop by in an hour or so? Would that work?"

"I'll heat up that jambalaya," said Carmela. "And chill a bottle of wine."

"You might want to chill two bottles," suggested Ava. "And while you're at it, better wipe that yellow glop off your dog's chin."

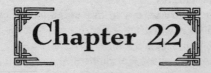

Chapter 22

CARMELA and Ava chatted their way through dinner, helping themselves to extra large servings of Carmela's very excellent jambalaya, slices of prune bread, and sipping the crisp white Vouvray they'd uncorked. They talked about Baby's party, the strange tissue paper–looking dress that a woman by the name of Magdalen Dilworth had worn, and about the Swedish crystal chandelier Jekyl Hardy had apparently found for a song at an antique sale over in Destrehan. They even skirted around the issue of the amazing disappearing Shamus but never did attack it head-on.

Now, with the dishes piled in the sink and the second bottle of wine uncorked, they were ready to get down to it.

"You found something out about Shamus today," began Ava. She was lounging at the little dining table while Carmela made a pretense of rattling dishes in the sink. "How did this all come about?"

Carmela abandoned the dishes and came over and sat

down across from Ava. "I paid a little visit to Glory Meechum, Shamus's sister," said Carmela.

Ava made a face. "Always a challenge dealing with the
queen of the harpies."

"Actually, Glory wasn't in *that* bad a mood," said Carmela. "I've seen worse."

Ava shivered. "Tell the story."

"Well, long story short," said Carmela, "I talked Glory
Meechum into escorting me to the Crescent City Bank
office and letting me snoop around inside Shamus's office," said Carmela.

Ava took another sip of wine. "And what incredible
findings were unearthed from his inner sanctum?" asked
Ava. "Gold from Carthage? Tutankhamen's Treasure?"
Ava paused dramatically. "Wait just a minute, that stuff
is already in the British Museum, isn't it? Silly me."

Carmela pulled the stolen file from her handbag, un-
folded it as best she could, and handed it to Ava. "I found
that," she said.

Ava set her glass of wine down, uncrumpled the folder.
"You didn't find it, you pilfered it."

"Well, yes," admitted Carmela.

"Good girl," said Ava as she opened the manila folder.
"And who exactly is this Theriot fellow?"

"Part owner in a real estate company," said Carmela.
"Trident Realty."

Ava nodded, then spent a good three or four minutes
poring through the documents. Finally, she frowned, then
looked up at Carmela. "What?" said Ava. "I don't see any
connection."

"Neither do I," replied Carmela.

Ava stared blandly at her. "Then why did you steal it?
Or is this just a practice exercise for some far grander cat
burglar caper?"

"The thing of it is," said Carmela, "I *know* there's some

important tidbit of information in that file. But I'm just not seeing it."

"Okay," said Ava. "Let's try to be analytical and completely emotionless about this, which is no small task when you're of the female persuasion and have just downed a few glasses of wine."

"Agreed," said Carmela, taking another sip of wine.

However," continued Ava, "let's try to recall every single detail concerning this entire Shamus mess. Going back to the absolute very beginning."

"The very beginning," agreed Carmela.

"We were at the parade . . ." Ava prompted.

"And saw Jimmy Earl Clayton collapse on his float," said Carmela.

"And then right after that, all sorts of strange rumors started flying," said Ava. "About Shamus."

"It was like someone was feeding them," said Carmela. "Busily fanning the flames." She hunched forward and stared at Ava. "And then Bufford Maple wrote a nasty column implicating Shamus."

"Right," nodded Ava. "It ran the day of Jimmy Earl's funeral, which I'm sorry I missed since, aside from Baby's party, it seems to have been one of the pivotal social events of the season."

"Then Hop Pennington, one of the property managers from Trident Realty, called and tried to muscle me around," recalled Carmela. He said Bartholomew Hayward from next door wanted my space."

"Oh no," said Ava, dismayed. "They can't do that. That's the absolute *perfect* space for you!"

"Don't I know it!" responded Carmela. She was still ticked off by Hop Pennington's macho power play attempt. "And get this, afterwards I called and schmoozed the receptionist at Trident Realty. And I found out that the company is owned by Bufford Maple and Michael Theriot."

"Bufford Maple penned the nasty column, and now we have Michael Theriot's bank folder in front of us," finished Ava. "With a turndown from Shamus."

"Right," said Carmela.

"But people get turned down for these kinds of loans all the time," said Ava. "That's not a reason to try to pin a murder on somebody. Unless, of course, *they're* the murderers and they need a handy pigeon to foist the blame on."

"I hate to think of Shamus as a pigeon," said Carmela.

Ava stared at her. "What do you think of him as?"

Carmela shrugged. "I don't know. My soon-to-be ex, I suppose."

"A couple weeks ago a very smart and together lady I know referred to him as a cad, a rat, and a louse."

Carmela squirmed uncomfortably.

"It's happening, isn't it?" said Ava, emitting a huge sigh.

"What's happening?"

"You're starting to feel *sorry* for him."

"I—" began Carmela.

"Don't!" admonished Ava. "This changes *nothing*. Shamus is still the man who boogied on out of your life with no just cause. He's still the man who left you in the lurch. You know," said Ava, peering carefully at her, "Shamus *could* be a murderer. He's secretive enough. And he's colossally hotheaded."

Ava's harsh words cut Carmela to the quick. *Shamus a murderer? My Shamus? Well, the man who used to be my Shamus? No, I still don't believe it. Or maybe I just don't want to believe it.*

"Up until this afternoon, I harbored a funny feeling about Dace Wilcox. I thought that he might be a suspect in Jimmy Earl's demise," said Carmela. "When I ran into him at the Marseille Ball, he pretended he really didn't know Shamus. Then later on at the shop, CeCe and Tandy discovered an old photograph that proved Dace *did* know Shamus. In fact, the two of them were in the same fraternity together. And then when we started talking about Dace, Gabby said that Dace Wilcox had been talking to Jimmy Earl right before he climbed up on his float."

"Hmm," said Ava. "Dace Wilcox. Yes, you mentioned him before. He's kind of a wild card in all this, isn't he?"

"And let's not forget about Granger Rathbone," said Carmela. "He's been harassing me *and* trying to locate Shamus. Plus I found out that Granger Rathbone is very tight with Jack Dumaine. Might even be working for him on the side."

"This *is* getting complicated," acknowledged Ava.

"I also have a slight confession to make," said Carmela. "I *followed* Jack Dumaine last night. That's where I disappeared to," admitted Carmela.

Ava's eyebrows shot up. "Followed him as in *tailed* him?" asked Ava. "PI style?"

Carmela nodded.

"Jeez, you really are a squirrel," said Ava.

"Thanks a lot," said Carmela.

"So where did our boy Jack run off to?" asked Ava.

"To the Calhoun Motel over near the airport," said Carmela. "Where he met up with one Rhonda Lee Clayton. She'd already reserved a trashy little motel room and was obviously expecting him."

"What?" Ava squawked. "Big Jack Dumaine had a clandestine rendezvous with Rhonda Lee? Jimmy Earl's *widow?*"

Carmela nodded, pleased that she'd been able to arouse so much outrage from Ava. "What do you think it means?" she asked excitedly. Maybe Ava could offer some insight as to this strange alliance.

Ava's face was a mixture of curiosity and shock. "It means the two of them are either thick as thieves or else that love is completely blind."

Chapter 23

IT was a show of solidarity that warmed Carmela's heart. Baby and Tandy were standing on the sidewalk outside Memory Mine, waiting for her when she arrived for work Monday morning.

"Hey, talk about a surprise!" exclaimed Carmela. "I didn't think anyone would show up today!"

"We didn't want you to be alone," said Tandy.

Carmela's smile immediately slid off her face. "What's wrong?" she asked.

"She hasn't heard the news," said Baby to Tandy. "I *told* you this would come as a complete surprise."

"What's going on?" asked Carmela. Watching the two women fidget, Carmela was growing more and more nervous.

"Del heard a rumor via the old boy's grapevine," said Baby.

"About what?" asked Carmela, instantly on the alert. She knew that, as a high-profile attorney, Baby's husband was privy to all sorts of inside information.

"Now don't come all unglued, sweetie, but Shamus has been hauled in for questioning again," finished Tandy.

Carmela put a hand to her mouth. "Oh no." Her voice was a hoarse whisper; the ring of keys she had clutched in her hand suddenly clattered to the pavement. *They found Shamus*, she thought to herself. *Or at least caught up to him.*

Tandy knelt down to scoop up the dropped keys. "Let me get those," she said.

Carmela turned to face Baby. "What else did Del say? Did he know if the police had any hard evidence against him?"

"Shush, dear." Baby put a hand on Carmela's shoulder. "That's all we know for now. Just that Shamus is being questioned again. Del has court all day today, so he'll be able to keep an ear open. Plus he knows where I'll be. He promised to call if there's any news."

Tandy put the key in the lock, fought with it for a couple seconds, then finally wrestled the door open. "C'mon, Carmela," she said in her characteristic upbeat, no-nonsense style. "There's really nothing you can do. So the best thing is to just stay busy."

Promptly at 9:00 A.M. Gabby came marching into Memory Mine and handed Carmela a steaming cup of café au lait that she'd fetched from the Merci Beaucoup Bakery down the street. Carmela, sitting at the back craft table with Tandy and Baby, murmured a quiet *"Bless you"* as she accepted the cup.

Unsnapping the white lid, Carmela took a sip of the hot, steaming coffee. "This really hits the spot," she declared as Gabby continued to stare at her silently. She took another sip. All the while, Gabby's eyes never left her.

"What?" asked Carmela finally. *"What?"*

Their antennae suddenly up and sensing an impending

problem, Tandy and Baby squirmed at the sudden tension developing between Gabby and Carmela.

"Stuart says I have to quit," said Gabby quietly.

Gabby's words hit Carmela like a bolt from the blue. "Gabby, what are you *talking* about? Why on earth would you quit?"

Gabby hung her head. "Stuart thinks it's for the best. Until this whole mess is resolved."

"This whole mess meaning . . ."

"Well . . . Shamus and everything," stammered Gabby.

"And this is *Stuart's* idea, not yours?" said Carmela, peering up at her.

Gabby's pleading face spoke volumes. "Oh, Carmela, you *know* I don't want to leave you in the lurch like this." Gabby looked like she was about ready to cry.

"Don't you think you should make up your *own* mind?" Carmela asked her gently.

"Honey," said Tandy, suddenly interjecting herself into the conversation, "are you suddenly experiencing a tremendous hormonal imbalance at your tender young age? I mean, what *is* this all about? Why on earth would you be doing this?"

"Because I promised Stuart that I would love, honor, and obey him?" ventured Gabby, her voice quavering wildly.

"Obey!" snorted Tandy. She glanced around the table, realized she had overreacted a bit, decided to try to diffuse the situation. "Is *that* all! Thank goodness, I thought we really had ourselves a big hairy *problema* here."

Baby, ever the diplomat, gave a gentle laugh. "Isn't that the cutest," she said as she continued to thread pink ribbon through the top of a scrapbook page that she'd just punched with little *V*s. "Spoken like a new bride. All sweet and innocent and still agog over the joys of marriage."

"But so misguided," added Tandy. This time she leveled a somewhat more accusing gaze at Gabby.

"Sakes, yes," agreed Baby. She gently took one of Gabby's hands in her own, focused her baby-blue eyes on the girl. "Honey," said Baby, with all the sincerity she could muster, "you're a married woman now. You have to learn how to *handle* your man."

"But Stuart thinks—" began Gabby again.

"It doesn't matter what *Stuart* thinks," snapped Tandy. "What do *you* think?"

Tears were streaming down Gabby's face now. "Carmela," she implored, "*help* me! You know I don't want to quit for good. Just for a while. Until things blow over."

Carmela leapt from her chair and swept Gabby into her arms. "I know that, dear," she told her. "Don't worry about it, okay?"

Gabby continued to sniffle. "It's just that . . . well, somebody broke into our house last night while we were over visiting Stuart's cousin. And now Stuart is mighty jittery."

"Oh no!" said Tandy. "Why didn't you say something sooner? Now *that's* a different story."

"Dear lord," said Baby, clapping a petite hand to her chest. "Did you-all lose your valuables? Your silverware and jewelry and such?"

Gabby continued to sob. "Some jewelry, yes. My ruby ring and the cameo I inherited from my grandmother. But the worst of it is that our house looks like we were positively *invaded!* The robbers emptied out all the drawers and messed things up pretty bad." Gabby wiped at her streaming eyes. "It looks like a hurricane blew through. I have no idea where to even start."

AS IF CARMELA DIDN'T HAVE ENOUGH GOING on in her life, business was positively booming at Memory Mine this morning. A gaggle of tourists had come pouring in, delighted to have found a dedicated scrapbooking store.

"We're from a little town in Ohio," said one of the women excitedly, "and we don't have a real scrapbooking store."

"Right," echoed her chubby friend who had just picked out a pair of scallop-edge scissors along with a pair that would create a lacy Victorian edge. "We have to pick stuff up at the mall whenever we can. Or drive up to Dayton when they have their scrapbooking conventions."

There's gotta be something strange in the ozone, Carmela marveled to herself. *My assistant quit, everything's in turmoil, and suddenly customers are pouring in here like crazy.*

"Tandy," called Carmela, as she tried to ring up three customers at once even as she was trying to explain molding mats to another. "Do you by any chance know how to operate a cash register?"

Tandy's eyes grew big. "Me? Uh . . . no." Obviously, it had been more than a few years since Tandy had held down a job.

As the door flew open once again, Carmela's first thought was, *We stuff one more body in here, and the fire marshal's gonna shut us down.*

But it wasn't another customer, it was Ava. She took one look around, saw the panic on Carmela's face, and plunged right in.

"You want to put that on your charge card?" she drawled as she plucked the Visa card from the hand of a woman hovering near the cash register. "No problem, sugar."

Sure enough, within five minutes, Ava had cashed out half of the customers and was now showing a die cutter and some alphabet templates to two other women.

"You're a lifesaver!" Carmela whispered to Ava when she had a spare moment.

"Where on earth is Gabby?" asked Ava. "She call in sick today?"

"Not quite," said Carmela.

Ava rolled her eyes. "Oh, oh, *that* doesn't sound good."

"It's not," Carmela told her.

BY NOON THINGS HAD SETTLED DOWN, AND Carmela, buoyed by her windfall of business, had phoned a nearby deli and had salads delivered for everyone. She, Ava, Tandy, and Baby sat munching them now at the back table. They rehashed events at Baby's party, still awe-struck by the food and giggling over some of the more colorful characters who had been in attendance.

"So tell me about the incredible disappearing Gabby," Ava finally prompted as she carefully spooned vinaigrette over her spinach and citrus salad.

"She just up and quit," pronounced Tandy.

"Well, it wasn't quite *that* abrupt," said Baby. "Her husband sort of strong-armed her into it."

"Plus her house was broken into," said Tandy, gesturing with a forkful of greens.

Ava shook her head. "This crazy city. They feed us all sorts of statistics that are supposed to convince us crime is on the *decrease*, then you hear something like this." She shook her head again. "Poor Gabby. She's having a tough time right now, but I think she'll be back."

"I *know* she will," said Carmela confidently. "Gabby loves this store almost as much as I do."

"We all love it," declared Baby.

"Ava," said Tandy, "what about *your* store? I would think you'd be jumping right about now. I mean, tomorrow's the big one . . . Fat Tuesday!"

"Tyrell's at the store today. He's even better at working the crowd than I am." Tyrell Burton was Ava's sometime assistant, a twenty-two-year-old African American who was also a grad student in history at Tulane. Tyrell's great-grandmother was purported to have emigrated from Haiti and been known to dabble in voodoo lore. Needless to say, Tyrell took great delight in his rather strange pedigree and never tired of spinning a few good yarns for the tourists.

"But the *real* reason I stopped by," said Ava, "was to give you a heads up on something." She paused, unsure of just how to relate her story. "The thing of it is, Carmela, I just stopped over at Bultman's Drug Store to pick up some photos I left to be developed."

Carmela nodded. She'd used Bultman's many times herself before she'd switched to digital photography a month or so ago. Bultman's was just down the block from Memory Mine and awfully handy. She still sent a lot of her customers there, since Bultman's offered photofinishing in both matte and high gloss.

"So I picked up my photos from that fellow Dirk who's always at the counter," continued Ava. "You know, the one with the pierced tongue and bowl haircut?"

Carmela nodded. She knew Dirk. Everybody knew Dirk.

"Anyway, he asked about you," said Ava.

"What about me?" said Carmela, stabbing at an oversized crouton.

"Well," said Ava, "here's where the story starts to get a little strange. It seems that someone had just been there ten minutes earlier asking if there were any photos for you."

Carmela gave Ava a quizzical gaze. "Somebody tried to pick up my photos?" *What is this all about? Jekyl Hardy trying to do a good deed, maybe?*

"According to Dirk, this *person* said they were running errands for you and wanted to know if your photos were ready."

"But I didn't drop anything off to be developed," said

Carmela. "Now that I've gone digital, all I have to do is *print* photos off my computer." She thought for a minute. "And I *still* haven't used up all the shots on my Leica."

The last time I used that camera was the night Jimmy Earl died, thought Carmela.

"I know that, honey," said Ava patiently, "but the point is, somebody was trying to pick up your photos." Ava paused. "You don't think that's a trifle strange?"

"I don't think it's strange at all," said Tandy. "I leave my film all over town. I'd be *delighted* if one of my friends volunteered to pick up my finished photos."

Carmela shrugged. "I don't know, Ava. In the scheme of things, it doesn't seem worth worrying about." She stood up and stretched. And, as if on cue, the front door burst open and four women with delighted grins lighting up their faces poured into her shop.

"Good afternoon," Carmela called to them. "Welcome to Memory Mine."

Chapter 24

CARMELA'S scrapbook for Saint Cyril's Cemetery was coming together nicely. Over the past week, in stolen moments here and there, she'd put together the introduction page as well as two double-page spreads. The material the Preservation Society had provided her with had been rich, indeed, and Carmela was quite pleased at how good everything was looking. In a couple days she would present her initial work to Donna Mae Dupres and her cemetery preservation group and, hopefully, get their final blessing to complete the project.

"Carmela, what *are* you doing with those photographs?" asked Tandy. She had watched Carmela take two perfectly good photographs, a black-and-white photo and a color photo, then cut them both into strips. Now, Tandy's curiosity had gotten the better of her.

"Oh," said Carmela, "it's a fun technique I picked up at a scrapbooking convention last year. You take a color photo that you like and also have it printed in black and white. Then you cut *both* photos into strips and weave them together."

"What?" said Baby, her interest piqued. "This I have to see."

"Here," said Carmela, laying the photo strips out. "What you do is alternate strips, see? A color strip, then a black-and-white strip, then a color strip again. When you weave the photo back together, you achieve a kind of checkerboard result. Or mosaic. It doesn't really matter what you call it, the results are just wonderfully effective."

"Wow," said Baby, watching as Carmela's deft fingers wove strips from the two photos into a single, finished piece.

"Isn't that a great effect?" asked Carmela. "The color strips make it look contemporary, but the black-and-white strips give it an aged feel."

"I love it," said Tandy, "but how do you keep all the various strips in place?"

"Turn it over gently and use some photo-safe adhesive tape," said Carmela.

"Saint Cyril's is going to absolutely *love* this," said Tandy. "Can I look at the rest of what you've done?"

"Sure," said Carmela. She slid the pages she'd already completed and carefully encased in plastic sleeves across the table to Tandy.

Together, Tandy and Baby studied Carmela's handiwork. They were obviously impressed.

"You know what you're missing?" asked Tandy, rubbing at the tip of her nose.

"What's that?" replied Carmela.

"You don't have any photos of the oven crypts."

Oven crypts were walls of crypts with front openings that looked something like bread ovens. When they were first built, they housed the final remains of indigents. Today, however, the oven crypts were much in demand by ordinary families. Coffins were slid into these so-called ovens and, after a couple years of New Orleans's heat and humidity, a sort of natural cremation took place. The contents and the coffins were reduced to almost nothing. The human remains were then swept back into a kind of pit in the rear of the oven crypt and the pieces of the coffin removed. The real estate, such as it was, was now available for yet another occupant.

"I *thought* I had some," said Carmela, as she shuffled through the various envelopes of photos that the Saint Cyril's group had given her. After a fairly thorough search, however, it appeared she *didn't* have any photos of the oven crypts.

"And you're right, Tandy," said Carmela. "The oven crypts *are* historically significant. Some of them are even older than the family and fraternal organization crypts."

"Plus they form the outside walls that surround Saint Cyril's," Baby pointed out. "That's important, isn't it?"

"I'd say it's critical," said Carmela. "Which means I'd better stop by Saint Cyril's tomorrow morning and shoot a few photos. I just hope it doesn't rain." Carmela noted that the day had started out partly cloudy and was rapidly becoming overcast. Fact was, the weather forecasters *were* predicting rain for Mardi Gras day tomorrow.

"I hope it doesn't rain on our parades!" declared Baby.

"But if it does rain, your photos might turn out nice and eerie," suggested Tandy. "Very funereal."

"The problem is," said Carmela, studying her pages, "I'm not exactly shooting for eerie. Saint Cyril's Cemetery Preservation Society specifically requested historic."

"I suppose a preservation group would look at it that way," allowed Tandy. "Most of the time, folks are so rabidly obsessed with our cemeteries and the notion that New Orleans keeps its dead so close by, you sometimes *forget* there's a historic aspect."

"It's those darn vampire stories," said Baby, shaking her head. "Just way too much vampire lore and mythology. Outsiders probably think we walk around with garlic wreaths strung around our necks."

* * *

TANDY PASTED A FINAL RAGGEDY ANN STICKER
on her scrapbook page. She'd titled her page, "When I
Grow Up . . ." and below her headline of colorful, bouncing type had created a photo montage of Julia, her two-
year-old granddaughter, interspersed with Raggedy Ann
stickers depicting the beloved doll in various astronaut,
karate, and nurse costumes. "Uh-oh," she said, glancing
up toward the front window. "Incoming."

Carmela looked up just in time to see Rhonda Lee
Clayton, Jimmy Earl's widow, pulling open the door to
her store. She winced and jumped out of her chair. The
set of Rhonda Lee's jaw and the fiery look on her face
told her this wasn't going to be pretty.

"I don't think Rhonda Lee's here to make a scrapbook,"
said Baby in a low whisper.

Rhonda Lee Clayton launched into her tirade before the
door swung shut and whacked her on the backside.

"I'm going to shut you down if it's the last thing I do!"
Rhonda Lee screamed at Carmela. Rhonda Lee, dressed
in a long, black skirt and oversized sweater, suddenly
seemed to bear a striking resemblance to the Wicked
Witch of the West.

"Rhonda Lee, take it easy," cautioned Carmela.
"What's got you so upset?"

"Upset? Upset?" shrilled Rhonda Lee. "I'm more than
a little *upset!*" Her normally pale face had two rings of
color high on her cheeks, making her look even more
hysterical.

Tandy, never one to be left out of a good catfight, decided to interject herself into the fray. "Hey Rhonda Lee,
how do?" She gave a friendly wave from where she sat
at the back table.

"Stay out of this, Tandy," Rhonda Lee snapped. "This
is between me and Carmela!"

"Rhonda Lee," said Tandy sharply, "don't go postal on us." She stood up and advanced on the screaming woman. "You're a lady, remember? Ladies don't go postal."

"I'll do whatever I want!" spat back Rhonda Lee. "My husband is *dead!*" She turned wild eyes on Carmela. "And it was *your* husband who killed him!"

What is this, wondered Carmela, *some kind of delayed stress reaction?*

Now it was Baby's turn to wade into the fracas. "For heaven's sake, Rhonda Lee," said Baby, adjusting the silk Hermes scarf draped about her neck, "you are *so* over the top. Ya'll know Shamus wouldn't hurt a fly. Besides," she said, adding a modicum of logic, "he's a Meechum. And you know the Meechums are a good, upstanding New Orleans family."

I wouldn't be so sure of that, Carmela thought to herself.

"Of course Shamus didn't have anything to do with poor Jimmy Earl's death," said Carmela, putting a real note of authority in her voice this time. No way was she going to back down to *this* woman.

Rhonda Lee dug in her purse for a hankie, then dabbed at her eyes. "My life is *ruined*," she moaned. "My *daughter's* dreams are completely shattered. And all because of Shamus Meechum." Rhonda Lee gazed about Memory Mine with a wild look in her eyes. "I'll shut you down!" she declared again. "As God is my witness, I'll shut you down! Then you'll see what it's like to have *your* life in shreds!"

Carmela gazed at Rhonda Lee with what could only be called bemused pity. In fact, she might have allowed herself to be halfway intimidated by this woman's threats if she hadn't just seen Rhonda Lee grinning ear to ear in the doorway of a room at the Calhoun Motel two nights ago. Opening the door of her somewhat *déclassé* motel room to the likes of Jack Dumaine, the partner of her dearly

departed husband. On the other hand, Rhonda Lee *had*
just lost her husband, which meant she should still be
accorded a small amount of leeway. Very small.

But Rhonda Lee was fixated on how she was going to
ruin Carmela. "I'll put you out of business," she cried
again. "Have the landlord padlock your door!"

As Carmela stared at Rhonda Lee Clayton and listened
to her rantings, she suddenly found herself wondering if
this was just an idle threat, or did Rhonda Lee really know
something? "Rhonda Lee," said Carmela suddenly, "do
you know who owns this building?"

That question halted Rhonda Lee in her tracks. Rhonda
Lee blinked, her nostrils flared, and her mouth opened and
closed like a fish gasping for air. "Whaaat?" she croaked.

"Do you know who owns this building?" Carmela
asked again. This time her voice rang out with even more
authority.

Rhonda Lee was temporarily derailed by Carmela's
bravado. And she also seemed to interpret Carmela's
question as some sort of *trick*. She clenched her jaw
tightly and pulled herself up to her full height, which was
difficult, Carmela noted, when you were only five foot
two. "I can find out!" Rhonda Lee spat at her. "I have
friends."

I'll just bet you do, thought Carmela. She almost said,
Like Jack Dumaine? She would have loved to see the look
of utter surprise on Rhonda Lee's face, but she held her
tongue instead. No sense revealing her cards at this stage
of the game. Especially when she wasn't sure what game
was even being played out here.

"Rhonda Lee," said Carmela slowly, wondering if she
could somehow get a piece of the puzzle to click into
place, "do you know anything about Jimmy Lee being
involved with Bufford Maple and a fellow named Michael
Theriot?"

"What is she *talking* about!" shrilled Rhonda Lee to

Tandy. "Will somebody *please* tell me what she's babbling about?"

Rhonda Lee was so worked up that every time she spoke, spit flew out of her mouth. It wasn't pretty, although at this point, it was starting to seem pretty darn funny.

Baby put a hand on Rhonda Lee's shoulder. "Maybe it's time you get going, dear," she suggested in a gentle yet firm tone. Clearly, Baby had grown tired of Rhonda Lee's hysterics.

Tandy closed in on Rhonda Lee's other side. "Gosh, look at the time, Rhonda Lee. Don't you have to be somewhere? Sure you do."

They escorted Rhonda Lee to the front door of the shop, trying to usher her out as gently as possible. Carmela remained standing where she was. Her friends were doing a masterful job with what had been a totally whacked-out situation. For that she'd be eternally grateful.

There were a few more muffled exchanges, then the front door banged shut. Tandy turned and threw her hands in the air. "What a fruitcake," she declared.

"Bonkers," said Baby. "Absolutely bonkers."

Is she really? wondered Carmela. *Or does Rhonda Lee know something but is just too upset to piece together what she knows?*

AS CARMELA WAS ABOUT TO FLIP THE LIGHT switch and lock up for the day, the phone rang.

Sighing, she contemplated not even answering it, but her conscience got the better of her. *Hey lazybones, it's a business, remember?*

She groaned and reached for the phone. "Good afternoon," she said. "Memory Mine Scrapbooking."

"Carmela?" came the voice on the other end of the line. "Hi, there. It's Alyse Eskew at the Claiborne Club."

The Claiborne Club, thought Carmela. *Lucky me. The club that isn't sure they want to admit any new members right now. I guess Alyse's remark about that has really stuck in my craw, as my momma would say.*

"Hello Alyse," said Carmela with not much enthusiasm.

"I'm glad I caught you," Alyse purred, "I know how busy you are."

"Mm-hm," replied Carmela.

"Say Carmela," asked Alyse, "do you still have that list we faxed you?"

Carmela's mind was blank for a moment. "The list?" *What list is Alyse babbling about?*

Alyse gave a nervous titter. Obviously, this conversation wasn't all that pleasant for her, either. "You know, the one you used when you created all those adorable place cards, then hand-lettered the names onto them?"

Carmela was suddenly confused. "You wanted the list *back*? I'm not sure I even have it anymore." *Probably tossed the darn thing out,* she thought to herself.

Then Carmela added, more out of curiosity than anything, "Isn't that luncheon being held tomorrow?"

"Yes, but we're just tidying up loose ends," Alyse assured her. "Trying to keep our records in order."

"Sure," muttered Carmela. "Whatever. If I run across it, I'll pop it in the mail to you."

Carmela dropped the receiver back in its cradle, feeling distracted. *Who cares about a dopey list when Shamus is probably still downtown being beaten with a rubber hose? Give me a break!*

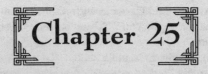

Chapter 25

RAIN lashed at the windows, pounded on the roof, gushed in torrents down the drain spouts. Cozied inside her apartment, Carmela figured that tonight's big Orpheus parade would *have* to be declared a washout. How could the floats and bands even survive in weather like this?

In fact, with this much rain pouring down, New Orleans would be lucky if Canal Street didn't flood completely and revert to being a real canal again! Carmela was so focused on the storm that when someone pounded on her door, she wasn't even sure if she was hearing right.

But when she finally threw the door open, there was Ava, looking soaked and disheveled.

"Didn't you hear me out there?" Ava grumped. She shed her raincoat like a snake shedding its skin, then did another little shake and dance that left a large puddle on the floor.

Carmela rushed to get her a towel. "I'm sorry," she apologized. "The storm was making so much noise I couldn't tell *what* was going on."

"Pour me a glass of wine, and all is forgiven," said Ava, deciding that she'd pouted long enough. Plopping into one of the chairs that surrounded Carmela's small wooden dining table, Ava ran long fingers through her tousled hair and gazed at the colorful papers and tags that were spread out on the table. "What's all this?" she asked.

Carmela set two glasses of wine down. "Tags," she told her friend. "I'm trying to put together a sample scrapbook page that's really an assembly of tags with photos mounted on them."

Ava studied the montage Carmela had assembled so far. It was really quite striking, all sorts of travel photos mounted on tags and then pasted on a terrific map background. She squinted. The map had to be either the Caribbean or Hawaii. She wasn't exactly sure which, since she'd popped her contacts out a few minutes ago.

"I swear," said Ava taking a sip of her wine, "I believe you could incorporate toilet paper rolls into a scrapbook page and make it look good."

"Now that *would* be a challenge," admitted Carmela. "But you didn't brave thunder and lightning to pay me a social call tonight, did you?"

"Aren't you the little psychic," said Ava. "Let's just wrap a turban around your head and call you *Madame* Carmela. Set you up in business in the back of my store. But, no, you're right. Tandy called earlier. She was worried about you and asked me to stop by and check on you."

"Did she tell you what happened after you left?"

Ava nodded. "That Rhonda Lee Clayton is truly certifiable. I can't believe you didn't just haul off and smack her one."

"I thought about it," admitted Carmela. "But mostly I just felt sorry for her."

"I'm surprised you didn't inform her in no uncertain terms that her little secret is out of the bag. I think it's shameful the way she's carrying on with her dead husband's partner."

Boo crept over to lie next to Carmela, and she dropped her hand to rub the little dog's furrowed head. "I think Rhonda Lee knows something," said Carmela.

"Knows what?" asked Ava, yawning.

"I think if Rhonda Lee could pull herself out of her hissy fit, she just might be able to put two and two together and figure out who killed her husband," said Carmela.

Ava stared at Carmela. "Yeah? Then why doesn't she just boogie on down to police headquarters and yak her little head off? Start *cooperating* with them?"

"Because Rhonda Lee doesn't know what she knows," said Carmela.

Ava blinked. "You think Rhonda Lee's little pea brain actually knows something but she doesn't know *what* she knows?" Ava repeated. "Is that what you're saying?"

Carmela nodded thoughtfully. "Pretty much."

"Are we talking repressed memory syndrome?" asked Ava. "Like that episode we saw on *Oprah*?"

"I wouldn't say it's that clinical," said Carmela. "But I do think that Rhonda Lee Clayton, in her own stumbling, bumbling way, just might know why Jimmy Earl was killed. She just hasn't put the pieces together."

"Assembly required," said Ava. "She ain't no Nancy Drew."

"You got that right," said Carmela.

"But you, on the other hand," said Ava, "are foaming at the mouth to take a crack at a perfectly good mystery that really could stand to remain unsolved. You want to figure out every precise little detail." Ava raised one eyebrow at Carmela. "You'd just love that, wouldn't you?"

Carmela rubbed at her temples as though she suddenly had a headache. "Ava, don't."

"You really don't need to keep picking away at this,"

Ava told her, "out of misplaced loyalty to that hairball Shamus."

"We've been over this before," said Carmela tiredly. "Maybe I *am* an idiot, but I still feel compelled to help him."

"So you can negotiate a better settlement," said Ava. "Really stick it to the Meechums when you start divorce proceedings."

"Yes . . . no," said Carmela.

Ava stared at Carmela, then shook her head. "I can tell by the look on your face, you've still got it bad for him, don't you?"

Carmela didn't say anything. She just felt defeated. Defeated and tired. All this intrigue was swirling around her, and she didn't seem to be able to make heads or tails out of anything. Hell, she didn't even have a *date* these days. Rhonda Lee thought *her* life was in shreds, and she at least had a *paramour*. Two nights after she tucked old Jimmy Earl into the family crypt at Saint Cyril's, she was out catting around. No Heartbreak Hotel for her, just a hot night at the Calhoun Motel!

"Don't you ever watch those TV shows where a bunch of clever, witty women sit around talking about how great it is to be independent?" asked Ava. "Didn't you ever think how nice and self-respecting it would feel to actually *be* one of them?"

"Listen to *you*," said Carmela. "First thing you do when you meet a man is interrogate him, try to determine if he's got the makings for a perfect matrimonial candidate."

"I daresay I'm not *that* obvious," said Ava.

Carmela folded her arms and stared back at Ava. One corner of her mouth twitched.

"I *am*?" screeched Ava. "Oh, no. You think so, *really*?"

* * *

AFTER AVA LEFT, CARMELA MOPED ABOUT HER apartment. Somehow the tags didn't seem all that intriguing anymore for the travel layout. Maybe she should start over, she decided. Try to do a sample page using torn pieces from old maps and then integrate some luggage templates.

At ten minutes to eight, Carmela snapped on the TV and turned to one of the local cable channels. Regular programming had been preempted tonight so they could cover the Orpheus parade. The newscaster, sent out to do a remote broadcast, was huddled pitifully beneath an enormous striped umbrella that rocked precariously in the gale and threatened to blow away. Yet the newscaster, Fred something, continued to reassure his TV audience that the Orpheus parade was *still* going to roll. In fact, Fred was fairly certain that this single stalled cell that was delivering such a walloping rain to New Orleans would soon rumble on over into neighboring Mississippi.

Carmela was just about to fix herself a grilled cheese sandwich when the phone rang.

"Hello?" she said.

"Carmela dear, I suppose you're planning to stay in." It was Jekyl Hardy.

"Absolutely," replied Carmela. "How about you? You're not going to the Orpheus parade are you? I figured it would be canceled, but now they're saying it's still going to roll."

"Word is the start time's been delayed an hour. Apparently the National Weather Service is making all sorts of optimistic predictions."

"So I heard."

"They're holding all the floats in the den, plus they packed in a bunch of bands and marchers, too. It's absolute bedlam. But they're still going to roll, come hell or high water."

That's Mardi Gras for you, thought Carmela. *Act of*

God, act of war, and the parades still roll. At least it was something that could be counted on, like death and taxes.

"So the thing of it is," said Jekyl, "I'm sitting here in a restaurant over on Esplanade, sipping Bloody Marys and doing oyster shooters with some of my die-hard float-builder friends."

"Having a better night than I am," quipped Carmela.

"Don't be so sure," said Jekyl. "I think the vodka they're pouring is about two hours old. Anyway, I don't want to schlep my costume home in the rain tonight, so do you mind if I stash it at your store?"

"Be my guest," said Carmela. "You still have the key, right?" She'd given Jekyl a spare key a couple months ago, in case he needed to raid her stash of paper and ribbon for float-making supplies. Whenever he stopped by, he left a detailed list. Then she'd tally it up later and send him an invoice.

"Still got it," said Jekyl. "Will I see you tomorrow when I stop by to pick my costume up?"

"Not sure," said Carmela. "I'm officially closed, but that doesn't mean I might not be in the back room catching up on busywork."

"Okay, love, see you when I see you."

"Bye, Jekyl," said Carmela. As she hung up the phone, she suddenly decided she really was hungry. What did she have in her larder that would be even easier than a grilled cheese sandwich? Bowl of cereal? Cup of yogurt? Or had she fed the last of the yogurt to Boo?

Carmela ambled into her small kitchen and pulled open the door of the refrigerator. When the phone shrilled a few minutes later, she realized that she'd been standing there staring at the somewhat meager contents, balanced on one leg like a sand crane, completely tranced out.

Jekyl again, Carmela thought to herself as she reached for the phone. *He's gonna spin some farfetched story and try to coax me out into the night. He's probably worried that I'm home alone again,* she decided as she picked up the phone.

But it wasn't Jekyl Hardy's voice that greeted her. It was the slow, slurry voice of Rhonda Lee Clayton.

"Carmela," she said, her tongue sounding thick. "It's Rhonda Lee."

What's with this? thought Carmela. And then immediately wondered, *Has Rhonda Lee been drinking? Or is she just tooted up on medication? A little Xanax or a hit of Valium?*

"Hello, Rhonda Lee," said Carmela. She was about to say, *Well this is a surprise,* but decided not to. It would be too much of an understatement.

"Carmela," said Rhonda Lee. Her voice suddenly carried that ebullient tone that users often get.

"Rhonda Lee," Carmela repeated cheerily, suddenly unsure of what to say and starting to feel like a complete idiot.

"I might have been a little . . . uh . . . *harsh* today," said Rhonda Lee.

Rhonda Lee apologizing for her little tantrum this afternoon? Well, this is history in the making.

"I'm sorry . . . ah, Car*mel*a," said Rhonda Lee, carefully pronouncing each and every syllable. Rhonda Lee's voice suddenly sounded sleepy.

"Rhonda Lee?" asked Carmela. "Are you all right? Are you at home?" God forbid that this woman was out driving around playing Chatty Cathy on her cell phone.

"Fine, fine, fine," Rhonda Lee said in a drowsy, singsong voice. "Just hanging around the old homestead."

"Are you alone?" asked Carmela. It suddenly occurred to her that Rhonda Lee might have taken an overdose of something. *Like Jimmy Earl had?*

"My beautiful daughter is here with me," said Rhonda Lee, suddenly sounding slightly more lucid. She sighed deeply. "I'm okay. *We're* okay."

Is there a point to this conversation? Carmela wondered. *Or is this just a rambling apology?*

"Carmela," began Rhonda Lee, "I think you might have been right. . . ."

Okay, I'll bite, thought Carmela.

"Might have been right about what, Rhonda Lee?" asked Carmela.

"I went through some papers in Jimmy Earl's desk," said Rhonda Lee.

Carmela stood stock-still. *Ohmygosh.*

There was a sharp *clink* and then a *thunk.* Carmela figured Rhonda Lee must be helping herself to another drink.

"Are you still there, Rhonda Lee?"

A few seconds went by before Rhonda Lee answered her. "I'm here. I've got some . . . uh . . . papers."

"Could I see them, Rhonda Lee?" asked Carmela. "Will you let me look at them?"

"Sure."

It's that easy? thought Carmela. *She said "Sure" just like that?*

Yeah, but she's been drinking. Is drinking. So what do I do now? Strike while the iron is hot?

Carmela squinted toward the window. Rain was still pelting down outside. Not exactly a great night to be dashing over to Rhonda Lee's house.

"Can I come over now, Rhonda Lee?" asked Carmela. *Damn, how would she even get through the traffic on—*

"Now?" said Rhonda Lee, sounding startled. "No. Oh no. Tomorrow."

"I can stop by tomorrow?" said Carmela. *Get this confirmed; set up a specific time.*

"I'll come to *you,*" said Rhonda Lee. "At your store. Tomorrow . . ." There was a long pause as Rhonda Lee struggled to get the word out. ". . . afternoon," she finished.

"Rhonda Lee," protested Carmela, "it's gonna be a

madhouse down here in the French Quarter. It'd be a whole lot better if I . . ."

But Carmela was talking to dead air. Rhonda Lee had hung up.

Carmela stood with the receiver clutched in her hand. Tomorrow afternoon. She'd have to wait until Rhonda Lee Clayton stopped by Memory Mine tomorrow afternoon. But then maybe, just maybe, she'd start to get some answers.

Chapter 26

THE morning drizzle didn't seem to dim the enthusiasm of the Fat Tuesday revelers as tourists and locals alike thronged the streets of the French Quarter. Many wore rain garb with costumes peeking out; most had the ubiquitous *geaux* cups clutched in their hot little hands. And those in the know, which was just about everybody these days, were headed for Bourbon and St. Ann Streets, where the ladies on the second-floor balconies, lubricated by liquor and urged on by a crowd that often numbered in the thousands, would be jitterbugging and proudly displaying their ta-tas.

Carmela hadn't really planned to go in to her shop today at all, would have rather headed right for Saint Cyril's Cemetery to photograph the oven crypts. But Alyse Eskew's call late yesterday had set her teeth on edge and caused her to completely forget about bringing her digital camera home with her, so a quick trip to Memory Mine was in the cards.

Pushing open the door to Memory Mine, Carmela

flipped on the lights and kicked the door shut. What she'd
do, she decided, was grab the camera and hoof it the eight
or ten blocks over to Saint Cyril's Cemetery. If she was
really lucky, she'd be able to click off a few shots between
raindrops. Then she'd zip back here to the shop and download the photos to her computer. Viewing them on her
monitor, a fairly new Hitachi with great color resolution,
she'd know immediately if she had her shot. If everything
looked okay, she'd go ahead and print them out on special
photo paper. Then, she'd sit tight and wait for Rhonda
Lee Clayton to show up. That is, assuming the somewhat
mercurial Rhonda Lee was still coming and wasn't curled
up in bed nursing a hangover.

That was the plan for sure, Carmela decided, as she
dug in her desk drawer, searching for her little camera.

Pawing through a tangle of papers, disks, and scrapbook supply catalogs, Carmela swore that she was going
to get organized one of these days, even if it killed her.
She couldn't live her life in perpetual disarray, could she?
Maybe she should take up the art of feng shui; then at
least there'd be a Zen-like semblance of order to her dis-
order.

Where is that darn camera anyway? she wondered as
Jekyl Hardy's costume, hanging in the corner of her office, suddenly caught her eye. Seeing the red sequined suit
hanging there made her stop and smile. Jekyl's prized
devil costume. A sequined red suit complete with top hat
and glittery pitchfork. *People in New Orleans truly are
mad,* she decided. To spend all year planning for Mardi
Gras and then spend a month's salary or more on a costume was . . . what? Insane? No, it only looked insane if
you didn't live here. But, if you were born and bred in
New Orleans, that madness was forever in your blood,
was part of your visceral heritage. And, sure as shit, the
minute Mardi Gras was finished and Ash Wednesday

rolled around, you'd find yourself dreaming about *next* year's exotic costume or big party idea.

Her fingers skittered across the plastic edge of the camera. *Okay, here it is,* she told herself.

Now, is there enough space left on the card?

Carmela flipped the switch on and checked the counter. It looked like . . . what? Maybe twenty shots left?

That's it? What have I been shooting lately?

Carmela racked her brain.

Oh, wait a minute. Gabby used it the night she and Stuart went to the Pluvius den. And then I snapped quite a few shots a few days later at Jimmy Earl's funeral. And, of course, nobody's bothered to download any of the images to the computer yet. Well, it really shouldn't be a problem. After all, I only need a couple good shots, right?

As Carmela headed down Pricur Street toward Saint Cyril's Cemetery, she felt completely out of step with the rest of the world. Or, at least the world of the French Quarter. Because while she was heading out of the *Vieux Carré*, it seemed that everyone else was spilling into it.

The French Quarter was definitely ground zero today; streets were cordoned off for twenty blocks. And the few blocks surrounding Jackson Square and the French Market were pandemonium, pure and simple.

Yes, thought Carmela, *today the French Quarter is bursting with parades, marching bands, jazz groups, street performers, strippers, and a couple million costumed revelers. To say nothing of the oyster bars, jazz clubs, street vendors, horse-drawn jitneys, and paddle wheelers sitting over on the Mississippi.*

ST. CYRIL'S CEMETERY LOOKED ALMOST ABAN-doned, Carmela decided as she squeezed through the half-open front gates. No visitors in sight, no funerals in full swing. Just row upon uneven row of whitewashed tombs

that stood out in sharp contrast to the muddy earth. Rain
was still sifting down in a fine mist, and when lightning
pulsed from purple, billowing clouds overhead, the old
tombs seemed to glow with their own eerie brand of elec-
trical energy.

Carmela shivered. She'd never been here alone before.
And as familiar as she was with the many cemeteries
tucked in and around the city of New Orleans, she'd never
seen one this empty. So utterly devoid of any human life-
forms. Then again, she'd never visited a cemetery on Fat
Tuesday before.

Well, she decided, as she made her way down one of
the lanes, she'd snap her photos and get out. Luckily, the
rain *seemed* to be letting up a touch. So she just might
get a good shot of the wall ovens. Which were . . .

Carmela stopped in her tracks and gazed around. She'd
entered Saint Cyril's from the Prieur Street entrance, so
the wall ovens had to be . . . where?

Her eyes skimmed the tops of tombs, trying to determine just exactly where the wall ovens were located.

*If that was the Venable monument up ahead, then the
wall ovens should be to her left. Correct?*

Carmela hooked a left and threaded her way through
Saint Cyril's. This was one of New Orleans's oldest cemeteries, and many of the tombs clearly betrayed their age.
Stone faces of angels and saints that had been lovingly
carved more than a century ago had been melted by the
ravages of time. Many tombstones were badly cracked
and chipped and tilted at awkward angles. As Carmela
skipped by one row of tombstones, they appeared to gape
at her like broken teeth.

Her nerves may have been slightly frayed, but her sense
of direction was intact. Carmela spotted the wall ovens
from forty feet away.

Good, she breathed. *I'll take a couple quick shots and*

get out of here. It's way too creepy without anyone around.

Stopping at a large, flat tomb, Carmela set her purse down and pulled the camera out. She turned it on and checked the battery. The green glow told her everything was a go.

Putting the camera up to her eye, Carmela framed the shot.

No, I can get closer yet.

Keeping the camera to her eye, she moved a few steps toward the wall ovens, thinking how nice it was to finally be working with an auto-focus camera. So much easier.

She paused, rather liking the composition of her shot. The viewfinder told her she'd be able to capture three of the wall ovens head-on. It was a good shot. Told a complete story.

And that's what a good scrapbook layout is all about, right?

Holding her breath, Carmela was about to click the shutter when she heard a faint crunch of gravel.

She clicked the shot anyway, then whirled about quickly.

Nothing. Nothing but white, bleached-out tombs.

Am I hearing things? Probably. Gotta stop being so jumpy.

She put the camera to her face, deliberately hesitated, then fired off three more shots.

Still hearing things? No . . . it's just that . . . what?

Something *felt* different.

Like *what?*

Like the *air* had been disturbed.

Carmela was suddenly conscious of her heart beating a little quicker, the hair on the back of her neck suddenly beginning to rise.

You're crazy; there's nothing here, she told herself.

Still . . .

Carmela fired off five more shots, then got the hell out of there. Walked briskly to the Roman Street entrance instead of going back to the Prieur Street entrance. *Better to walk around the outside wall of the cemetery,* she decided, *even if it is the long way. There are people out here. Living people.*

Chapter 27

THE feeling that she was being followed stayed with her all the way back to her shop.

You're being paranoid, Carmela told herself. *Nobody's dogging your footsteps; nobody's brandishing an umbrella with a poison tip. Stop running old James Bond movies in your head!*

But even lecturing herself sternly didn't stop Carmela from glancing in shop windows to see what shimmering reflection might be hovering behind her. And once she even stopped dead in her tracks and turned around to scour the crowd. But all she saw was a marauding band of pirates, a couple people in goofy-looking bird costumes, and a person in a red-and-yellow clown suit.

Hardly, she told herself.

The phone was ringing as she pushed her way into Memory Mine. Leaning across the counter, Carmela swiped the phone off the hook. "Hello," she answered breathlessly.

"I thought you weren't gonna be there." It was Ava.

"If you didn't think I was going to be here, why did you call?" A fair question, Carmela decided.

"Don't know," said Ava. "Force of habit?" They *did* tend to call each other a lot.

"You finish all your masks?" asked Carmela. She knew there were at least a dozen different masked balls tonight and that Ava had been hustling her buns to get a couple last-minute orders finished.

Ava sighed. "Just barely. I'm still putting the finishing touches on one. Gold paint with lots of red and purple feathers. Very exotic and hot looking. Think Rio and conga lines. Then I'm gonna zip down to Canal Street and catch the Rex parade."

"Isn't Rex already rolling?" Carmela asked. She knew Rex usually hit downtown right around noon. That's when all hell broke loose.

"I was just listening to the radio, and the announcer said they're way backed up," said Ava. "Not all the Zulu floats have gone through yet." Zulu was the parade *before* Rex.

"So what else is new," said Carmela. *Will Rhonda Lee be able to make it to my shop at all? Maybe I should call Rhonda Lee at home, just to double-check. . . .*

"Oops, gotta go," chirped Ava. "Customers."

"Talk to you," said Carmela. She hung up the phone and stood there, gazing about her empty store. *Okay, what's next on the agenda? Oh yeah. Download the photos.*

It took her but a minute to pop the card out of her camera and insert it into her computer. Then she was clicking her way through the roster of photos that, up until now, had been stored on the camera.

The first shots, of course, were the photos Gabby took the night she and Stuart went to the Pluvius den.

The night of the Pluvius *parade*, Carmela reminded

herself. The night Jimmy Earl Clayton ingested his fateful dose of ketamine.

Gabby had taken the usual jumble of shots. Close-ups of Stuart talking with various people. A couple of Stuart hanging off a mermaid float. One with him cuddling up to the oversized mermaid. Gabby certainly was enamored of old Stuart, thought Carmela. Then decided her sour grapes attitude wasn't particularly cordial. Just because *her* marriage didn't work out all that well . . .

There were other shots, too. Shots that showed frantic volunteers putting finishing touches on a Poseidon float and a seahorse float. A couple that showed Jekyl Hardy looking like he was ready to tear his hair out. One close-up of a large silver papier-mâché octopus that had obviously just lost a tentacle. *Probably that's why Jekyl was tearing his hair out,* Carmela decided.

There was even a shot of Jimmy Earl Clayton. Standing with two other men, raising their glasses in a boisterous toast.

Interesting, thought Carmela.

The next few shots weren't so interesting. Wide shots. Mostly just photos that recorded the frantic last-minute activity in the den.

Carmela scanned them quickly, was about to delete the ones that weren't particularly good, when something caught her eye.

Who is that? Is that Dace Wilcox in the photo? Sure it is.

Carmela studied it.

Gabby had caught Dace Wilcox in profile. He looked like he was talking to a couple of the float builders.

Hmm. No. Nothing here.

Carmela flipped through a few more shots.

Here's a shot of Ruby Dumaine. With her philandering husband, Jack.

Carmela clicked to the next shot.

Ruby again. This time alone.

Doing what? Carmela hit a couple buttons to enlarge the photo. *Nope, that doesn't work. I need to enlarge just the lower right portion of the photo.*

She made a few adjustments on her computer. There, now she had it.

She stared at the photo, frowning.

Ruby was holding a drink out to Jimmy Earl's daughter, Shelby.

Okay.

Carmela forwarded to the next shot. In this photo Jimmy Earl had grabbed the glass and was waggling a finger at his daughter!

Carmela stared at the screen. *What was going on here?* She wasn't sure, but she had a feeling it might be bad *juju,* as Ava would say. Really bad.

Feeling discombobulated, Carmela stood up, stretched her arms overhead, blew out a couple deep breaths.

A jittery feeling had suddenly insinuated itself in her body. Nerves, a little hit of adrenaline, whatever you wanted to call it, had definitely gotten her going.

Carmela sat down in front of her computer again. She thought for a couple seconds, then pulled open the bottom drawer of her desk, started pawing through papers.

It was here before, she told herself. At least she *thought* she'd put it there.

She shuffled through the stamp catalogs again, a few old invoices that had been marked paid, flyers for scrapbooking classes that had come and gone.

Ah, there it was. The list of names for the Pluvius queen luncheon that Alyse Eskew had been so hot to trot over.

Carmela scanned the list, blinked a couple times, set it aside. She rubbed the top of her head in an unconscious gesture, as if trying to stimulate her brain cells.

What's so strange about this list? Something.

Carmela shook her head. *No, it's just a list. Nothing more.*

But the odd feeling persisted, and a germ of an idea was definitely rattling around in her brain.

Carmela picked up the list, studied it again. *Think,* she prodded herself. *What's off about it?*

A name is missing.

She bit her lip, thinking. *Whose?*

Shelby Clayton. Jimmy Earl's daughter. She had always been one of the front-runner candidates for Pluvius queen.

And in that same leap of consciousness, Carmela thought, *So what? Shelby Clayton dropped out of the running for Pluvius queen after Jimmy Earl died.*

Carmela slumped back in her chair, then immediately straightened back up again.

Hold everything! How can that be? I received this list long before Jimmy Earl died from his overdose of ketamine! Unless . . .

"Oh my God," breathed Carmela. There was a sudden pounding in her ears as it dawned on her what might have taken place.

Someone drew up a nasty plan to insure that Shelby Clayton wouldn't be a queen candidate!

Jimmy Earl hadn't been killed over a business deal at all! Jimmy Earl had been sacrificed so his daughter would drop out . . .

Holy smokes! Could that be right?

Carmela paced nervously about her store, thinking.

Okay, try this on for size, she told herself. *What if poor Shelby Clayton had been the intended target all along? And Jimmy Earl, her father, had simply gotten in the way?*

Carmela reeled at the idea. Strode back into her office, dropped into her chair.

Would someone commit murder just for the sake of

their daughter being named Pluvius queen? Was that possible?

Deep in her heart, Carmela knew it was possible. That it could happen. In Texas, not that long ago, a woman had taken out a contract on a sixteen-year-old girl just so her own daughter would be insured a slot on the cheerleading squad!

Crazy? Yeah. But there are lots of crazy people in the world.

The bell over the door sounded.

Rhonda Lee? Already? Oh, no, the poor woman. Can't let her know about this yet. . . .

Carmela looked up from her computer, her expression one of consummate grief and commiseration.

How am I ever going to—

Carmela was stunned to see a red and yellow clown costume materialize before her eyes.

What the—?

"Hello, Carmela." The flint-edged voice of Ruby Dumaine rang out in the stillness of the deserted shop.

Carmela's eyes turned to saucers; she tasted bile in the back of her throat. *Ruby. Oh no!*

Ruby Dumaine reached up and pulled a curly purple wig off her head. She flashed Carmela a supremely confident smile above the pistol she had pointed directly at her. Curiously, Ruby balanced the pistol in her hand with a confident, relaxed manner. It made Carmela think Ruby had done this before. That Ruby might be an old pro with a pistol.

Careful, a warning bell sounded in Carmela's head. *Don't want to mess with an old pro.*

"Ruby!" said Carmela, fighting to keep the panic from her voice. "What a surprise."

"Oh, I don't think you're all that surprised to see me here," said Ruby Dumaine. Her voice was smooth and dangerous. She edged into Carmela's office carefully, and her eyes darted toward Carmela's computer monitor.

"Well, isn't that sweet," Ruby Dumaine purred as she stared at the screen. "A lovely little photo show. Planning to immortalize me in one of your silly little scrapbooks?"

"Just reviewing a few shots," said Carmela, trying to stay cool. *Now what?* she wondered. *Got any great ideas? Noooo, not really.*

"Yes, let's run through those shots," said Ruby. "Let's see what that dim-witted assistant of yours really captured."

"You broke into Gabby's house," said Carmela, staring at her. Ruby Dumaine had slathered white greasepaint on her face and outlined her lips with coral lipstick. Not only did she look like a clown, she looked like a parody of an older woman who was hooked on using way too much makeup. The Tammy Fay syndrome.

Shit. And I'll bet Ruby was there in the cemetery with me, too. No wonder I came down with a bad case of the creeps.

"Of course I paid a visit to Gabby," said Ruby. "I figured she still had the camera."

"And then you tried to pick up my photos," added Carmela. Suddenly, the pieces of the puzzle were coming together with dizzying speed. And she didn't much like the picture that was emerging.

"I didn't realize you'd gone digital," said Ruby. "Silly me; guess I'm going to have to take the plunge into cyberspace myself."

Carmela also knew, with complete and utter clarity, that it had been Ruby Dumaine who strong-armed Alyse Eskew into calling her and trying to get the list back.

Nobody noticed that Shelby Clayton's name wasn't on the list? No, of course not. Ruby drew up the list with zealous glee and probably hadn't given a second thought to the fact that Shelby's absence from the list might be a dead giveaway. It hadn't occurred to Ruby until now. Now that things are getting a little too hot.

Dead giveaway, thought Carmela. *Ha-ha.*

"Know what else I did?" bragged Ruby Dumaine. "I talked that idiot Rhonda Lee into calling you last night."

"You did? How?" Carmela regretted her question the minute the words flew from her mouth.

But Ruby just smiled. "I have my ways. Suffice it to say she's just a drunken pawn, doesn't understand a thing. In fact, I'm sure she'll be thrilled to death when my own daughter, Swan, is crowned Pluvius queen tonight."

Thrilled to death. Once again, an interesting choice of words, thought Carmela.

Carmela mustered up her nastiest sneer. "You'll never get away with this!" she told Ruby with far more conviction than she felt.

"I already have," smirked Ruby Dumaine. "Now, there's just one final little item I'm going to enlist from you. In fact, it'll help me tie up an awful lot of loose ends." Ruby paused, flashed a horrible barracuda smile. "Your confession."

"What?" said Carmela, stunned.

"You're going to pick up your pen and write out your confession. About how Shamus killed Jimmy Earl Clayton and you gave him your very capable assistance."

"Dream on," said Carmela.

Ruby shifted the gun slightly to focus on the space between Carmela's eyes. *I've always been partial to that space,* Carmela decided. *Okay, fine, I'll pick up the damn pen and humor this crazy lady.*

Carmela searched around on the top of her desk. *Too messy,* she thought wildly. *Gotta get organized.* Her fingers hit a green plastic pen that lurked under a pile of papers. It was the pen with the disappearing ink. *Ahh . . . there you go! I finally caught a break.*

Ruby dictated a somewhat rambling statement, which

Carmela diligently wrote out word for word on a piece of plain white paper. Ruby scowled at Carmela's efforts, watching her over the pistol, moving her lips as she read the statement back. Then she gave a quick nod. "Sign it," she ordered.

Carmela signed it.

Ruby snatched the paper from Carmela's hands, folded it in half, and tucked it inside her red leather purse.

A clown with a designer purse, thought Carmela. *If this wasn't Mardi Gras, people would for sure know she was fruit loops.*

"Stand up," commanded Ruby. She gestured wildly with the pistol, and Carmela reluctantly scrambled to her feet.

"Is that your costume?" asked Ruby, gesturing toward Jekyl Hardy's devil suit.

"No," Carmela told her.

"Put it on anyway."

Carmela slid the jacket off the hanger and put it on. The shoulders were too big and the sleeves way too long.

"Excellent," said Ruby. "Trousers, too." She leaned forward with a stupid grin on her face. "Remember, dearie, it's Mardi Gras! We wouldn't want to rouse suspicion."

Carmela grabbed the trousers and stepped into them, pulling them up over her own black slacks. All the while she was hoping someone or something would intercede.

What was it that always saved the day in a Greek tragedy? Deus ex machina. God by machine. That was when a person or deity came crashing into the final scene to resolve a conflict. The Greek dramaturge's version of the cavalry arriving.

That single idea fueled Carmela's hope. Maybe Jekyl Hardy would show up to retrieve his devil costume. Or Ava would get worried and peek in the window. Or maybe Rhonda Lee would get it together and drop by for their chat. Unfortunately, Carmela noted, none of those possibilities seemed to loom large on the horizon.

"Is your car parked nearby?" asked Ruby. She was tugging the purple clown wig back on over her red curls. If she didn't look so terrifying, it would have been ridiculous.

"Not really," said Carmela.

"Where is it?"

"Um . . . in an alley off Esplanade Avenue," said Carmela. She decided it was better to tell the truth than lie about it. If Ruby decided to march her to her car, maybe she'd be able to figure out *the great escape* on the way. Flash a signal to someone. Or wrest herself away. Or get a bullet in the back of her head. No, she decided, the latter was not such a good option.

"Perfect," cooed Ruby. She hefted the gun again. "Let's march."

There was a famous quote that went something like, "Never argue with people who buy ink by the gallon." Carmela thought there should be another version that said, "Never argue with crazy people who carry guns." Because as Ruby marched her down the street, Carmela realized just how helpless she was.

Here they were, in the middle of Mardi Gras, for goodness sakes, and she couldn't do a thing.

"You live around here?" asked Ruby after they'd gone the requisite two blocks or so.

"No," said Carmela. *My apartment is barely fifty feet away, and Boo is in there all by herself. I'll die before I let Ruby near my dog.*

"You sure?" Ruby Dumaine cocked her head like an inquisitive crow, staring at Carmela with glazed eyes.

Carmela shrugged. "I just park my car here," she answered.

Ruby seemed to accept the answer at face value. *Good,* thought Carmela, *she's not as shrewd as she thinks she is. And she obviously didn't do her homework.*

Carmela showed her the old Cadillac.

"Perfect," said Ruby. "Unlock it, and let's get in. And don't try anything funny. I have very good reflexes."

I'll bet you do, thought Carmela.

Carmela inserted the key in the ignition, turned on the engine. It did its rough *tocka-tocka-tocka* for a couple minutes, warming up. "Where to?" Carmela asked as she buckled her seat belt.

"Back to Saint Cyril's," Ruby told her. She ignored her seat belt and half turned in her seat, focusing her hostile gaze on Carmela.

Carmela could barely contain her surprise.

Ruby waggled the gun in her face again. "Just drive," she said in a tired voice. "Don't piss me off any more than you have to, okay?"

Carmela negotiated the car out of her parking space, headed down to Barracks Street. Luckily, the streets this far over weren't blocked off yet, and she was able to head over to North Rampart, then hang a right to Prieur.

"That's it," said Ruby, catching a glimpse of the cemetery a few blocks away. "Go in the front entrance. The Prieur Street gate."

"Ruby . . ." began Carmela. "I don't know what you've got planned, but you'll never—"

"Honey, you don't know *what* I've got planned," Ruby spat out. She snaked a hand into her purse and fumbled around. She pulled out Carmela's confession as well as a large, rusty key.

Skeleton key? thought Carmela. *What's that for?*

Ruby saw the consternation on Carmela's face and favored her with a thin smile. "In case you don't know, the Dumaines also have a family crypt at Saint Cyril's. Six generations are interred there. And probably a few other various and sundry bodies as well." Ruby let loose a crazed chortle and gazed hungrily at Carmela. "I don't think one more body would put a strain on the accommodations. There's not all that much of you."

Carmela felt her hands go numb and her knees begin to tremble. *Ruby is going to try to force me inside the family crypt. If all goes well with Ruby's bizarre plan, I'll die of starvation, and there'll be nothing left of me. Barely a few bones.*

Ruby waved the signed confession at Carmela and jangled the key in her face. "Keep driving," she snarled, "don't slow down now."

Is this the key the tarot cards revealed for my future? Is this how my life is supposed to end?

Carmela's brows furrowed together. *No,* she told herself. *We all have a part in creating our own destinies. We just have to act on our impulses, take advantage of situations. That's what spells the difference!*

Carmela's right foot crunched down hard on the accelerator, and the old Cadillac shot ahead with a burst of speed.

"That's the spirit," roared Ruby. "Zoom zoom, hurry it along!"

Up ahead Carmela could see the wrought-iron gates of Saint Cyril's Cemetery coming into view. She'd walked through those gates barely an hour ago. Actually, she'd more or less *squeezed* through them, since the gates weren't completely open, more like standing ajar. When she'd arrived here earlier, she'd just figured the caretaker had hastily unlocked them, then been distracted by something.

That's it, thought Carmela. *I'll aim for the gates. I'll drive this big honkin' car right into the wrought-iron gates and send this crazy lady clear through the windshield!* Carmela clutched the steering wheel and tried to brace herself.

Good-bye, Samantha. Please forgive me. You've been a great car.

At the last minute, Ruby saw Carmela's plan written

on her face. "Stop it!" she screamed. "Don't you dare crash this—!"

Finally hearing fear in Ruby's voice, Carmela took a deep breath, even as she tried to relax every muscle in her body as her car slammed into the giant pair of black wrought-iron gates that loomed at the entrance to Saint Cyril's Cemetery.

The air was filled with screams, the sickening screech of grinding metal, and the high-pitched shatter of glass as the car gunned its way up one of the wrought-iron gates. Then, back tires still churning and burning rubber, the car began to roll to its side. As if in slow motion, passengers, papers, and bits of Mardi Gras costumes all tumbled wildly in the car. And the last thing that flitted into Ruby Dumaine's consciousness was the realization that the ink on Carmela's signed confession had somehow faded into oblivion.

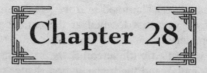

Chapter 28

SUNLIGHT. A white blur of a costume. And definitely a splitting headache.

Carmela was also cognizant of buzzing voices and soft footsteps padding around her. She knew she should try to open her eyes. But it all seemed too much. Too painful to even contemplate.

What's going on? Am I lying on the pavement in the middle of Mardi Gras with a bullet through my head? Is someone in a white chicken costume flapping about in a panic?

Carmela fought to open one eye. It fluttered mightily before she managed to get it to remain open and focus. The white chicken costume wasn't a costume at all; it was a nurse's uniform.

She decided to go for the other eye, too. *Live a little,* she prodded herself. *That is, if I'm still alive.*

Both eyes fluttered open, and she stared into the anxious faces of Tandy Bliss, Ava Grieux, Baby Fontaine and . . . Shamus? Oh my.

Carmela made a feeble effort to sit up, decided her head hurt too much. "I'm not dead?" she croaked. "This isn't heaven?"

"Close to it," said Ava kindly. "You're still in New Orleans."

"Mardi Gras?" rasped Carmela.

"The poor girl's delusional," sobbed Tandy.

"Quick, get her a sip of water," Baby directed the nurse. "Her throat is bone dry. Listen to that poor rattly little voice."

Ava clutched at Carmela's hand. "You're in the hospital, honey. You're going to be okay. No broken bones, but you're a little shook up."

"Samantha?" Carmela croaked again.

"Who's Samantha?" asked the nurse. "Was she the victim in the clown costume? The one they had to subdue?"

"Samantha's her car," murmured Ava. She smiled at Carmela, shook her head. "She didn't make it. Samantha was totaled. I'm sorry, kiddo."

Carmela sipped greedily at the water the nurse offered her. Then she licked her lips.

"Ruby?" she asked.

"Broken collarbone, broken arm, broken jaw," said Tandy, happy to deliver such dreadful news. "They've got her all trussed up."

"And in traction, too," added Baby helpfully. Her blue eyes were bright with tears.

"Here?" asked Carmela. She had to know. She'd been dreaming about Ruby Dumaine for the last couple hours. Sick, drug-induced dreams that had made Ruby seem larger than life. Like some rampaging *thing* that couldn't be stopped. Lying here, feeling completely helpless, Carmela didn't even like the idea she might be in the same *building* as Ruby Dumaine.

"No. They moved Mrs. Dumaine to the state hospital early this morning," said the nurse.

"Ladies," said Shamus, finally speaking up. "Could you give the two of us a few minutes alone?"

There were knowing glances all around, then Ava, Baby, Tandy, and the nurse shuffled out into the hallway and pulled the door closed behind them.

Shamus moved around to the side of Carmela's bed so he could be close to her. Carmela could smell his spicy aftershave. It smelled nice. Like their bathroom used to smell after he showered and shaved.

"I was so worried about you, darlin'." Shamus bent down and kissed her cheek gently. In his navy cashmere sweater and khaki slacks he looked like a college kid.

"I was worried about me," said Carmela. "Oh, no . . ." Once again she tried to struggle to a sitting position. "Poor Boo! She's been stuck in my apartment for—" Carmela began.

"Shhh, Boo's fine," said Shamus, patting her shoulder. "She stayed with me last night. At Glory's."

Carmela winced. "Glory'll make Boo sleep outside," she whispered. "She hates dogs."

"Honey . . . no." Now Shamus's fingers caressed the top of Carmela's bandage-wrapped head. "Boo slept on the bed with me all last night. She's fine, really. In fact, she's having the time of her life chasing the vacuum cleaner around."

"Is Ruby hurt real bad?" Carmela asked in a small voice.

"You banged her up pretty good," said Shamus. Carmela could tell he was trying to put a lighthearted spin on things, but his face was tight with concern.

"I thought Jimmy Earl was killed because of a real estate deal," said Carmela. "I thought Bufford Maple and Michael Theriot were involved."

"They *are* involved in a real estate deal," said Shamus, looking grim now. "Just not the one you were hell-bent on pursuing. Maple and Theriot are under investigation by the SEC for real estate fraud. Phony bonds and some mortgage flipping."

"What's mortgage flipping?" asked Carmela.

"It's kind of like a real estate ponzi scheme," explained Shamus. "You trade properties back and forth to avoid taxes and declare paper profits. Dace Wilcox has been investigating them for several months now."

"Dace?" said Carmela weakly. "I thought he might be involved with Jimmy Earl, too."

"He was, but as an investigator. Dace is a special agent for the IRS, although it's not widely known. Just as well to keep it under wraps."

Carmela settled back against her pillows. *Boy, did I have a wrong number with Dace! Who knew he was working on the side of justice?*

"What about Jack Dumaine? And Granger Rathbone?" asked Carmela.

"Apparently Jack hired Granger to try to figure out how much I knew. You see, I was the whistle-blower on the deal. Maple and Theriot also tried to tap Crescent City Bank for financing and, in reviewing some paperwork that came over from Clayton Crown Securities, a few things started to look hinky. Anyway, you kind of got pulled along for the ride." Shamus ducked his head. "Sorry about that."

"So Jack Dumaine was involved in this real estate fraud, too?" said Carmela.

"Yes, he was," said Shamus. "But apparently not Jimmy Earl. Strangely enough, Jimmy Earl seems to have been the innocent one."

"But Jack knew what Ruby did to Jimmy Earl? With the ketamine?" asked Carmela.

Shamus shook his head. "No. Jack was as shocked as we are. At least that's what he claims."

Carmela snuggled against her pillow, trying to digest all these layers of information. "Jack Dumaine and

Rhonda Lee Clayton are having an affair," she told Shamus. Her voice was still hoarse, almost husky sounding.

"You mentioned that the other night, remember?"

Carmela blinked. "I did?"

Shamus leaned over and kissed her on the forehead. The small part that wasn't bandaged. "You look so helpless lying there," he said, the words catching in his throat.

"I'll be just as helpless when I get out of here," said Carmela. "Poor Samantha . . . completely totaled." She sighed. "I really loved that old car."

"I know you did," said Shamus slowly. "Think you can get used to driving something else?"

"I suppose I'll have to," said Carmela. "Eventually."

"Why not right now," said Shamus. His right hand dug into the pocket of his khaki slacks and Carmela heard a faint, metallic *clink*.

Suddenly, a set of car keys dangled before her eyes.

"What's that?" Carmela asked warily.

"Keys to your new car," said Shamus.

She peered at him. A shit-eating grin was spread across his handsome face. *Oh no.*

"You bought me a car," she said. She was shocked. *What does this mean? He loves me, he loves me not? Oh, I wish my poor head didn't ache so much. If ever there was a time I needed to think straight, it's right now.*

"Don't think about it so hard," said Shamus, watching her closely.

Carmela sighed and closed her eyes. "Don't try to read my mind," she murmured, feeling slightly perturbed. She lay there for a moment until one eye peeked open, then the other. Now the slightest hint of curiosity danced in her blue eyes. "What exactly did you buy?"

"Mercedes." The pride was evident in his voice. "Five hundred SL."

Carmela was shocked. "No way!"

"I can see you in a Mercedes," said Shamus. "Classy woman, classy car."

"There's no way I can accept this." Carmela turned her head so she wouldn't have to look at the keys that dangled from his fingers.

This is nuts. Plus everything's happening way too fast. In warp speed, as a matter of fact.

"Look, you've got a concussion," Shamus told her. "You're not thinking straight yet. So just . . . think about the car. Okay?" His face shone with kindness and concern.

Carmela stared at him. Damn, he looked good. Cute, eager to please. Just like the fella she married that fine day at Christ Church. "Okay," she finally answered. "I'll think about it."

"Good." His hand brushed her shoulder. "Better get some sleep now. I'll stop by again later, okay?"

"Okay," she said and closed her eyes again, half aware of a whispered exchange at the door.

More than anything, Carmela wanted to drift off to sleep, but someone was standing at her bedside, plucking at the sleeve of her stylish polka-dot hospital johnny. She lifted a lid tiredly. It was Ava. "What?" she asked her friend.

"You're going to accept it, right?" said Ava expectantly.

Carmela shook her head. "I can't."

"Honey," said Ava, dangling the keys in front of Carmela's face. "The keys I have clutched in my hot little hand are for a Mercedes Five hundred SL. We're talking three oh two horsepower with a V-eight engine. Sticker priced at over eighty-five grand. Like it or not, you just grabbed the brass ring!"

"It doesn't seem right," said Carmela stubbornly. "Especially since Shamus and I seem headed for divorce."

"Now you're headed for divorce," said Ava. "Two days

ago, you were sticking by him out of loyalty."

"Shamus is a good man, and I love him dearly. But he's having trouble with the commitment part," sniffled Carmela.

"All men have trouble with the commitment part," answered Ava. She pulled a half dozen tissues from the box near the bed, stuck them in Carmela's hand.

Carmela held one up to her leaky eyes, sighed heavily.

"You know," said Ava in an upbeat, conspiratorial tone, "there are lots of mechanical devices on the market today that can bring pleasure to a woman. But the best by far is a Mercedes-Benz!" She gently placed the car keys in Carmela's hand.

Carmela closed her fingers around the shiny new keys. There was no denying it, a Mercedes-Benz *was* an awfully nice car. Beyond nice, actually. Bordering on splendiferous. She narrowed her eyes, gazed down at the keys. With the sun pouring in her hospital window, the keys looked like they were plated in twenty-four-karat gold. Like keys to a magical kingdom. The promise of something new and bright, like sunlight bouncing off Lake Pontchartrain.

She thought back to the tarot card reader at Baby's party. Maybe *these* were the keys in her future. *Could they be?*

"You think I should accept?" said Carmela, trying to stifle a yawn. *Damn, I'm feeling tired.*

"I think it would be *rude* not to," said Ava, doing a masterful job of maintaining a straight face.

Carmela's fingers closed tightly around the keys as she smiled up at Ava. "You know what?" she said, "I think you may be right."

Scrapbooking Tips
from Laura Childs

Words Add Impact

Be sure to add snippets of poetry, favorite sayings, or your very own jottings to your scrapbook pages. One easy way is to compose your words on a computer using a nice, funky type, then output those words on a sheet of see-through vellum. You can tear around your words to achieve a deckled-edged cloud effect or even cut the vellum into a square and lay it across your photo for a ghost effect.

Tag, You're It!

Have you seen the wonderful tags that are available in various shapes, sizes, and colors? They really add interest to a scrapbook page. You can paste smaller photos on tags, rubber stamp the tags, or add stickers if you want. And be sure to thread a piece of ribbon, lace, or raffia through the punched holes in your tags to complete the look!

Charm-ing Ideas

Tiny charms and other three-dimensional objects really make scrapbook pages come to life. Depending on the story your page is telling, think about adding tiny brass keys, old coins, paper butterflies, scrabble tiles, tiny beads and buttons, even little squares of foil that you've embossed.

Brush It Up

When using embossed papers as backgrounds, drybrush a little bit of gold acrylic paint over a few select areas to add elegant highlights.

Try Your Hand at Painting

Why not create your own scrapbook background page? Try painting a beach scene with white clouds, scalloped waves, and gentle, undulating yellow sand. Once you lay your summer photos over it and rubber stamp a fish and starfish, you might be surprised at how impressive your artwork looks!

Personalize Your Scrapbook Covers

Buy a simple album and make you own elaborate cover. Silk flowers and ribbons are easily glued on. You can use charms, beads, quilted squares, or a piece of needlepoint. Lace and dried flower petals also lend an elegant touch. Or get a yard of fabric and cover the entire book!

Adding Dimension to Your Scrapbook

A tiny mirror surrounded with lace, an old embroidered hankie, paper dolls, even a tiny locket or string of inexpensive pearls adds a personal touch and is very symbolic of a keepsake motif.

Scrapbooks Can Be More Than Just Scrapbooks

You can create a special book that you use for journaling, sketching, jotting down poems or special phrases, or even recording vacations, special events, favorite memories of your children, or your best recipes.

Favorite New Orleans Recipes

Carmela's Jambalaya

¾ cup chopped onion
½ cup chopped celery
¼ cup chopped green pepper
¼ cup minced fresh parsley
1 clove garlic, minced
2 tbsp. butter
2 large tomatoes, skinned and chopped
2 cups of chicken stock
1¼ cups water
1 tsp. sugar
½ tsp. dried whole thyme
½ tsp. chili powder
¼ tsp. black pepper
¼ tsp. Tabasco sauce
2 cups browned sausage or cooked ham
1 cup uncooked long-grain rice
1½ pounds fresh medium shrimp

Using a Dutch oven, sauté onion, celery, green pepper, parsley, and garlic in butter until vegetables are tender. Stir in tomatoes, chicken stock, water, sugar, thyme, chili powder, black pepper, Tabasco sauce, and sausage or ham. Bring to a boil, then stir in rice. Cover, reduce heat, and simmer for 25 minutes. While mixture cooks, peel and devein shrimp. Add to rice mixture and simmer uncovered for an additional 10 minutes. Yields 6 servings.

Prune Bread

5 cups all-purpose flour
8 tsp. baking powder
1 tsp. salt
1 tsp. nutmeg
¼ tsp. ginger
½ tsp. cinnamon
1 cup sugar
2½ cups chopped prunes
4 eggs, lightly beaten
2½ cups milk
½ cup shortening, melted

In large mixing bowl, combine flour, baking powder, salt, nutmeg, ginger, cinnamon, sugar, and prunes. In a separate bowl, beat eggs, milk, and shortening, then add to flour mixture, stirring until moistened. Pour into two 9" × 5" greased loaf pans. Bake at 350 degrees for 1 hour. Cool in pans for 10 minutes, then remove bread from pans and cool on wire rack.

Baked Oysters with Blue Cheese
(For the adventuresome eater!)

½ lb. peeled young potatoes
4 tbsp. milk
4 tbsp. olive oil
2 tbsp. chopped parsley
2 dozen fresh oysters with shell
Salt and pepper
2 egg yolks
4 tbsp. dry white wine
⅔ cup cream
3 oz. crumbled blue cheese

Cook potatoes in salted, boiling water until tender. Drain well and mash with fork, adding in milk, olive oil, and parsley. Open oysters and separate the bodies from the shell. Reserve the juice and set aside. Discard top shell, wash bottom shell carefully. Beat egg yolks together with wine in double boiler and cook until mixture doubles in volume. Continue to beat while cooking. In another pan, mix together cream and blue cheese. Bring to a boil for 2–3 minutes, then remove from heat. Add oyster juice and fold this mixture gently into the egg yolks. To serve: Fill oyster shells with mashed potatoes. Put oysters on top, and cover with sauce. Place under grill for 5 minutes until mixture becomes golden brown. Add salt and pepper to taste. Serve hot.

Fried Okra

1 pound okra
3 tbsp. all-purpose flour

2 egg whites
1½ cups soft bread crumbs
Vegetable oil
Salt

Wash okra and drain well. Remove tip and stem end, then cut okra into ½" slices. Coat okra with flour. Beat egg whites until stiff peaks form, then fold in okra. Stir in bread crumbs, coating okra well. Deep-fry okra slices in hot oil until golden brown. Drain on paper towels and sprinkle with salt. Yields 4 servings.

Ava's Favorite Rum Hurricane

2 oz. dark rum
2 oz. light rum
1 tbsp. passion fruit syrup
2 oz. apricot nectar
2 oz. strawberry nectar
2 tsp. grenadine
2 tsp. lime juice

Shake well with ice and strain into a hurricane-shaped glass filled with ice. Beware!

Carmela's Sour Cherry Cream Cheese Spread

4 oz. cream cheese
2 tbsp. chopped dried sour cherries

2 tbsp. slivered almonds
1 tsp. honey
1 tsp. fresh lemon juice
1 drop of almond extract

Mash softened cream cheese in a bowl; add in the rest of the ingredients plus a dash of salt. Spread on toasted English muffins or bagels. (Note: In a pinch you could use sour cherry jam.)

DON'T MISS THE NEXT
SCRAPBOOK MYSTERY

What could be more fun than an all-night crop at Carmela's scrapbooking shop? As ideas on rubber stamping, hand-tinting photos, and decorating album covers are shared, scrapbookers also help themselves to hurricane rum drinks, jambalaya and homemade praline pie. Spirits run high and the soft New Orleans night buzzes with excitement. But when Bartholomew Hayward, the shady antique dealer from next door, is found sprawled in the back alley with scissors jammed in his neck, it looks like the work of a very crafty killer!

Find out more about the
Scrapbook Mystery Series
and the Tea Shop Mystery Series
at www.laurachilds.com

And coming in August 2003

The English Breakfast Murder

Dawn is about to break at South Carolina's Halliehurst Beach and the members of Charleston's Sea Turtle Protection League are taking part in the annual "turtle crawl." As they help hundreds of tiny green loggerheads tumble safely into the surf, the dedicated volunteers congratulate themselves with a well-earned shore breakfast. But as the tea steeps and the gumbo simmers, a strange mass is spotted floating offshore. Donning mask and swim fins, Theodosia paddles out to investigate, only to discover a dead body bobbing in the waves. The hapless victim turns out to be Harper Fisk, a prominent Charleston art dealer and passionate collector of Civil War antiquities. Rumors of sunken treasure and gold bullion have abounded, yet nothing has ever been found near Halliehurst Beach. But now Theodosia begins to wonder—did Harper Fisk finally stumble upon something? And was he killed because of it?

High Praise for the
Tea Shop Mystery Series

**Named to the Paperback "Bestseller List"
by the Independent Mystery Booksellers**

**Each has been an "Editor's Select Choice"
by the Literary Guild's Mystery Book Club®**

"Brilliantly weaving suspense and tea knowledge."
—*In the Library Reviews*

"Engages the audience from the start . . . Laura Childs provides the right combination between tidbits on tea and an amateur sleuth cozy that will send readers seeking a cup of *Death by Darjeeling*."
—*Midwest Book Review*

"This mystery series could single-handedly propel the tea shop business in this country to the status of wine bars and bustling coffeehouses."
—*Buon Gusto,* Minneapolis, MN

"Joins the growing trend of cozies that give food depictions and recipes a close second billing to the mysteries."
—iloveamystery.com

"Just the right blend of cozy fun and clever plotting."
—Susan Wittig Albert, bestselling author of *Mistletoe Man*

"As brisk and refreshing as any brew!"
—*Romantic Times Magazine*

"Will warm readers the way a good cup of tea does."
—*The Mystery Reader*